RESONANCE OF LOVE

LOVE

愛的迴盪

DEDICATION

To my mother, Yang, Xiejin (楊謝盡).

"Trees wish to be calm, but the wind does not stop blowing. The son wishes to repay his parents, but the parents cannot wait."

漢·韓嬰·韓詩外傳·卷九: 「樹欲靜而風不止，子欲養而親不待也。」

ACKNOWLEDGEMENTS

I would like to express my deep appreciation to the following people: Nancy Hauser for initial editing of this novel, Axie Breen for her cover design, my proofreaders Colin Borsos and Jamie Urquhart; and James Norman for his final editing, formatting, and help in publishing this novel. Finally, I would like to thank the friends who read and expressed their opinions on the story.

PREFACE

I was born in 1946, one year after the end of World War II. China, under the rule of Guomingdang (國民黨, Chiang's Party), was still celebrating its victory against Japan and preparing to rebuild the country. At the same time, Gongchandang (共產黨, The Chinese Communist Party), with Russia's military and material support, began to enlarge its Manchuria territory and invaded southward with the intention of taking over all of China.

During this time, many large-scale civil war battles were taking place within China. Due to severe corruption within Chiang's government, inefficient military discipline, and a lack of weapons, Chiang's troops were defeated constantly and pushed ever further south.

In Taiwan, after Chiang's Party took over control from Japan in 1945, the conditions were getting worse every day. Corruption amongst politicians, police, and government workers; poor military discipline, a loss of social morality, military requisitioning of the few supplies and food stores available, language barriers, severe inflation, an extreme shortage of food, serious unemployment, discrimination by the Party against Taiwanese people, and an unfair employment system all added to the harshness of daily life. The atmosphere of hate among the native Taiwanese against Chiang's government and the foreign province refugees from Mainland China was ramping up rapidly. This eventually triggered a revolutionary riot against Chiang's government from February 27th to May 16th of 1947. Chiang's forceful military suppression of the revolt was estimated to have caused 18,000 to 28,000 deaths and led to the ever more hostile atmosphere in Taiwan against those refugees escaping from Mainland China.

Within just a couple of years, Chiang had lost all crucial battles in China. He retreated to Taiwan in 1949. The entire situation in Taiwan was chaotic and people were terrified that the Chinese Communist Liberation Army might soon cross the Taiwan Strait and take over Taiwan as well. Life was very difficult due to the lack of food coupled with the sudden increase in population. It was estimated that a total of 1,210,000 people escaped from Mainland China to Taiwan by the end of 1949; this was equal to 13% of Taiwan's population at the time.

I was the second of nine children in a typical Taiwanese family. Life was very difficult with so many children. Most people were struggling for survival. Food was short and the government, for its war against the Communists, levied almost all living supplies. Growing up in this environment, in one way you felt hostility against Chiang's government and those foreign province refugees who were pouring into your homeland; in the other way, you felt pity, and were sorry for those innocent refugees who were just looking for a safe place for their families.

Since I grew up in this background, I could really comprehend and feel the hardship at that time. Therefore, I have always wanted to write a story based on these experiences to help the young generation today understand how fortunate they are. They should appreciate the peace and harmony they are able to have today.

Dr. Yang, Jwing-Ming
YMAA CA Retreat Center
Miranda, California
June 30th, 2018

HISTORICAL BACKGROUND

5/8/1945

Germany surrenders and World War II in Europe ends. However, the war in the Pacific continues.

8/6/1945

The United States Air Force drops 1st atomic bomb on Hiroshima (廣島市).

8/8/1945

The Soviet Union declares war against Japan.

8/9/1945

The U.S. Air Force drops 2nd atomic bomb on Nagasaki (長崎市).

9/2/1945

The surrender of Imperial Japan announced and formally signed on September 2nd, 1945 on board the USS Missouri in Tokyo Bay. World War II ends.

10/5/1945

Chiang, Kai-Shek's general, Ge, Jing-En (葛敬恩中將) arrives in Taiwan to arrange the takeover after the Japanese surrender.

10/17/1945

Chiang, Kai-Shek's general, Chen, Kong-De (陳孔達) and his Seventy Army (七十軍), a total of 3,000 soldiers on an American transport ship under cover and protection from their American allies, arrive from Ningbo of Zhejiang Province (浙江寧波), China in Jilong Port (基隆港), Taiwan and enter Taipei City (臺北市). More than 300,000 Taiwanese people welcome the troops on the street. The people welcoming Chiang's troops are very surprised and disappointed when they see the disorderly soldiers with their clumsy clothes and shoes marching through Taipei's streets. Compared with the highly disciplined Japanese soldiers in their clean and neat uniforms, what the Taiwanese see is beyond comprehension for some. However, many of them understand that the poor condition of these soldiers is the result of eight long years of war.

10/25/1945

Chiang, Kai-Shek's general, Chen, Yi (陳儀), represents Chiang to take control of Taiwan.

10/26/1945 – 2/27/1947

After the takeover, conditions in Taiwan continue to grow worse every day due to corruption amongst the politicians, police, and government workers; poor military discipline, a loss of social mores, the requisitioning of living supplies for military use, language barriers, severe inflation, an extreme shortage of food, serious unemployment, discrimination against Taiwanese people, and an unfair employment system. The atmosphere of hate against Chiang's government and foreign province people escaping from Mainland China rapidly worsens.

2/27/1947-5/16/1947

Revolutionary riot against Chiang, Kai-Shek's government. Suppression of the riot results in an estimated 18,000 to 28,000 deaths. It is called the 2-2-8 incident or revolution (二二八事變). After this, many Taiwanese turn hostile against the new foreigners coming from Mainland China.

9/12/1948 – 11/2/1948

First crucial, main battle between the Communist Liberation Army and Chiang's troop, Liaoshen Campaign (遼瀋戰役). Chiang's troops are defeated badly.

11/6/1948 – 1/10/1949

Second crucial, main battle between the Communist Liberation Army and Chiang's troops, Huaihai Campaign (淮海戰役), also called the Battle of Xufeng (徐蚌會戰). Chiang's troops are again defeated badly.

11/29/1948 – 1/31/1949

Third crucial, main battle between the Communist Liberation Army and Chiang's troops, Pingjin Campaign (平津戰役). Chiang's troop are completely defeated and lose more than 521,000 soldiers. Chiang's party loses hope to regain any of the lost territories.

5/2/1949

Complete retreat of Chiang's Party, Guoming Dang (國民黨), from Shanghai.

5/27/1949
The Communists take complete control of Shanghai.

10/2/1949
The American Government announces its recognition that the Republic of China (Taiwanese Government) is the sole representative of China.

10/3/1949
Chiang, Kai-Shek flies to Taiwan from Canton City (廣州市).
It is estimated that a total of 1,210,000 people fled from Mainland China to Taiwan by the end of 1949; this represents 13% of Taiwan's population at the time.

6/25/1950 - 7/27/1953
Korean War Period.

6/30/1950
Land reform in China causes 2,000,000 to 4,500,000 deaths.

1/26/1953
Land Reform in Taiwan. Land is taken from landlords and distributed to tenants.

11/1/1955 - 4/30/1975
Vietnam War Period

8/23/1958 - 10/5/1958
Jinmen Cannon Battle (金門砲戰). An estimated 31,757 cannon balls fall on Jinmen Island. It is also called the 8-2-3 Cannon Battle (八二三砲戰).

10/26/1971
The Republic of China (Taiwan) is forced to withdraw from the United Nations.

2/21/1972
President Nixon visits China.

4/5/1975
  Chiang, Kai-Shek dies.

9/9/1976
  Mao, Tse-Tung dies.

1/1/1979
  Communist China and America establish formal relations.

PRELUDE
前奏

Before dawn, dew clung to the grass and leaves on the battlefield. You could hear some ravens calling in the distant woods. The sound was desolate and sorrowful on this otherwise peaceful morning – as if the ravens could sense some huge disaster about to happen that would make your breath come short and your heart beat faster. It was the serenity before the big storm.

***

Chiang's army, which had occupied the hills two weeks ago, continued to have its advantage in this battle while the People's Liberation Army was forced to stay on the exposed, flat ground. Though Chiang's army had this strategically advantageous position, their situation was getting worse due to the lack of a continuous stream of reinforcements and supplies. On the other hand, the People's Liberation Army was getting stronger with the addition of more soldiers and more cannons. From their view of the fighting from the top of the hills, all of Chiang's higher-ranking officers knew that, sooner or later, their enemies would take over these hills and win the battle. While they were talking about future strategies, a new volley of cannonballs started to fall near their headquarters. Within just a minute, hundreds of cannonballs landed on the top of the hills. This was the third attempt by the People's Liberation Army to take over these hills.

Immediately after the cannonballs fell, countless soldiers from the People's Liberation Army launched another assault. When their enemies were within shooting range, Chiang's troop fired the limited cannons they still had. Soon their ammunition would be exhausted. After thirty minutes or so, due to the strong resistance and firepower of Chiang's army, the People's Liberation Army retreated and prepared for its next assault. At their enemies' retreat, thousands of Chiang's soldiers immediately entered the field to search for any weapons and ammunition left behind. They would need these since their supplies were quickly running out.

Lin, Hanmin (林漢民), a major in Chiang's army, quickly led his soldiers into the field to begin collecting weapons and ammunition. They all knew they didn't have very much time. As Hanmin's search brought him further down the hill, he suddenly saw a soldier of the Liberation Army stand up. Without hesitation he raised his gun and pulled the trigger, since he did not want to give the enemy a chance to shoot or throw a grenade at him.

As Hanmin pulled the trigger he thought, "That face looks so familiar." He wondered at that even as he saw the enemy fall. Then he noticed that one of the enemy's legs had been wounded earlier in the battle.

Hanmin hurried over to the enemy he had just shot and searched the man's pocket, finding a photo - the same family photo that Hanmin carried at all times. Suddenly he realized that this enemy he had just shot was his own elder son. Shock gripped him. He could not believe what had happened.

Hanmin lifted up his son's head and called his name in a loud voice. "Jiaxiang (家祥), Jiaxiang! Wake up, Jiaxiang! Alas, my heavens. What have I done?" he wailed. His body trembled in anguish. He called again, "Jiaxiang, Jiaxiang! This is your Die (爹, Dad). This is your Die. Please, please, wake up!"

Hanmin hugged his son's head to his chest and cried. When he felt the body moving, he put his son's head down and grabbed the arms. His son looked up at him. Jiaxiang's breathing was very weak.

"Die! Die! I ... I ..." Jiaxiang closed his eyes and his life was gone.

"My heavens! What did I do? Wake up! Wake up, Jiaxiang!" Hanmin couldn't help himself crying out loud and nearly going crazy.

"I shouldn't have encouraged him to go to Dongbei (東北, Manchu) to study. Obviously, he was recruited by the Communist Party and became one of them." Hanmin sat on the battlefield holding his son and regretting everything deeply while all around him forces on both sides prepared for the launch of another attack.

CHAPTER 1
FLEE FROM CALAMITY
逃 難

NANJING HOME 南京家

This was May 3rd of 1949. In this military housing unit, there was a small kitchen, a small study, a family room, and two bedrooms. The home was simple but comfortable. Wanping (婉萍), the lady of the house, picked up a photo on the table and showed it to her younger son.

"Jiaming (家明), look at this photo. You were still young at that time," Wanping said with a bit of sadness in her voice.

"Niang (娘, Mom), that was four years ago. I was only 19 years old." Jiaming looked at his mom with a smile.

"Remember the day we took this photo?" Wanping asked. "The war with Japan had just ended."

"Yes, Niang. The day Da Ge (大哥, Big Brother) went to Dongbei (Manchu) to study when he was 21 years old."

"I was very upset that he left. But he said that he was lucky to be accepted by Shenyang Dongbei University (瀋陽東北大學)."

"Yeah, I remember. Die (Dad) was also home at that time, so we went to have a photo taken while we were all together. It was expensive to have done. I am glad that all of us have a copy, Niang," Jiaming said.

"Your Die said it was good for your brother to experience life. Actually, he encouraged him to go. I miss him very much. He is my first born," Wanping said.

"Niang, I wonder why we have not received any letters from him in the last two years."

"I don't know. It's difficult to receive mail during wartime. Just

wish that he is well! You know your Die is a major in Chiang's army. He must be very busy now. We also don't have any news from him! I heard that the People's Liberation Army has already taken over most of Northern China."

"Niang, that is true. What should we do now? If the situation gets any worse, the Liberation Army will reach Nanjing in a couple of weeks. I also heard that since Die is a high-ranking officer of Chiang's army, if the Liberation Army catches us, our fate will be very miserable," Jiaming expressed his concern.

The Chinese Communist troops, The People's Liberation Army, had just defeated Chiang's last, mass defense in Pingjin (平津) on January 31st of 1949. After this final battle, Chiang's troops lost all hope of regaining their lost territories, or even just defending themselves. The commander of the 35th army, Guo, Jingyun (郭景雲) committed suicide. Chiang's troops continued retreating to Southern China, Taiwan, or Hainan Island (海南島).

Five days later, Jiaming looked at his mother with panic and worry. "Niang, we have to make a decision now! The time is urgent. They're saying that the Liberation Army is only two days away. If we don't go now, we will be captured."

"I wish your Die were here. I don't have any idea of what to do. I think the best thing is to run away from Nanjing. I received a notice from Nanjing military headquarters yesterday that if we wish to leave and go to Taiwan or Hainan, they have trucks to take us to Shanghai tomorrow. They have been evacuating all of the military families over the last few days. We are assigned to tomorrow's group if we wish to leave."

"Niang, we can't hesitate. If we don't go, we may die when the Communists arrive. You know, President Chiang was forced to resign on January 21st and since then the whole country is in chaos. We must run, Niang."

RUNNING AWAY FROM HOME 逃離家鄉

They packed as quickly as they could. Since they didn't have much in the way of valuables in the house, they just took with them some important documents and some old jewelry that would have to serve as their money. Paper currency held no value now. As Jiaming was going through his father's small office, he found a pistol and a dozen bullets in the desk drawer. He hesitated for a while, then made his decision and put them into his bag. Since the situation was so chaotic, he was afraid some bad guys might try to rob them. But if he had this pistol and bullets, he might be able to save them from being robbed or killed. He did not tell his mother about this though, since he did not want to cause her concern and frighten her.

The next day they were on the way to Shanghai on military trucks. There were at least another 100 people riding together in four trucks. Before they left, one of the military officers told them that the Liberation Army was only eight hours away from Nanjing.

Along the way, they saw thousands of people fleeing from Nanjing on foot. All the roads and paths were crowded with refugees. Occasionally, they saw trucks carrying wounded soldiers pass them. Their own group of trucks moved slowly through the crowd. They could hear people crying and see the panic on people's faces. Once their trucks had gotten beyond the walking throng, they picked up speed and went as fast as possible.

Soon, however, they came upon another big group of refugees, and then another. Although they had to travel a distance of only 280 km, it took them nearly six hours to reach Shanghai. By then it was already 4 p.m. According to the original arrangement, they were assigned to board a ship on Shanghai Pier #2. When they arrived, they could see thousands of people crowded around the pier looking for a chance to board the ships. Unfortunately, previously, on January 27th, the two biggest ships, Taiping Lun (太平輪) and Jianyuan Lun (建元輪) had collided with each other while carrying people between Shanghai and Taiwan. Thousands of people had drowned. The loss of these ships significantly reduced the transport capacity available for evacuation. The pier was in total chaos. On people's faces, you could see their expressions of worry, sadness, fear, and anxiety. There were only a few large ships and a limited number of smaller motorized fishing boats available. Fishing boats without motors would not be able to carry people the long distance to Taiwan, Hong Kong, or Hainan Island.

Wanping and Jiaming waited for two hours in the military building on Pier #2. Eventually they were notified that due to too many military service men and families trying to leave, there was no space for them to board any ship. It was recommended they go to Pier #4. It was thought they might have a better chance there. The worst part was that there was no transportation to take them, and they would have to make their way on foot. Everything was in disorder and people were panicked.

With deep disappointment, Wanping and Jiaming began to walk to

Pier #4. The sky got darker and darker as they went, and soon it began to drizzle. It seemed that even nature would not show mercy to all these unfortunate refugees crowded on the piers with only the smallest fragments of hope in their hearts. Many of those who were rich had been able to hire private boats and had already either gone to Taiwan or Hong Kong.

On the way to Pier #4, Jiaming heard a few people arguing.

"Should we go to Hainan Island? I heard there will be a boat available tomorrow morning," one person said.

"No! No! Hainan Island is too close to Mainland, it can be taken over easily by the Liberation Army," another person said.

"We should go to Taiwan. With Taiwan Strait, the Communists will not be able to cross easily. We must go to Taiwan!" the third person argued.

"It does not matter where we go, sooner or later, the Liberation Army will take over unless Chiang receives military aid from foreign countries. The only safe place in my opinion is Hong Kong since it is under the rule of the British Government," an older man expressed his opinion.

Actually, no one was sure where the safest place was to run to or to hide. Soon the Liberation Army would wipe out all of China. Everyone was panicking, but especially the rich landlords, Chiang's old officers, and the military families who followed Chiang.

After Wanping and Jiaming had moved apart from the group that had been talking, Jiaming asked his mother, "Niang, what do you think? Should we go to Hong Kong or Taiwan?"

"Jiaming, Hong Kong is too small and cannot squeeze in so many refugees. It will have problems sooner or later. Furthermore, I believe your Die will follow Chiang's troop to Taiwan. If that happens, we can reunite with him in Taiwan."

Jiaming nodded his head in agreement with his mom's opinion and trudged on. After about an hour of walking, he asked her, "Niang, are you tired? It will be another hour before we get through this crowd and reach Pier #4." Jiaming was very concerned for his mother since all their clothes were getting wet in the constant drizzle.

"Jiaming, I am okay. We cannot stop! We still don't know if we have a chance to board the ship at Pier #4," Wanping replied. She knew that she was tired, but Jiaming was also tired, especially since he was carrying the bags. She looked at Jiaming with all the love and concern of a mother.

Halfway into the walk toward Pier #4 the rain got heavier.

Wanping and Jiaming were squeezed in amongst the crowd. Except for a very few people, most of the refugees had not carried umbrellas when they ran away from home. Many of them sat on the wet ground now, not knowing what to do. There were a few sheltering eaves on the warehouses around the piers, but the spaces under these were already crowded with people. There was not enough room under them for even one tenth of the people that were present. Fortunately, the temperature was not as cold as it might have been on this day in May.

"Niang, there is Pier #4! We can see it from here now," Jiaming said with excitement and encouragement.

When they were nearer, Wanping and Jiaming could see that, again, there were thousands of people crowded at the pier. Their hope started to dim. They immediately searched for a temporary military service station. Due to the rain, the station had been moved from its original outside location to the far corner of a building under an eave. As they approached the station, Wanping noticed a young lady who was alone and had curled herself into a corner near the door of the building. She was shivering with cold in her wet clothing. She looked sloppy and dirty.

For some reason that could not be explained, Wanping stopped and asked the young lady with concern, "Are you alone? Are you sick?"

"Da Niang (大娘, Big Aunt), I am lost! I became separated from my family in the crowd two days ago. I am sick and weak." The young lady lifted her head and looked at Wanping with tears in her eyes. Now, Wanping could see her face more clearly. Somehow, Wanping pitied her and felt touched for this young lady.

Wanping used her hand to feel the young lady's forehead; it was burning with fever. She was obviously very sick. Wanping worried about what would happen to her, especially as it was getting darker and colder with the coming of evening.

"What is your name? My name is Wanping and this is my son, Jiaming."

"Da Niang, my name is Peng, Xiaohua (彭曉華). I am from Zhenjiang City (鎮江市) of Jiangsu Province (江蘇省)," the young lady replied. She was grateful for Wanping's concern.

"Stay here! I will see if I can find some medicine for you," Wanping said.

"Niang! Where can we find medicine? There is no doctor around here," Jiaming asked with concern. He also wished he could help this poor lady.

"Let's check in first. That is most important. We need to register our spaces as soon as possible."

Wanping and her son went to the service station and produced the documents that proved they were the family of a military officer.

"How many members of your family are here?" the officer asked.

Before Jiaming could reply, Wanping said, "Three. It will be my son, my daughter-in-law, and me. My name is Wanping, my son is Jiaming, and his wife is Xiaohua. She is very sick now and is staying there at the corner of that building." Wanping used her finger to point to the place where Xiaohua had taken refuge.

While the officer was writing their names down, Wanping looked at Jiaming with a smile. Jiaming knew what his mother was doing. She had found a way to help Xiaohua.

"There is a fishing boat leaving tomorrow at dawn around 6 o'clock. You will have spaces in this boat. You have to be here on time otherwise the boat will leave without you. This boat can only take 50 people maximum," the officer said.

"Thank you very much. Thank you very much, Officer!" Wanping and Jiaming were very happy to know they had a chance to leave in the morning. They considered themselves very lucky, considering how many people were waiting for a space.

Before they left the station, Wanping asked, "By the way, Officer, do you know where I can get some medicine for my daughter-in-law? She has a very high fever."

"If you enter the building, in the right corner, there is a temporary medical center. Talk to the doctor," the officer replied.

"Thank you very much, Officer," Jiaming responded and bowed with appreciation.

Wanping and Jiaming quickly went back to the place where Xiaohua stayed.

"Xiaohua, I hope you don't mind going with us tomorrow morning. I found a way to get you on board with us."

"Da Niang! I don't know how to thank you. You are my life saver."

Xiaohua looked at Wanping and couldn't help the tears flowing freely down her face. She knew it was almost impossible for any laymen to board a ship or boat unless they were very rich.

"Jiaming, please stay here with Xiaohua. I will go in to ask the doctor for medicine."

Jiaming nodded his head. After his mother left, he took the small towel he had brought in his bag and went to a faucet next to the building. He wet the towel and returned, then proceeded to gently wipe all of the dirt off Xiaohua's face. Xiaohua just stared at him through her tears. She could not believe there were still people with such good hearts in this kind of situation. After Jiaming had cleaned her face, he could see that she was a very simple and good-looking lady.

"Why don't you wipe the dirt off of your hands," Jiaming suggested, giving Xiaohua the towel. He felt uneasy touching the lady's hands when they had just met.

Xiaohua took the wet towel and wiped her hands. She and Jiaming did not talk very much but sat quietly together in the shelter of the building. A few minutes later, Wanping returned.

"We are lucky. There was not too much medicine left. There is only one doctor and many patients," she said. "The doctor said to take two pills now and two more six hours later," Wanping instructed as she gave Xiaohua the medicine.

Jiaming took a bowl from one of their bags and went to collect some water for Xiaohua. At the same time, Wanping removed a few clothes from another bag.

"After you take the medicine, you should change your clothes. All yours are wet and that's not good for a sick person. These are my clothes. Since your body is almost the same size as mine, I think they will fit. There was a hidden place inside next to the medical center. You can change there."

Although Xiaohua felt hot from her fever, she could not stop shivering due to the cold air and her wet clothes. The day was completely dark now, and the temperature was dropping very quickly. Rain fell relentlessly, and it seemed that there was no hope of it stopping any time soon.

Jiaming returned with water and gave it to Xiaohua. She took it and used it to swallow the medicine.'

"Jiaming, can you stay here to protect this place?" his mother asked. "If all of us leave, others will take it immediately. At least there is no rain under the roof here."

"Sure, Niang!" Jiaming sat down with his bag next to him.

Wanping helped Xiaohua to stand up and slowly walked her into the building. Twenty minutes later, when they returned, Xiaohua looked very different wearing the clean and dry clothes. She also felt warmer. However, the best warm feeling deep in her heart was Wanping and Jiaming's care and concern for her. Together, the three of them arranged the small area Xiaohua had claimed so that they were able to lie down for the night. They were all exhausted.

"Niang, I am very hungry. Can we finish the dried food we brought?" Jiaming asked.

"I am hungry too. Xiaohua, are you hungry?"

"Da Niang, no! I have not eaten for nearly two days, but I feel weak and have no appetite. I am just tired."

"Rest! All you need is rest now. We will save some food for you when you have your appetite back," Wanping said.

"Thank you, Da Niang." Xiaohua impulsively reached her hands out to grab Wanping's. They felt like mother and daughter.

After Jiaming and Wanping had eaten some of their precious stores, they put their bags under their heads so no one would steal them when they fell asleep.

They had slept for just a few hours when they were awakened by some noise. It was 5 o'clock in the morning and people were rushing here and there getting ready to board the ships or boats. Two middle sized ships and 12 fishing boats would be leaving this morning from Pier #4. Fortunately, the rain had stopped, apparently passing through during the night, and the sun would rise soon.

Jiaming and Wanping woke Xiaohua. She seemed to be in better spirits after the dose of medicine and a night of sleep. However, she was still weak, and had a fever. Wanping helped her take her second dose of medicine.

The three of them searched the pier for the boat with number 11 on it. Although it was only 5:30 in the morning, there were many people already in line and waiting. They took their own places in line quickly. They knew if they did not get on the boat soon most of the nice deck spaces would be taken.

At 6:15 a.m. on May 10th, a military officer came to Pier #4. One by one he checked people's documents before permitting them to board. Once Wanping's group had passed inspection, her heart filled knowing that now they would have hope for their future. The trio quickly found a space on deck where they might avoid the strong winds once they were on the ocean. According to what was being said, if they were lucky, the boat would take only ten hours to reach Jilong Port (基隆港) on the north of Taiwan.

Since Xiaohua was still weak, once they were aboard and settled Wanping encouraged her to sleep and rest again. The sun would be high soon, but it was still a bit chilly and moist in the early morning air, so Wanping covered her with Jiaming's coat. Xiaohua felt comfortable and warm and fell asleep within a few minutes.

The boat cast off around 7:15 in the morning; however, there were so many ships and boats leaving from different piers at the same time that it took them nearly an hour to make their way from Huangpu

River (黃浦江) out onto the sea.

Once the sun was up, people took their wet clothes out of the bundles they carried, draping them wherever they could find a place to let them dry. Suddenly, Xiaohua woke up sobbing from a nightmare.

"Are you okay, Xiaohua?" Wanping, who had been sitting next to her asked, reaching out to reassure her.

Xiaohua could not help hugging Wanping in return. After she calmed down, Wanping gave her some food.

"You must be very hungry since you have not eaten for a couple days," Wanping said.

"Da Niang, thank you! I don't know what would have happened to me if I had not met you and Da Ge (大哥, Big Brother)." She looked at Wanping with tears in her eyes.

"Tell me about yourself and your family, Xiaohua," Wanping urged with kindly interest.

Xiaohua's Story 曉華身世

Xiaohua traced her memory back only a few days earlier to May 3rd. Xiaohua's 72-year-old grandpa, Peng, Zhaoyang (彭朝陽), was in the living room with the entire family: his wife Meiying (美英), 70 years old; his son, Zhigang (志剛), 48; daughter-in-law, Xiuzhen (秀珍), 46; and their two children, Xiaohua (曉華), 20; Ronghua (榮華), 9.

"Listen to me, everyone! Our neighbor, Old Zhang (老張), told me that the People's Liberation Army is only a few days away from here. We must find a way to care for ourselves. He told me that we will have a serious problem when the Communists come since we own land." Zhaoyang made this pronunciation with panic and worry clearly showing on his face.

"Die, but the land was purchased through generations of our family's hard work and savings," Zhigang said.

"The Communists will not care about that. From what they said in their propaganda, they will take over the land from all landlords and give it to the tenant farmers. They may also punish landlords seriously. Our doomsdays are coming." Zhaoyang could not help that his eyes turned red with anger and sorrow.

Xiaohua's 9-year-old brother did not really understand the situation. All he knew was that something serious was going to happen to his family. He could feel their worry and panic all around him. The room was quiet for several minutes.

Zhaoyang pondered deeply, then finally broke the silence. "Zhigang! You have to take your wife and two children and get away from here. This place will turn into hell in a few days. I heard many people, especially those who are rich, have already run away to Taiwan or Hong Kong."

"But, Die, won't you and Niang go with us?" Zhigang asked.

"No! No! We are too old and will only slow you down and hinder your escape. All we worry about is you, Xiuzhen, and your two children. Besides, we are not young anymore and cannot take such a long journey. It would only kill us sooner."

"No, Die, no! I would rather die here together with you instead of running away," Zhigang cried with tears in his voice. "When the Communists come, they will give you trouble, Die!" he implored.

"Listen to me, my son. Your mom and I are too old for this kind of long journey. It would just kill us for sure. Furthermore, we don't have too many years to live and we don't want to leave here. I also don't believe that the Communists will give two old folks trouble. There is no benefit or advantage to them. However, you and Xiuzhen are still young. Your two children, my lovable grandkids, you must take them away from here. Time is urgent. You don't have too much time."

"But Die! I cannot leave both of you here alone."

"Listen to me, my son. Your mother and I will go to your sister's home. She can take care of us. Her husband is not a landlord or Chiang's soldier. We should be okay there."

Without saying a word, Zhigang stood up and went to stand in front of his parents. He knelt down with tears in his eyes. When Xiuzhen saw it, she brought Xiaohua and Ronghua forward to also kneel down on the floor next to her husband and before Zhaoyang and Meiying. It was a gesture of loving respect as well as sorrowful resignation. The entire family was full of sadness. Their departure would have to be very soon, and they knew they might not see each other in this life again.

Zhigang's family packed only three bags. Zhigang would carry the heavier one with their money: thirty-five 200gm bars of gold bullion and some silver. His wife and daughter would carry dried food, drink, and clothes. Nine-year-old Ronghua was still too young and would need to be looked after all the time.

Early the next morning, on the 4th of May, Zhigang brought his wife and two children before his parents to say good-bye. Again, they knelt down on the ground in tears.

Zhaoyang lifted them up, saying, "Go now! It may take two or three days to walk to Shanghai. Buddha blesses you." He and his wife waved their hands and urged their son and his family to leave. Their sadness was hard to endure. They stood next to the door till they could no longer see their departing family.

The street was full of refugees. All of the faces were full of worry and fear. The distance from Zhenjiang City to Shanghai was about 250 kilometers. Normally, it would take a healthy person walking at a steady pace three days to reach Shanghai. However, with women and children, and carrying whatever possessions they had, making it in that time would be questionable. The journey would be very hard and tiring.

As Zhigang and his family walked, they heard the other refugees expressing their own fears and alarm. Some people were discussing the situation, saying, "I heard the Communists would only give trouble to those who are rich, especially landlords. We are poor tenant farmers; they won't harm us. As a matter of fact, I also heard it was our day to see the sunshine and the hope of a great China under Communism."

"That's not true. I heard they killed people in cold blood," another said.

Nobody was sure what was going to happen.

"One thing is for sure, as I heard and read from their propaganda, is that they would only give trouble to landlords. This is the day for the tenant farmers' revolution," someone else confirmed.

Zhigang and his family followed the crowd and moved away from the city as quickly as they could. To prevent the young boy from getting lost in the crowd, Xiuzhen kept a firm hold on his hand as she followed her husband. She asked Xiaohua to follow them as closely as possible. She kept turning her head to make sure Xiaohua was still with them. There was no public transportation running. Unless you had private transportation, it was nearly impossible for anyone to get away quickly except by walking. There were no cars to be hired, even with gold. Furthermore, if a car was available, there was no gas for it.

Millions of people lived inland. A couple of weeks ago, once they knew that Chiang's army had lost three critical battles, people had begun to run toward the shore. They all hoped to find a way to get to Taiwan or Hong Kong.

After a whole day of walking, everyone was tired. Like a river swelling in size from its tributaries, the size of the refugee group continued to swell as more and more people joined in from side roads. Before long the group, including the old, young, and children, numbered at least 2,000.

On the second day, many people had already run out of whatever food they had brought. Some people were very kind and shared what they had. Some other unlucky ones could not find food and went hungry.

Zhigang gave his two children some of the dry food they had brought with them the previous morning. He and his wife, though, did not eat but endured their hunger, and tried to make what food they had last as long as possible. It would be at least two more days of walking at this slow pace. Everyone was hungry, thirsty, and tired.

On the third day, some people got up early in the morning to continue their journey. But some elders were too tired to engage another day so soon. Finally, Zhigang and his family took up their bags and started walking again, following the group already moving down the road. By noon, everyone's food was running out. There was no place to buy or to beg for food. Everyone in the group just looked at each other in hopeless despondence. In reverse of when they had started out, now, people started dropping out along the side of the road as they became too exhausted to keep going. By late in the day, there were only about 600 left in this group.

The refugees tried to comfort each other but there was no respite. In another two hours it would be dark. They knew they needed another day or more of walking before they would reach Shanghai. In the meantime, everyone was getting more tired, hungry, thirsty, and weak.

"Hey, everyone! There is a stream here!" On the far end of the group, a young man was shouting. When everyone heard of this, they rushed to the stream and drank the water.

While they were drinking, "Hey! Everyone! Look! There is an abandoned sweet potato field next to the stream. If we dig, we may find some sweet potatoes left in the ground," an old man said.

The possibility of food gave everyone a glimmer of hope. Without hesitating, they went to the field and started to dig with their bare hands.

"I found one," someone shouted.

"I also found one," another yelled.

Though the potatoes they found were very small, everyone smiled since they knew some food could be found in the field. They hunted diligently to find as many leftover sweet potatoes as they could before it became too dark to look.

"Wow! This sweet potato tastes so good. I never realized that it could be so tasty," one person said. Everyone laughed.

Zhigang and his wife, with Xiaohua's help, also found some sweet potatoes – enough to hold back their starvation temporarily.

Near dusk of the next day, Zhigang's family were finally drawing closer to Shanghai City. Once again, the crowd multiplied, from their group's 600 to 1,000 to countless numbers. People were pouring into Shanghai from everywhere, looking for a way to get out of China.

The day got darker and darker and the great mass of people were squeezed together. Suddenly, a few gunshots were heard. Everyone panicked, thinking the Communists had entered Shanghai. The mass surged forward as people began to run. Zhigang and his family also ran, pushed along by the group. Suddenly, Xiaohua felt her right shoe come off. Someone had stepped on her right foot and she was pushed forward a few steps. She quickly turned back to search for her shoe. After five minutes she finally found it, but in the meantime, she had lost sight of her parents and brother.

Xiaohua cried out in alarm and called for her parents, but her voice was covered by the noise of the panicked crowd. She kept being carried forward faster and faster. After 20 minutes, she still could not find her family. She began to cry and did not know what to do.

"Niang must have noticed that I am missing. They will look for me. I should just wait here instead of roaming around," Xiaohua thought. She squeezed her way through the crowd over to the side of the road and stood on top of a pile of abandoned furniture. She hoped, from there, she would be able to see her parents, or be seen by them. But all she could see was a huge crowd that kept moving forward by its own momentum, and then split in two directions at a junction in the road. Half of the crowd went to the left and the other half was pushed to the right. She still had not seen her parents when darkness fell. She was completely lost and separated from her family.

Xiaohua did not know what to do. She did not have any gold. All she had were the few clothes in the bag she carried.

"Niang! Die! Where are you? My heavens! What should I do?" She was so scared. After waiting for an hour, Xiaohua realized she had no hope of finding her parents, and she began to follow the crowd once again. She did not know which road would take her to Shanghai. When she asked, no one was sure. She had been walking with the crowd for nearly four hours when it began to rain. She used her jacket to cover her head, but in just half an hour her body was completely soaked. The crowd walked till midnight. Finally, they reached the Shanghai port.

Xiaohua was cold and wet, and by the morning she was shivering with fever. She knew she was sick. She hadn't slept the whole night. Frustrated, sad, frightened, and weak, she found a corner of a building, tucked herself in the shelter of an eave, and sat there.

"I will die soon if I don't have help," she thought.

But there was no one able to spare his or her time to look after her. Everyone was worried and frightened. So, there she stayed till she met Jiaming and his mother, Wanping.

CHAPTER 2
UNKNOWN FUTURE
未知的未來

SURVIVING IN TAIWAN 台灣求生

On May 10th of 1949, the fishing boat arrived at Jilong Port in northern Taiwan. It was getting dark and everyone was tired and hungry by the time they landed. Nothing on shore was organized. Everything was in chaos. Once the passengers got out of the boat, some Taiwanese volunteers were there to help and offer them some food. Fortunately, it was not raining, and the weather was warmer in Taiwan than it had been in Shanghai. All the people could do was wait until the next day and hope the situation would improve. Nobody knew what the future would be. The worst of it was that Xiaohua's fever had returned once the medicine was finished. Jiaming and Wanping could not find any help for her, especially more medicine. There were too many refugees, and nothing was in order. Xiaohua's fever remained high the whole night. Jiaming used a rag with cold water and placed it on Xiaohua's forehead repeatedly to try to keep her temperature down. They did not sleep that night.

The next morning some military trucks arrived and called for any military families who had just escaped from Mainland China. Jiaming immediately reported to them and showed the officer in charge his family's documents. He, his mother, and Xiaohua were placed on a truck with a few other families and taken to a primary school about five miles away. There, they were allotted three cots in the school's auditorium. They were also offered some rice and sweet potatoes. Before the officer left, he gave Wanping NT$100 to use as temporary survival funds. Wanping felt so lucky that they were taken care of. She knew there were so many other non-military families, refugees without resources, who still did not know what to do or where to go.

Unfortunately, no doctors were at the shelter and Xiaohua's situation worsened. Wanping kept asking the military servicemen where she could find a doctor.

"Madam! There are only a few doctors and they move from refugee camp to camp to treat people. Some doctor will be here after tomorrow," a soldier said.

"But my daughter-in-law's sickness is getting worse and worse. Isn't there any way to see a doctor?" Wanping cried in frustration and worry.

"I am sorry, madam. There are thousands of people waiting for doctors. You will have to wait."

Xiaohua did not eat and most of the time she was only barely conscious. She was very weak, and her breathing came in heavy gasps. This made Jiaming and Wanping very anxious.

Finally, after two days, a doctor arrived. There were many patients among the refugees waiting for the doctor's arrival. Jiaming went to the medical tent right away, pushing his way through to get to the doctor.

"Doctor! My wife is in critical condition. She is dying. Can you please come and take a look at her?" Jiaming appealed to the doctor with eyes that were red and wet. The doctor could see how urgent the situation was.

"Okay, I will look at her first. Please just give me a few minutes. I have not eaten since this morning and there are so many patients. I slept only five hours last night," the doctor said.

Jiaming waited outside of the medical tent patiently. After ten minutes the doctor stepped out of the tent and walked over to Jiaming.

"Show me where your wife is. What is your name, young man?" the doctor asked.

"Jiaming, Doctor. I am Lin, Jiaming."

"You may call me Dr. Tang. I am Taiwanese and speak only a little bit of Mandarin."

Jiaming took the doctor very quickly to where they were staying. Wanping was so happy that Jiaming was able to get the doctor there to see Xiaohua first. She bowed to Dr. Tang with hope in her eyes.

Doctor Tang checked Xiaohua's tongue, measured her temperature and took her blood pressure. After that he took his stethoscope out from his medical case and listened to Xiaohua's front and back while she coughed.

"She has serious pneumonia. She needs special care immediately, otherwise she may die," Doctor Tang said.

After hearing what the doctor said, both Jiaming and Wanping were sad, filled with worry, and anxious. They had known that Xiaohua's sickness was serious but had not expected it would be this bad.

"What should we do, Doctor?" Wanping asked with tears in her eyes.

"The medicine available through the military here cannot save her. She needs penicillin as soon as possible. There is a Taiwanese doctor in downtown Jilong, Doctor Lin. Take her to see him and see if he can help. Penicillin is an antibiotic medicine that was discovered only in the last few years. The supply is limited, but he may have some there," Doctor Tang said.

"How can we find Doctor Lin?" Jiaming asked.

"When you go downtown, just ask for him. He is well known; everyone knows him. Here are some medicines that can help your wife in the meantime. Have her take some now and again in four hours. I need to go now." And with that, Doctor Tang left with his assistant.

Without hesitation, Wanping and Jiaming helped Xiaohua to stand up and walk from the primary school. Outside they found a few tricycles for hire and went to secure one.

"Doctor Lin! Doctor Lin! Please," Jiaming said as he tried to communicate with the tricycle drivers. But the drivers did not know Mandarin and most of them just looked blankly at Jiaming. Fortunately, one of the drivers recognized that Xiaohua was sick and realized they were looking for Doctor Lin. He smiled at them and showed them to his tricycle.

"Thank you! Thank you very much," Wanping said. Even though the driver did not understand what she said, he knew what she meant.

Thirty minutes later they arrived at a private doctor's clinic. Jiaming paid their driver and took Xiaohua in immediately. They registered and waited another 25 minutes for Xiaohua's name to be called. All three of them entered the doctor's office. It took only a moment for the doctor to realize they did not understand the Taiwanese dialect. Unfortunately, the doctor did not know how to speak Mandarin. He solved this by taking out a pen and some paper. Since all Chinese writing was the same in the entire country, they would communicate with each other through writing.

The doctor took a detailed inventory of Xiaohua's situation, then wrote: "She needs antibiotic medicine right away, but penicillin is very expensive. Will you be able to afford it? I am sorry that I cannot afford to pay for her medicine. However, if you are able to pay the cost of the penicillin, I can treat her without charge."

Doctor Lin recognized that they were refugees from Mainland China. He was willing to extend his kind hands to help them, but he could not afford the high cost of penicillin either.

Wanping wrote back, "Please go ahead and treat her. I will bring money tomorrow to pay for the medicine. How much will it cost?"

"It will be probably around NT$600. Just hope her situation is stable after treatment. If not, it will cost more. I need to keep her here tonight to watch over her. Come back tomorrow and see if her condition has improved. I will give her the penicillin right away."

After the doctor gave Xiaohua a shot, a nurse took her to the backroom where she would stay the night under observation. Wanping and Jiaming said good-bye to her and stepped out of the clinic.

"Niang, we don't have enough money to pay for the medicine. What should we do?" Jiaming asked with concern.

"I brought some jewelry with me when we left the Mainland. I just don't know how much it's worth though. Let us go back to pick up the jewelry and see if we can sell it in jewelry shops."

In order to save money, they walked back to the primary school. Wanping searched through the bags they had packed in their hasty departure so many days ago until she found the pieces of jewelry that her mother had given her when she was married. Then she and Jiaming walked back downtown to search for jewelry shops. After hunting for a while, they found three. They asked the owner of each shop to give an estimate of the value of all Wanping's jewelry, then chose the highest offer and sold it. It came to NT$750.

"Jiaming! It is enough to cover the medicine. I just hope that after treatment, she is okay. If she is still sick, then we will be in big trouble," Wanping said anxiously.

Since they were near the doctor's clinic, they decided to find a cheap lunch, and then bring food back to the clinic for Xiaohua. They hoped she would be able to eat something. Once they arrived at the clinic, however, the doctor was busy treating other patients.

Wanping wrote a note to the nurse at the reception window, "I would like to pay NT$500 for Xiaohua's treatment now. I will pay the balance when the treatment is completed." After she showed the note to the nurse, she gave her NT$500.

Again, Wanping wrote, "Can we look in on Xiaohua? How is she?"

"After treatment this morning, she has calmed down. She is in a deep sleep. It is better to let her rest without disturbing her. Come back tomorrow. Hope that she is better tomorrow," the nurse wrote back.

"Here is some food for her. When she wakes up, please give her some food. She has not eaten for a couple days," Wanping wrote.

The nurse nodded her head with a smile. They thanked her and left.

First thing the next morning, Wanping and Xiaohua went back to the clinic. This time they were able to see Xiaohua, whose fever was under control. She had even begun to eat some food. This made Jiaming and Wanping very happy. While they were there, the nurse came into the room and gave them a note from the doctor.

"After taking the medicine, she is on the way of recovery. I would like to keep her here for another two days and watch her progress. I don't believe you have a good environment at the shelter for a patient. She needs rest, especially for these next couple of days," the note said. The doctor knew the conditions in the refugee camp would not be healthy for a patient trying to rebuild her strength.

"Thank you very much, Doctor. You are a very kind man. Heaven blesses you," Wanping wrote back.

Wanping and Jiaming stayed to visit with Xiaohua for half an hour, then left her to her much-needed rest.

They went to see Xiaohua again the next day. Then the third day when they arrived at the clinic, the nurse told them that the doctor wanted to see them again.

Once Wanping and Jiaming were in his office, Doctor Lin wrote, "Xiaohua is more stable now. She needs a lot of rest and good nutrition. She will be okay in a couple of weeks. But there is one thing that I have to tell you. One-third of Xiaohua's lungs have already been damaged. This one-third of the lungs may be crystallized in the future. That means her lungs' capability will be only two-thirds that of normal people. Please be careful in the future. You may take her home today. The nurse will also give you some prescriptions for you to take home. Follow the directions and give her the medicines until they are finished."

"Thank you very much, Doctor! We will appreciate your kindness forever," Wanping wrote back. Doctor Lin extended his hand and shook Wanping's and Jiaming's warmly.

When they checked Xiaohua out of the clinic, the nurse told them that no further payment was needed. Actually, the doctor had offered them some help privately. Wanping and her little family were so thankful to know that there were still many kind people in the world. This kindness was especially important and appreciated during these times made so much more difficult by war.

Once they had returned to the school where they were staying, they discovered that a lot of people were gone, having been relocated to a temporary village. The village had been quickly built in the space of a week in order to help the refugee military families have a place to settle down. Wanping and Jiaming, though, did not know where this village was. In the afternoon, a military officer came to see them.

"We are relocating all military families to a military village. If you want to join them, we will take you there in the early morning tomorrow. Please get everything ready before we pick you up," the officer said.

Since Wanping and Jiaming did not know where else they could go, they agreed and thanked the officer. That evening was spent packing so they would be ready. The next morning a truck arrived. They, along with all their belongings and five other families, climbed into the back. The truck left Jilong City and drove toward Taipei City. Along the way they were told they would be relocated to a village called Muzha, an eastern suburb of Taipei City. The truck took a route that connected Jilong to Muzha without passing through Taipei.

As the truck neared the military village, Jiaming and Wanping saw a very beautiful, large rice field next to a mountain. Between the field and mountain, there was a nice, clean creek with many willow trees along its bank. They watched some white cranes land in the tops of bamboo trees growing next to the rice field. The scene was so peaceful and serene. Then they saw a small hut next to the creek about half a mile away from the main road. They did not know why or how the hut had come to be there. They guessed that perhaps it was a hunting hut that had been used by the Japanese for hunting. While they were appreciating the calm beauty of the scene, their truck arrived at its destination. The new military village was only about two miles from the creek and its little hut.

Within an hour of their arrival, Wanping, Jiaming and Xiaohua had been placed in a temporary cottage. In the village, thousands of these cottages had been built for the military refugees and almost all of them were already occupied. It was very crowded and noisy. At the end of each month, they were told, they would receive NT$200 from the government since Jiaming's father was a high-ranking officer in Chiang's government. This pension payment would continue until the officer's spouse, Wanping, passed away. It was a relief to learn of the pension. Without an income, Wanping's little family could not last long.

After a while, though, life in the village became unbearable. Although Xiaohua had been getting stronger each day since they were able to use some of the pension money to buy more nutritional food for her in the free market of the village, it was also true that they often saw fights and arguments amongst the people living in the village. In this kind of situation, where the space was cramped and resources were slim, it seemed everyone had become more selfish and greedier. They also discovered there were many thieves in the village.

One afternoon, Jiaming approached his mom while Xiaohua was sleeping.

"Niang!" he said, "I don't feel comfortable living in this crowded place. There is no peace and harmony here."

"What option do we have, Jiaming? It seems we are stuck here with the others until a further development," Wanping said.

"Remember that beautiful place at the foot of the mountain we saw the other day? It is not too far from here. I want to go there and see if we might be able to live there by ourselves," Jiaming said.

"Are you sure we can survive if we move there?" Wanping asked curiously.

"Niang, I will take a look first this afternoon and see if it is possible," Jiaming replied.

That afternoon, Jiaming left the village and walked along the public road back toward the creek they had seen the day the truck had brought them. It took him about 40 minutes to walk the two miles to the creek. Then, he walked along a small path next to the creek until he came to the hut they had seen. The hut was about 8 feet by 8 feet. Some daylight illuminated the interior through holes in the aluminum sheet that made up the roof.

"It is small, and many places are rotten. This hut must have been built many years ago," Jiaming said to himself. Inside he saw two wooden beds on each side of the hut, and at the corner near the entrance there was a small cooking stove. Jiaming stood right in front of the hut and faced the creek. The view of the large rice field filled him a warm, peaceful feeling. "It seems this hut does not belong to anyone. I think I can improve it to make it habitable," he thought.

To get to know the area better, Jiaming followed a wider path that ran along the rice field. After two miles or so, he came across a few farmhouses, and a little bit farther on in his investigations he discovered another stream, bigger than the creek next to the hut. In addition, there was another big rice field on the other side of stream. It seemed that this stream was the main water supply to many rice fields on both sides of it.

Jiaming walked for another hour or so until he felt he had gotten a good idea of the environment near the hut. "I believe living here would be better than living in the military village," he thought.

Jiaming turned his steps back toward the village and, on his way, he began to plan how to move to the creek and how he would re-build the hut. The more he thought about it, the more excited he became. When he returned, Wanping and Xiaohua were waiting for him with a dinner of sweet potatoes and pickles; meat was too expensive for them to afford. As soon as he saw them, he told them about what he'd found.

"Niang! Xiaohua! I think we should move to the hut we saw the other day. I was there today and took a survey of the nearby area. I believe we will be happier there," Jiaming said.

"Well! Let us experience it and see if it is habitable there," Wanping responded.

Xiaohua was happy to move out of the military village. She also had not felt comfortable living there.

Jiaming knew that the next day a truck was going to Taipei City. Jiaming asked the driver if he would take his family to the creek area two miles from the village. Since it was on the way to Taipei City and the truck was empty, the driver granted his request and took them there in the morning.

As Jiaming, Wanping and Xiaohua left the truck and walked toward the hut, they could see some fish swimming in the creek. The sight of fish swimming in the clean water made them very happy. The place was so beautiful, with a mountain on one side of the creek and the rice field on the other.

Once she saw the hut, however, Wanping expressed her doubts.

"Jiaming, are you sure that we can live here? Does this place belong to someone? Can this hut be used for living? It looks like much of the wood has rotted and the roof was leaking."

"Niang, we will see once we move in. We will know if this place belongs to someone. We can always move back to the military village if needed. As to the rotten wood and leaking roof, I can repair them in a few days," Jiaming replied.

With that, they decided to move in and see what happened.

Over the next few days, Jiaming used some of their limited money to buy wood and some aluminum sheets in the village. He also bought nails and a hammer, cookware, and utensils. These items were common and easy to find since a lot of farmers used these materials. He fixed the beds and made them stronger. He also made another portable bed for himself. Then he repaired the oven with some abandoned bricks he found in the village. Finally, he reinforced the structure of the roof.

Once the hut was made livable, Jiaming bought some food and vegetables. He gathered dried branches from the ground for cooking. Then he took stock of their new situation. He realized that the money they had was getting low and there were still 15 days before the next pension payment. Jiaming had to find a way to make money quickly.

The problem was that they were strangers here, and most Taiwanese were not happy about the presence of Chiang's government or the recent influx of people from foreign provinces. Furthermore, there was another major obstacle - he could not speak the Taiwanese dialect while almost all Taiwanese did not speak Mandarin.

One day when he was in the village, Jiaming found many pieces of abandoned wood and a few sheets of aluminum. He knew from the scraps that some farmer must be repairing or rebuilding his cottage or storage room. He was very happy with his find and took the scraps home one by one. After a few trips he was exhausted from all of the walking and carrying the materials to the hut. He realized that he could not keep moving objects like this. It was too difficult and tiring for him.

When he came to the village again the next day, he discovered a small two-wheeled trailer that had been abandoned next to a tool shop. He asked the owner of the shop if he could buy the trailer. The owner had just bought a new one and was ready to get rid of the old one.

Since it was difficult for them to talk to each other, the owner wrote on a piece of paper, "If you want it, I can sell it to you for NT$30. You will have to replace one of the tires, though. It was leaking. A new tire will cost you about NT$15."

When Jiaming took his money out and counted it, he had only NT$40. He felt awkward and a little bit embarrassed. The owner of the shop noticed and nodded his head to indicate that Jiaming could have the trailer and a new wheel even though he was NT$5 short. Jiaming thanked the owner and borrowed the tools to replace the tire. He was so happy as he headed back to the hut, pulling the trailer behind him.

On his way through the village, Jiaming saw many more objects that he thought would be useful to him. As he went along, he put each discovery on the trailer. He kept doing so for a few days. Then he found out there was a shop in the village that purchased discarded metal and bottles, then sold the recyclable materials back to factories at a profit. Once he realized this, Jiaming began to collect discarded metals and bottles from garbage piles. Also, in the garbage dumps he found many other useful things such as old clothes, a comforter, a blanket, etc. He brought all his discoveries home where Wanping and Xiaohua would wash them in the creek. After being dried under the sun, the items were clean and useful again. With this new enterprise they had two income sources: scavenging and the pension payment. Now they could at least live without having to go hungry.

After Wanping's family had been living in the hut for a couple of weeks, the villagers in the area noticed there was a foreign province family among them, and soon word was passed to the landlord on the other side of creek.

"There is a foreign province family that has moved into the hut on the other side of the creek next to our land. I don't like it. I don't like strangers, especially those foreign province people!" the owner of the farm, Zunxian, said to his family during dinner one night.

This hatred between Taiwanese and foreign province people had arisen because of the February 28, 1947 revolutionary riot against Chiang's government when many Taiwanese were killed. It had been forbidden by the government to talk about this event, but it was well known by the general public and remembered bitterly, especially by the older generations. Furthermore, Chiang's retreat from Mainland China had resulted in more than 1.2 million people pouring into Taiwan within a very short amount of time. Almost instantly, 13% of the population in Taiwan was made up of refugees. This caused many social problems that were exacerbated by the many bad people also entering Taiwan and committing crimes.

"Zunxian, that piece of land belongs to no one! It was public land belonging to Xizikou Mountain (溪子口山). It was the government's property during the Japanese period," Zunxian's father, Jianhong (健宏), said.

"I don't care! I just don't like it. I will gather a few local rowdies in the village to give them trouble and push them away," Zunxian said angrily.

"Zunxian, listen to me! Life is not easy for them! They are refugees and have lost their home on the Mainland. You should be more merciful to them. In this case, Buddha will bless you and the Heavens will protect you," Zunxian's mom, Shufen (淑芬), said.

Zunxian was not convinced. He just did not like strangers around his property, especially strangers from Mainland China. There was too much hatred between Chiang's government and the Taiwanese people.

"Zunxian, please listen to me! Not all those people are bad. Just think if we were in their position. They don't bother us, and we should not bother them," his mom said again.

Zunxian's father kept quiet since he did not like foreign province people either. But what his wife said was also right. We should have compassion and a merciful heart.

"Zunxian! I say just leave them alone and see what happens in the future," the old man said.

Since Zunxian's father said so, Zunxian did not insist on following through with his idea. He decided instead to watch them closely and see how the future developed.

A BRIEF WEDDING 簡單的結婚

Two months after they had moved into the hut, Jiaming built another small room next to the old one. He also built a firm wooden bed for himself. His mother and Xiaohua then shared the new room and he stayed in the old room.

One morning during breakfast Wanping said, "Jiaming! Xiaohua! Listen to me. If both of you agree I would like to be your matchmaker. I would like to see both of you get married. In this case, we will be a real family."

After listening to Wanping, Jiaming and Xiaohua simply bowed their heads very low without saying anything. In Jiaming's heart, he had known he liked Xiaohua from when he first saw her in Shanghai. To Xiaohua, Jiaming was her lifesaver, and a good man, which was hard to find. When Wanping mentioned it again, Jiaming responded.

"Niang, we have been treating each other like brother and sister already," Jiaming said.

"Think, Jiaming! We are in a very different country and we need to build a family here. Furthermore, I am getting old. I wish to see my grandkids before I die," Wanping said. "What do you think, Xiaohua? Will you marry my son?" Wanping persisted, looking at Xiaohua.

Xiaohua kept her head down but nodded a few times.

Jiaming was very excited. Wanping proposed having the wedding on February 6th, the day of the Chinese New Year. This was an auspicious date that would bring happiness. When the day arrived, Jiaming bought some red candles, incense, a chicken, some other meats, and vegetables. It was an especially happy day for everyone. After placing these tributes on an old table that Jiaming had found in his scavenging a few weeks earlier, Wanping lit the candles and burned the incense. She gave Jiaming three and Xiaohua three. First, they knelt down to the ground in front of the door and thanked the Heaven and the Earth. Next, both Jiaming and Xiaohua knelt down in front of Wanping and touched their heads to the ground three times. This completed a simple but solemn ceremony. Heaven and Earth were their witnesses. Jiaming and Xiaohua were husband and wife.

Wanping was so happy - she felt this was the happiest day she had had all year. That evening, Jiaming moved into the new small room he had just built and Wanping moved back to the old room. It would be a new, happy Chinese Year of the Rabbit.

AN UNEXPECTED INCIDENT 意外事件

Sixty-five-year-old grandpa, Jianhong (健宏), was taking his five-year-old grandson, Nianxiong (年雄), from a neighbor's home back to their home. It was drizzling out as they walked. Half way to their house the sky opened up and rain poured down in torrents. The water level of the stream beside them rose up quickly and ran more swiftly. Grandpa and grandson rushed to get home. The old man was using one of his hands to hold his umbrella and the other hand to hold his grandson's hand. The bridge over the stream was narrow, made from only three logs of wood. As they were crossing it, suddenly the boy slipped and fell into the swift flow of the stream.

"Help! Help! If someone is there, please help. Oh, my heavens!" the old man yelled in a panic as he watched his grandson being rapidly carried away by the roiling current. He wanted to jump in to save his grandson, but the water was deep and fast, and he knew he was too old. Furthermore, he did not know how to swim. He did not know what to do.

Jianhong cried out again, "Help! Help! Someone, please help!" He kept shouting as tears ran down his face.

Due to the rain, Jiaming had decided to stop his scavenger work early that day. He was walking on the path along the stream to go home when he saw the old man waving his hands and shouting on the bridge. Although it was too far away for him to hear what the old man was saying, he could tell from the man's agitated manner that something alarming was happening. Then he saw a boy in the stream flowing directly toward him and knew exactly what had happened. Immediately, he put his things down, and jumped into the stream just in time to catch the boy as he was tumbled along by the water. Due to the strong current, however, Jiaming was now also carried away with the boy clutched in his arms. It was not till nearly 50 yards later when, finally, Jiaming was able to grab hold of a branch of a willow tree that had fallen into the river from the bank. With a firm grip on the tree and an arm wrapped around the boy, he climbed up the bank from the stream.

Jiaming laid the unconscious boy on the path next to the bank and knelt down beside him. He was trying to revive the boy as the old man hurried toward them from the bridge. Jianhong's eyes were filled with tears. He did not know if his grandson was still alive. When he arrived, he saw Jiaming was trying to revive his grandson by pushing on the boy's stomach and then pressing his Renzhong cavity (人 中 穴). Jianhong watched anxiously with worry and apprehension. Finally, the boy spat out a great deal of water from his stomach and gradually opened his eyes.

As Nianxiong became aware of his surroundings he realized a stranger was holding him. Seeing his grandpa standing next to him, he cried out, "A Gong! A Gong (阿公, Grandpa)!" and extended his arms toward his grandpa.

Jianhong immediately scooped up the boy. "My dear grandson! Thank heavens you are okay!" he cried through his tears. The rain continued to pour down on them, so that the old man who had stayed out of the stream was just as wet as the two who had been in it.

Suddenly, the old man knelt down in front of Jiaming and, using the Taiwanese dialect, said "Duoxia! Duoxia (多謝, many thanks)!"

Jiaming knew what it meant even though he did not know much of the Taiwanese dialect. Immediately he grasped the old man's arms to lift him from where he knelt. The old man's and Jiaming's hearts were together, and the distance between a foreign refugee and a local Taiwanese suddenly disappeared.

Jiaming escorted them home before returning to his cottage. He did not mention the event to either his mom or Xiaohua. He did not want them to worry about it.

Grandpa Jianhong, though, told everyone in sight once he got home. After explaining what had happened to his wife, son, and daughter-in-law, they all realized that if they had forced Jiaming and his family out from their temporary home a few months ago, their precious little boy would have died for sure that day. They began to comprehend what the grandma always said, "Good heart with good deed will always receive good Baoying (報應, i.e. karma) and blessing from Buddha."

The sky was clear the next morning. The temperature had risen a few degrees to give people a pleasant warm feeling. Jiaming was getting ready to leave home for his daily scavenge when the old man arrived with his son, Shen, Zunxian (沈尊賢). They had brought a rooster with them.

"Duoxia (many thanks)! You saved my son's life," the farmer, Zunxian said in Taiwanese and tried to give Jiaming the rooster and a red envelope containing money.

"No! No! Da Bo (大伯, Great Uncle). Please don't be so polite," Jiaming responded in Mandarin and refused to accept either the chicken or the money.

In spite of their language barrier, Jiaming and Zunxian understood each other perfectly. Wanping and Xiaohua, quietly watching, did not know what was going on since Jiaming had not mentioned this incident to them.

Zunxian and his father continued to insist until, finally, Jiaming accepted the rooster but refused the money. While they talked, Zunxian and his father observed their surroundings. They had never come near this place before. Naturally, they did not know the poor, miserable living conditions Jiaming's family lived in. There was no door to the cottage, but just a few pieces of rotten, wooden boards that stood for walls and a few aluminum sheets as the roof. A tiny corner functioned as a kitchen. More wood boards were used for beds. All of these were squeezed into a very tiny place. From what they saw, Zunxian and his father felt very sorry about how Jiaming and his family were mistreated by the local Taiwanese.

"We shouldn't misjudge all the people from Mainland China due to a few bad guys. There are many good people with good hearts," they thought. Zunxian and his father left with a new understanding and a greater appreciation of their neighbor's struggle, and with the nice warm feeling of a new friendship.

Since then, the two families always greeted each other when they passed each other. Word quickly spread to the other neighbors who also came to have a different view of this family. When they met on the road, instead of ignoring or shunning the other party, they tried to communicate with each other. One day, early in the morning, Zunxian came to visit Jiaming with another person. This person spoke Mandarin.

"Ninhao (您好)! My name is Dexin (德信). Zunxian wants me to tell you that he would like to hire you and your wife for farm work, especially in the busy farming season."

Jiaming was surprised to meet a Taiwanese that could speak Mandarin so well. However, he was so happy that finally through Dexin, he would be able to communicate with Zunxian's family.

"How can you speak Mandarin so fluently? There are few Taiwanese who know how to speak Mandarin," Jiaming asked with curiosity.

"I went to the Mainland for business with my father many years ago before the Japanese invasion." Dexin smiled with pride that he could speak Mandarin.

Dexin went on to explain that Zunxian wished to hire them to help with the farming. Springtime had arrived and Zunxian would need many workers.

"But I don't know anything about farming," Jiaming explained.

"Zunxian said it does not matter. You and your wife can begin with simple things and learn. By no time, you will be an expert in farming," Dexin responded.

Jiaming knew that this was an attempt by Zunxian to help them improve their poor financial condition. Zunxian did not need to hire them - there were plenty of Taiwanese around and available to work. Deep in his heart, Jiaming appreciated the offer very much. He knew this would help his family significantly. He nodded his head with a smile and looked at Zunxian with deep appreciation.

"Zunxian would like you to begin tomorrow morning. You know, the busy season has just started," Dexin said.

"Thank you very much! My wife and I will be there tomorrow morning. How early should we be there, may I ask?"

"All farmers usually begin their work right after dawn. Can you make it?" Dexin said.

"No problem! We all get up early and Zunxian's farm is just next to us. We'll be there on time tomorrow morning."

After Zunxian and Dexin left Jiaming looked happily at his mother and wife. "Working on the farm is better than scavenging," he said. "The best part is that it seems the local community has accepted us. This will improve our relationship with our neighbors and give us better hope for the future." Jiaming was delighted that their future would be improved.

Next morning at dawn, Jiaming and Xiaohua went to Zunxian's house. Jiaming knew the way from when he had taken Zunxian's father and son home a couple of weeks ago. Zunxian invited them in to have breakfast. Though Jiaming and Xiaohua had already eaten before they came, they did not refuse since this would offer them a chance to get to know the farmer and his family better. Breakfast was simple with some eggs, rice soup, and some pickles, but there was plenty of it.

Using a mixture of talking combined with hand gestures, everyone somehow managed to communicate with each other without too much trouble. While Jiaming and Xiaohua were paying close attention to this language that was new to them, Zunxian's family and a few other workers were also interested in learning some simple Mandarin. The atmosphere was filled with harmony, cheer, and laughter.

Xiaohua was assigned to work with a few other women doing some light work such as sorting the seeds to select the big ones for planting. She was also responsible for helping cook for the men who worked in the fields. Three large meals and two light meals were served each day. Jiaming went to work with the strong men in the field. He learned how to coordinate with others very quickly. In just a few days, Jiaming and Xiaohua were able to fit into the routine on the farm very smoothly.

Time passed quickly. While they were working there, Zunxian's wife, Xiumei (秀美) often gave Jiaming and Xiaohua some extra food and vegetables to take home. This kindness helped Jiaming's family significantly. By the end of April, as was Taiwanese custom, the owner of the farm, Zunxian, held a banquet for all his workers. This planting season would last for one more month. After that, they would not need as many people to operate the farm for maintenance. The next busy season would start four months later. Since Taiwan was located in a tropical area, farmers could grow rice twice in the north and three times in the south. Jiaming's mother, Wanping, was also invited to the banquet. This was the first big feast they had had since they arrived in Taiwan.

After dinner, every worker received their payment in an envelope. When Jiaming and Xiaohua received their envelopes, their eyes turned red. This was the first payment they had earned from formal work. They waited to open their envelopes until they got home. Jiaming found there was NT$400 in his, while Xiaohua had NT$300. They all knew that Zunxian had paid them more than the other workers. Usually, for this kind of work, a man would earn about NT$300 while a woman would receive only NT$200. This was a lot of money to them.

When Jiaming was working as a scavenger, he only earned about NT$5 per day. Jiaming used some of the money to buy building materials to improve the condition of their cottage, especially the leaking roof. They also began to save money for the future. They knew that after one more month, when the season was over, they might not have the farming job anymore.

In just a few months, Xiaohua had already learned some of the Taiwanese dialect and was able to communicate with the local people without a problem. This helped her to develop good relationships with them. In turn these good relationships, along with the sewing skills she had learned from her mother, made it possible for her to accept jobs making clothes for her neighbors. Most of the time, she went to her customers' homes and worked there, but occasionally she took the work to her own home.

One day when Jiaming was working on the farm, he was asked to retrieve some farm tools from the storage room. When he entered the room, deep in a corner he saw an abandoned bicycle with both tires flat. The bicycle appeared to have been there for a long time. During the lunch break Jiaming approached the farmer.

"Mr. Shen, I saw there is an old bicycle in the corner of the storage room. Is it possible for me to borrow it?" Jiaming asked.

"Ya! I forgot about it already. It has been there for more than five years. It belonged to my father's Japanese friend. After the Japanese surrendered, and before he went home, the friend gave it to my father. I don't think it can be ridden unless you fix it. If you want it, you can have it," Zunxian said.

"Really? Many thanks. This would help me quite a lot. I will fix it." Jiaming bowed to Zunxian with appreciation.

After he finished his farm work that day, Jiaming took the bicycle to a shop and bought two new tires. Once he had fixed the bike, he rode it home. He was so happy. Having the bike to ride shortened the time it took him to get around by at least half when he travelled. Furthermore, he found he could tie his trailer to the back seat of the bicycle when he went out to do his scavenging. This made the work faster and easier so that he was able to cover a much wider area. Now that he had the bicycle, his scavenging income increased significantly.

About two years later the Taiwanese government implemented a land reform program that took away most of the privately held land from the landlords. Each landlord was allowed to keep only five to ten acres of land. The government paid the landlords for their loss based on a very low price, and then distributed the taken land to tenant farmers who applied for it. Though this program was set up very differently from the land reform in Mainland China a couple of years earlier that had caused an estimated 2 to 4.5 million deaths, still the reform in Taiwan caused a lot of complaints and resentment.

Naturally, Zunxian's family also lost most of the land they had inherited from their ancestors. The need for helpers to work the farm was significantly reduced. In spite of his loss, Zunxian still found ways to help Jiaming so his family would have some extra income. But once again, the main source of income for Jiaming returned to relying on his scavenging.

One day when Jiaming came to the rich village to scavenge, he found a mid-sized bicycle at the public dump. One of the wheels was missing and the one that was left was flat. At first, he thought about selling it to a metal collector, since the metal of this bicycle could bring him at least NT$30. He hesitated for a while, and in the end took the bike home on his pulling trailer.

"This can be fixed. When we have extra money to buy another wheel, I can fix it. Then this can be used by Xiaohua when she goes to work," Jiaming thought. He took it home and put it outside of the cottage under the roof.

New Hope 新希望

Since they had arrived in Taiwan, whenever they could, Wanping and Jiaming would inquire through all the military units to see if there was any information to be found about Hanmin. After five years of searching, they were pretty sure that Hanmin (漢民) was not in Taiwan. Otherwise, the military authority would have a record of it, especially since he was a high-ranking officer.

After the Korean War ended on July 27th of 1953, more than 14,000 prisoners of war who had either surrendered to or were captured by the American military had chosen to come to Taiwan and join Chiang's force in the fight against Communism. According to what was known, almost all of them were originally soldiers of Chiang's who had, earlier in the war, either surrendered or been captured by the Communists in the wars between Chiang's army and the Liberation Army. The Communists had put them in the front line as a sacrifice in the Korean War against American troops, since the Communist Party did not really trust them. These anti-communists (反共義士)

arrived in Taiwan on January 23rd of 1954. Two days later, Jiaming came back from his scavenge with some exciting news for his mother.

"Niang! According to the newspaper, more than 14,000 of President Chiang's old soldiers arrived in Taiwan, from Korea, two days ago," Jiaming exclaimed. His right hand was holding an old newspaper he had found in his scavenging. Since this was not a busy farming season, he had once again returned to earning some income that way.

"Really? That is good news. We may find some information about your Die from them." Wanping felt her excitement rise along with a new hope that she might at last find her husband, Hanmin. After thinking for a few minutes, she decided to ask her son to go look for word of him.

"Jiaming, I know we need you here to earn money to survive," she said, "but can you go to Jilong Port and try to see if you can find out any news? We may be lucky to find some comrades of your father among them."

"Niang, how would I find them though?"

"From the document we have, your Die was the commander of first Ying (營, Battalion) of first Tuan (團, Regiment). This Tuan belonged to second Lü (旅, Brigadier) of second Shi (師, Division). This Shi was under the command of 35th army unit General Guo, Jingyun (郭景雲)."

"I cannot remember all of this. Can I take the document to town and make a copy of it? I also believe if I have the copy of the original, it will be more convincing when I ask around," Jiaming said.

"Yes, you may. But remember this document is very important. Without this document, we will lose our identity. Take care of it carefully," Wanping replied.

Jiaming took the document in its large envelope and went to town with it early the next morning. He knew there was a new copy shop in the town from when he scavenged there. At the shop he made a copy and then rushed back home with excitement at the possibility that they might have a chance to know what had happened to his dad.

Jiaming said good-bye to his mother, then went to the Taipei train station and took the train to Jilong Port. By train the trip was only 90 minutes. Once in Jilong, he asked and searched around until he found the military center that was responsible for taking care of a few groups of anti-communists. He went into the office and approached one of the military service men there.

"Sir, would you please help me?" Jiaming asked. He explained to the officer that he was looking for his father and showed him the copy of his document.

The officer replied, "We don't know yet. It is still all chaotic. There are more than 14,000 of them. We are trying to sort it out. There are all kinds of people inside. We need to check them clearly before we relocate them."

"How long will it take, sir?"

"Probably a few weeks or possibly even months. We will have a better idea after everything is sorted out. Give me the document and I will make a copy to keep. Also give me your address. When I have any information, I will write you a letter," the officer said.

Since there was no other choice, Jiaming gave the officer the document and waited while he left with it. After five minutes or so, the officer returned.

"Write down your address on this paper. I will submit it for you," the officer instructed.

Since Jiaming's cottage did not yet have an assigned address, he gave the officer the address of Zunxian, whom he had worked for. This task done, Jiaming returned home with some disappointment. It was nearly midnight by the time he arrived home. His mother and Xiaohua were still awake and waiting anxiously for his return.

"Niang, they told me that they have not managed the settlement yet for these soldiers. I gave them Mr. Shen's (沈先生) address. They said they would notify us when they had any news."

Wanping also felt disappointed, even though she had known that the chance of learning anything was slim. "You better tell Mr. Shen about this so when they receive letter they are not surprised," she said.

"Yes, Niang. I will tell them tomorrow."

SAD NEWS 傷心的消息

Time passed very slowly. Both Wanping and Jiaming waited and waited anxiously and patiently. The combination of worry, excitement, and anxiety tortured Wanping. She could not sleep peacefully and was often awakened in the middle of the night by nightmares. When she woke up, she couldn't help thinking about the past and crying. She worried and missed her husband and eldest son very much. Her hope diminished with each week that passed. This affected her health, which very quickly deteriorated. Jiaming and Xiaohua worried about her, but they did not know what to do. They just tried to comfort her as much as they could.

Finally, nearly six months later, one month after farming season, Mr. Shen came to see them one afternoon. When he arrived, Jiaming and Xiaohua were out working and were not home. Mr. Shen talked to Wanping using the poor Mandarin he had learned.

"I just received this letter this morning. I hope this is what you are waiting for," he said.

"Thank you, Mr. Shen. Thank you very much." Wanping's hands shook as she received the letter from Mr. Shen. She was excited as well as nervous.

After Mr. Shen left, she opened the letter, which said, "There was a soldier name Wang, Chengde (王承德), who belonged to the 35th army unit. He may have the news you are looking for. He has been relocated to Hualian (花蓮) county for highway construction."

Wanping cried out loud at this news. Attached to the letter was another note containing the name of the soldier and his address. She couldn't wait for Jiaming and Xiaohua to return. When they did, she told them with excitement, "Jiaming! We may have a clue to find your Die," and she gave Jiaming the letter.

"Niang, we must go to Hualian to talk to this Mr. Wang! Hualian is on east side of Taiwan and it would take at least two days for the trip. Do you want me to go alone or will you come with me?" Jiaming asked.

"I will come with you. But we cannot leave Xiaohua alone at home," Wanping said.

"Niang, please don't worry about me. I can take care of myself. Just go with Jiaming and hope there is good news there," Xiaohua said.

"No! No! That's too dangerous in these days. It is not quite peaceful yet." Jiaming spoke with worry and deep concern in his voice.

"If all of us go, do we have enough money for traveling?" Wanping asked.

"Niang, it will exhaust more than half of our savings. But I think this is important and we should all go together. If Xiaohua stays home by herself, I will be worried to death."

Xiaohua listened to Jiaming's words and was happy to hear them. She knew Jiaming loved her deeply, even though he was not a romantic person and did not express himself. He was simple, pure, innocent, and always shy. She kept her head down. The fact was, she also worried about how she could pass two days by herself.

The next morning, they all took off together. Since there was no railroad from Taipei to Hualian at that time, they had to take a bus. After nearly eight hours and a few bus transfers, finally, they arrived in Hualian. It was late in the day and they knew it would be hard to find Mr. Wang's lodging place. They found a cheap hotel to stay in overnight. Though it was reasonably comfortable, Wanping was kept awake the whole night with anxiety and worry.

They rose early the next morning and asked for directions to the highway construction site. Another bus brought them there and they finally arrived around 10 a.m. At the office of the construction head-quarters, they asked after Mr. Wang and explained to an officer the purpose of their visit.

"Madam, I am sorry to tell you that all of the workers are in a field right now that is at least one hour away by car. They will not be back to the dormitory till tonight. Furthermore, you cannot go there. It is too dangerous," the officer told them.

Upon hearing this, Wanping eyes filled with tears. The officer saw it and could also see how frustrated his three guests were.

"Let me contact the manager of the construction site and see if he approves Mr. Wang's absence today. He can return when there is a car coming back here this morning. But I am not sure when he can be here," the officer said.

"Thank you very much, sir. You are so kind," Jiaming replied with great sincerity. He also was sad to see his mother's disappointment.

The officer picked up the phone and called the construction site. He explained the situation to them and conferred with them for a bit, then turned back to Wanping.

"They told me they would pass the message to the construction manager. Hope we have good news in an hour," he said.

Wanping nodded her head gratefully. They were shown to a wait-ing room where they sat as patiently as they could. About a half hour later the officer came to see them.

"Good news. Mr. Wang has received approval from the construc-tion manager. He should be here by noon."

"Thank you again for your help, officer!" Wanping said, bowing to him.

Around 11:30, they saw a worker come in to the waiting room.

"Hi! I am Wang, Chengde. They told me you were looking for me."

Wanping answered him, "Yes. I hope I can ask for some news about my husband from you. You belonged to the 35th army unit in the past, right?"

"Yes, Madam. What is your husband's name?"

"Here is his name and ranking, Mr. Wang," Wanping said, giving him the military document about her husband.

When Mr. Wang looked at the document, he was surprised and

looked at Wanping with astonishment.

"Your husband is Major Lin, the Commander of First Ying of First Tuan. I heard about a lot of good deeds he had done during the war. He was a hero in many of our eyes."

"Do you have any news about him? Please, Mr. Wang," Wanping asked anxiously. Jiaming and Xiaohua stood close by, listening carefully.

"Mrs. Lin, actually, though I belong to the 35th Army Unit, I was in a different division. All the information I have about him was from one of the war prisoners like me. His name was Dong, Mingjie (董明傑). He belonged to Major Lin's division."

"Do you know where Mr. Dong is, Mr. Wang?" Jiaming asked.

"No. I met him three days before the start of the Korean War. In total, we had about 12,000 soldiers either captured or surrendered to the Communists at the end of the Battle of Pingjin. In the Korean War, he and I were assigned in the same group to attack the American army. He was killed in the attack. Before he was killed, we talked whenever we could. You know, as prisoners of the Communists, we were forbidden to talk to each other. However, whenever we saw a chance, we talked about the past. One thing we talked about was Major Lin."

"Please tell me what he said, Mr. Wang." Wanping looked at him anxiously.

Mr. Wang hesitated a little bit and his eyes turned red in sorrow. He did not know how to say what he knew in a way that would give Wanping some comfort.

"It was a tragedy, Madam, a tragedy!" Mr. Wang shook his head and did not know how to continue. It was just too sad to talk about.

Wanping could sense the unfortunate bad news. However, she looked directly into Mr. Wang's eyes and pleaded with him, "Please tell me. I need to know."

"The tragedy was on January 8th of 1949. When the Battle of Pingjin was at its hottest point, Major Lin accidently killed his eldest son."

This shocked Wanping and Jiaming. They could not believe what they had just heard.

"What! How did it happen?" Wanping couldn't help interrupting.

"Major Lin's son was in the Liberation Army and wounded in the Communists' third assault. After the Liberation Army retreated, Major Lin took his soldiers to scan the battlefield and collect weapons and ammunition. Suddenly, he saw a soldier of the Liberation Army stand up. Without hesitation, he pulled the trigger. Later, he discovered that this soldier was his elder son."

When Wanping and Jiaming heard of this they cried unashamedly, their tears flowing freely down their faces.

"My heavens! How could this happen?" Both of them were extremely disheartened and sad. Xiaohua did not know how to comfort them. In fact, she also felt very sad as the whole situation had made her think of her own lost parents and brother.

Mr. Wang broke off his story in the face of the anguish filling up the room. His eyes teared up in sympathy, but he was at a loss to know how to comfort them.

Wanping struggled to control herself. "Mr. Wang, please go on," she said through her tears.

"Mr. Dong said, Major Lin was so sad, and they could see his eyes were red all the time. It seemed that he had been crying when others weren't looking. Two weeks later, our troop was completely defeated by the Liberation Army. Communists had taken almost all of the territory. All we could do was fight and run at the same time. Mr. Dong told me that their unit of about 300 soldiers was running from the Communists who were giving chase. They all knew that they would be captured or killed in the next 20 minutes. When they reached a bridge, Major Lin ordered everyone to run as fast as they could. He took the machine gun and set it up at the entrance of bridge. He stayed behind to hold back the Liberation Army for at least 30 minutes. He sacrificed himself for his soldiers. On January 31st, the commander of 35-unit, General Guo, Jingyun (郭景雲), committed suicide."

When they heard of this, they all cried out loud. It was the only way to release their deep sorrow. Mr. Wang's eyes also filled with tears.

"He is our hero, you know, a real hero. He saved at least 300 people's lives that day. We will remember him forever." Mr. Wang did not know what else to say. He felt so sad. He stood up and bowed deeply to Wanping, then left.

Wanping and her little family sat for a while in their deep sorrow. They all knew now that there was no hope to ever see Hanmin and Jiaxiang again. Even their loved ones' dead bodies would be forever beyond their reach. They felt deeply the cruelty of the war that had ripped so many families apart.

There was nothing left to do, nothing left to learn. Dejected, they left the construction site to return to Hualian. It was late afternoon by the time they got back. As they had not eaten since breakfast, they bought some buns on the street to take back to the hotel. It was too late to go back to Taipei. They would have to stay at the hotel one more night. The next day they returned home in great sorrow. The only good to come from the trip was that now they knew what had happened to Hanmin and Jiaxiang and would no longer wonder about them constantly.

New Born and Wanping Passes Away 新生命與婉萍的過世

The sad news had brought huge shock and disappointment to the family, especially Wanping. Whenever she thought of her husband and eldest son, her eyes turned red. Her deep sorrow and the thought of missing them gradually affected her health.

One early morning in September 1955, a heavy mist of fog covered the mountain and the rice field. Cranes could be heard calling in the distance. When Wanping got up and got ready to prepare breakfast, she discovered Xiaohua vomiting next to the stream.

"Are you okay, Xiaohua? Don't catch cold in this chilly morning," Wanping said with concern and went to stand beside Xiaohua.

"Niang, I don't know what is happening! I just feel like I have to vomit." As Xiaohua said it, her face was very pale.

From the symptoms, Wanping suspected that Xiaohua might be pregnant but she was not 100% sure. Not wanting to mention it until she was certain, Wanping just comforted Xiaohua and told her to rest.

"I will take care of breakfast this morning. You just rest."

"Niang, I am sorry." Xiaohua felt guilty that she could not help to prepare breakfast.

Xiaohua's symptoms continued and after a couple of days, Wanping was pretty sure that Xiaohua was pregnant. She was so happy about the prospect of a grandchild, but at the same time she worried about their living conditions.

"These are not good conditions to raise up a child," she thought.

As soon as Jiaming came back from working at the farm, Wanping gave him the good news.

"Jiaming! You are going to be a father! Xiaohua has a baby in her stomach," Wanping said with a smile.

"Really? Really, Niang?" Jiaming exclaimed happily and went to hug his wife. Xiaohua was happy but also embarrassed. Jiaming had never expressed his emotions so openly before. She could feel how happy Jiaming was.

Time passed very quickly. While the whole family was excited about the new life, Wanping's health was rapidly deteriorating. Jiaming took his mom to see a doctor but the doctor did not help much.

He said she needed to rest more and sleep more; too much stress and lack of sleep would worsen her condition. Her heart was weakening fast and this had triggered some irregular beating.

By the end of May, Jiaming and Xiaohua were back working on the farm during the busiest plowing season. One day they returned from work with a request for Wanping.

"Niang, can you give a name to the new born? Xiaohua and I will be very happy if you would name the child," Jiaming told her.

"Well, how about Mingde (明德) if it is a boy and Suyue (淑慧), if a girl?" Wanping replied.

"Thank you, Niang. Those are good names." Jiaming and Xiaohua were delighted. But when they saw their mom's face covered with tears, "Niang! Are you OK?"

"I just wish your Die and Da Ge (大哥, Big Brother) were still alive and here with us," she cried. She missed her husband and elder son so much.

At midnight on June 15ᵗʰ, Jiaming was awakened by the sound of Xiaohua moaning. "Are you OK? Xiaohua?" he asked.

"I believe it is time. The baby is coming!"

Jiaming was excited and worried all at once. Wanping, who was already awake due to her sickness which kept her in constant pain, sent Jiaming to get help.

"You have to go to find the midwife, Mrs. Chen, right away. She lives a few houses away from the police station. Go quickly," Wanping said with excitement in her weak voice.

Jiaming ran very quickly to find the midwife to deliver the baby. It took him twenty minutes to get there. In the meantime, Xiaohua's labor pains had shortened from ten minutes to six minutes apart. Unfortunately, Wanping was too weak to offer much help. All she could do was worry and wonder why Jiaming and the midwife had not come back yet. Her heart beat faster and faster. It took nearly an hour for Jiaming to return with the midwife, who could not walk very quickly. By the time they arrived, Xiaohua was yelling in pain and Wanping was pale faced and breathing in short puffs.

The midwife immediately took a look at Xiaohua's situation while Jiaming went to Wanping to comfort her. Finally, Wanping began to calm down and breathe normally. In just another hour, Jiaming and Wanping heard a baby's crying. They were so excited. Jiaming came out of his mother's small room to find the midwife waiting for him.

"Congratulations! You have a son," the midwife said to Jiaming. She then told him how to take care of both the baby and the new mother. Jiaming paid her NT$50 and she left. The whole family was full of joy.

"Thank heavens! You have an offspring. You are a father now, Jiaming," Wanping told him.

Jiaming could see how happy Wanping was. Her face glowed with the satisfaction of a grandmother. "I wish your Die and Da Ge were here," she said again sadly. "Go to take care of your wife, I am okay."

Jiaming went into his room and sat next to Xiaohua where she lay on the bed holding the newborn in her hands. Jiaming just looked at her, letting the expression on his face and the tears in his eyes show the deep love and appreciation he had for her.

"Xiaohua, sorry for your suffering. We have a son!" he said with wonder.

Xiaohua could see how happy Jiaming was and basked in the moment. It was so seldom that he let his emotions show on his face.

Five days later, when Jiaming went to Wanping's room for breakfast, he discovered that she had passed away with a smile on her face while she was sleeping. It seemed that she was happy to see her grandson before she died.

Since they did not have much money for a funeral, Jiaming just buried his mother near the foot of the mountain where they could visit her easily. He missed his mother so much. In her honor, other than the formal name his mother had chosen, he also gave the baby a nickname, Nianci (念慈), which meant, "yearning mother." Since then, the boy's parents and close friends called him Nianci whether in school or in public, though his formal name was Mingde.

CHAPTER 3
NEW LIFE, NEW HOPES
新生命，新希望

HOPE FOR THE FUTURE 未來的期望

After Wanping passed away, life for Jiaming's family became very different. First, they lost the pension payment from the government. Second, income from working the farm was greatly reduced since the land reform policy had been carried out. Now, their main sources of income once again relied on Jiaming's scavenging and Xiaohua's tailoring at home. Sometimes, Jiaming would catch some fish, crab, shrimps, and clams from the creek. When the dry season arrived and he could catch more seafood, he would sell it in the market place. But he needed to be very careful as there were also many poisonous snakes living in the creek.

To counteract his sadness after Wanping's passing, Jiaming often held Nianci and carried him to the place about 100 yards from the hut where many willow trees grew. There he would sing a song and rock Nianci until he fell asleep. He also often brought Nianci to Wanping's gravesite and would sit there with him for a long time. He just missed his mother so much.

Occasionally, Jiaming was still hired to work at Zunxian's farm, especially during the plowing and harvest seasons. He knew that, actually, Zunxian did not need the extra help since he did not have a lot of land anymore. Zunxian just wanted to assist him as much as possible. In addition, more and more landowners were using machines to cultivate their land now instead of human power. Xiaohua continued receiving tailoring jobs here and there. Both of them put all of their hope and love into the new child.

When Nianci had learned how to walk and run, Jiaming had a lot of fun teaching him how to walk and run uphill, downhill, and along the narrow paths of the rice fields. This helped Nianci's balance and feeling of rooting. Nianci always had a good time with his father. Sometimes, Xiaohua would join their chasing game, but she could not last long. Her breathing would grow short and her face turned red with exertion easily.

When Nianci was four, the most interesting thing to him was watching his father catch fish, crab, shrimp, and clams. However, since he was small, and it could be dangerous in the flowing water, with the possibility of poisonous snakes around, Jiaming did not want him to enter the water. Instead, Nianci would stay with his mother along the path and watch Jiaming while he worked in the stream. Whenever Jiaming caught a big fish or a crab, everyone laughed and was happy. The three of them lived in isolation from the outside world with great happiness.

When Nianci was five, Xiaohua taught him how to sing and told him some old stories she had learned from her grandma. She remembered those days as the happiest time for her and her brother, Ronghua, as they sat next to their grandma and listened to her old stories. Xiaohua missed her family so much, especially her parents. She did not know where or how they were. She wished her mother could see Nianci. That would be the most joyful reward, just to see her mother's laughter and happiness.

Jiaming, whenever he had time, also liked to tell Nianci about his father, a tough military officer with great discipline who put all his love into his country. Nianci grew up under his parents' influence into a wise and thoughtful boy. He liked to sit alone among the willow trees. When Jiaming was out scavenging and Xiaohua was busy making clothes, he would go to the willow tree area, close his eyes, feel the air, listen to the water, and sing a song. By the age of six, he had already learned how to be independent.

One day, after Jiaming finished some garden work, he noticed the bicycle he had brought home seven years earlier. He had almost forgotten about it. The bicycle was mottled with rust. He thought again of selling it to the metal collector. Then he had a second thought.

"The frame of this bicycle is still strong. I may be able to fix it. Nianci will love to learn how to ride a bicycle."

Jiaming put the bicycle in his pulling trailer and took it to a bicycle shop in town. There he bought a wheel the same size as the other. He put new tires on the wheels. Then he bought a rust remover and took everything home. After he cleaned the bicycle, though it was not like new, it was still nice. Nianci watched with great curiosity as his father worked on fixing the bicycle. He sat next to his father and examined everything he did.

"Nianci! This is for you. It is your birthday gift this year," Jiaming said.

"What? I thought it was for Mom."

"Well! You can share with your mom. How about that?"

Nianci had always been taken by the sight of his father or other people riding their bicycles. He had wished he could learn how to ride a bike one day. Now, he couldn't believe that he had his own bicycle.

After Jiaming fixed the bike, he took Nianci to a flat field at the foot of the mountain. There he taught him how to keep his balance. Unfortunately, the bicycle was still too tall for Nianci, so Jiaming figured out a way to teach Nianci how to push the peddles whenever they came within reach of his feet. It took Nianci almost a month of practice before he could ride it comfortably. Once he had mastered the bicycle, he was so happy: now he had a toy that could quickly take him far from his home!

SCHOOL 上學

When Nianci was seven, according to new laws he was required to enter primary school. The law made it compulsory for any child to complete both primary and junior high school.

"Nianci, tomorrow I will take you to school. You will make many friends and learn how to read and write. It is very important for your future. I will come to pick you up when school is over. Hopefully, after a few weeks, you will know how to come home by yourself since I will not be able to pick you up every day. Understand?" Jiaming told Nianci at dinner one day. Zunxian had received a notice from the government a few days earlier about Nianci's schooling and had just brought the notice to them this morning.

The next morning, Jiaming took Nianci with his bicycle to Muzha Primary School. This was a completely new and foreign environment for Nianci, and he did not know what to expect. After his father left, he already felt lonely and sad. However, he hid his feelings because he did not want to cry in front of the other students. After a few days, he found he was always alone and could not find any friends in school. Later, he realized that he was one of the few foreign province students in the school, and that all the foreign students were despised and disliked by most of the Taiwanese students. It seemed that the hatreds and prejudices of the parents had been passed down to the next generation.

Soon, the foreign province students formed a group. They played with each other separately from the Taiwanese students. Often, the two sides argued and fought.

"You, foreign province pigs! You have killed so many Taiwanese, taken over our land, and abused us." This kind of language was often heard in the groups' arguments at school.

Nianci did not feel like joining them; he did not want to argue or fight. Instead he often sat alone and could not wait to go home each day. In his solitude, his mind kept pondering many things including hate, love, justice, righteousness, and compassion. These were concepts he had heard about from his parents' stories.

"Who am I? What will I do in the future? Will I be a useful man for society?" These questions kept hanging in his mind. Soon he had developed a habit of pondering and placed his feeling on others. He was more mature than the other kids.

It was not until six months later that Jiaming realized the problems Nianci was having in school. In an effort to help, he began to teach Nianci some of the Taiwanese dialect he had learned while working at the farm. Mandarin was the official language used in school and all students were required to learn it. In fact, to enforce this policy, often when a student was caught speaking the Taiwanese dialect, he or she would be punished. Behind the teachers' backs, though, almost all Taiwanese students spoke their own language.

Time passed quickly. Nianci learned the Taiwanese dialect from his father and from listening to the conversations of the Taiwanese students around him. He practiced the dialect out loud so that when he spoke, there was no accent and he could sound just like a native Taiwanese.

By the time he was in his second year of primary school, due to his fluent Taiwanese dialect, Nianci had begun to make more and more friends especially those kids from his village.

On Sunday, Jiaming usually stayed home so that he could have some precious time with Nianci. He missed all of the time he used to be able to have with his son. Since Nianci had started school, they seldom found time to talk and play with each other. On this Sunday, before breakfast, as usual, they woke up early. They always enjoyed the early morning air. Jiaming and Nianci walked to the willow trees while Xiaohua was preparing breakfast.

"Nianci, I hope you are enjoying school," Jiaming inquired with concern.

"Yes, Papa! I learn how to read and write. See I am able to write a short letter now. I know how to use a brush. I really like calligraphy. It offers me a peace and calm and at the same time teaches me how to focus," Nianci said.

Jiaming was shocked to hear what Nianci said.

"This kind of saying should not be from an eight-year-old boy. I cannot believe that he is so mature already," Jiaming thought. After they had sat down on a log under the trees, Jiaming carefully introduced a new type of lesson for his son.

"Nianci, you know your Yeye (爺爺, Grandpa) was a high rank military soldier. When your da bo (大伯, great uncle) and I were in high school, he told us, 'The most important thing for surviving in a battle is a high level of awareness and alertness. These two things can not only keep your life safe on the battlefield, they can also provide you important tools to survive in society and understand the meaning of life.' Is this too deep for you to understand, Nianci?" Jiaming asked.

"Papa, I would like to know more. I am always questioning myself, why am I here? What is the meaning of life? How do I find all these answers? Papa, I need to know! How do you build a high level of awareness and alertness?" Nianci asked.

Jiaming could see that his boy was so precious since he had already thought about these questions that were usually asked by children who were much older, at least in their teens.

"Nianci, the mind is the key to everything. My father told me that your mind could make you happy, make you sad, become a great person, or become a bad guy. If you are able to understand your mind and know how to control it, then you will have your life in your hands," Jiaming said.

"The key of this control is focus. When you are focused, your spirit will be high and when this happens, your awareness and alertness will be sharp," Jiaming continued.

"Papa, what is spirit? I've heard of it often, but nobody has told me what it is?" Nianci asked.

"According to Chinese belief from Yi Jing (易經, The Book of Change), there are two dimensions that live together in nature. One is called the Yang World (Yang Jian, 陽間) and the other is the Yin World (Yin Jian, 陰間). The Yang World is the material world that we can see all around us, while the Yin World is the spiritual world that we cannot see but can feel. The Yang World is the manifestation – the physical appearance of the Yin World. While we know a lot about the Yang World, we still don't know anything about the Yin World. That is why all religions have been trying to interpret the Yin World. Unfortunately, this has been misused and has become a tool for controlling people. Do you understand?" Jiaming asked. He was afraid that Nianci would not be able to comprehend such a complex concept at his young age.

"I will think about it, Papa! But how can I feel the spirit and raise it? You said focus. What does that mean?" Nianci asked.

"The way you focus is not from thinking. When you think, your thinking has dominated and manipulated the action. When you think, you are planning and using your intelligence to make things happen. This is not real focus. Real focus is from deep feeling, not thinking," Jiaming explained.

"I am confused now. If you are not thinking, where does the action come from?"

"The subconscious mind, Nianci! The subconscious mind is more truthful than the conscious mind, and it can only be reached through deep feeling. Our subconscious mind has memory but is not able to think like the brain. This subconscious mind resides at the center of the head where two red dots exist. Chinese Daoists call it Niwang Gong (泥丸宫). The most powerful thoughts in your mind originate from this center and you have to reach it through deep feeling," Jiaming explained.

"But, how do you reach it, Papa?"

"Through meditation. When you pay attention to this center, all thoughts generated from your conscious mind will disappear. For example, reflexes are generated from this subconscious mind through feeling. The most powerful action is the action of no action and the most powerful thought is the thought of no thought." Jiaming did his best to explain from what he remembered. When his father had taught these concepts to him Jiaming was already in his teens. At the time he had been very confused. Now that he was older and had more experience, he could see and feel what his father had been talking about.

"Papa, does that mean that the action of no action and the thinking of no thinking is the instincts that people talk about?" Nianci asked.

"Yes, when you have reached this level, all your actions and thoughts are initiated from your instincts. That is where the alertness and awareness originate. They are not from the conscious mind."

"How do I develop these, Papa?" Nianci asked with curiosity. Even though he did not understand half of what his father said, all of what his father was telling him was firmly taking root in his mind.

"For example, when you see a leaf moving, you pay attention. The eyes give you the connection between your mind and the object. However, once you are connected, place your feeling into the action of the leaf instead of thinking about it. Then, you will feel how naturally the leaf follows the breeze and acts accordingly. Once you feel the wind, then you will feel how the wind is made to move. All these are natural events that exist around us. However, we humans, like to interpret things through thinking and dominate the situation. That is why we have lost our natural instincts and our feeling of nature is shallow," Jiaming said.

"It is just like when you walk you don't think about walking and when you eat you don't think about eating. You just feel it like a fish swimming and a bird singing. There is no thinking about the subconscious actions. When you practice this for a long time, your feeling will be deeper than others, and naturally your alertness and awareness will be higher. My father told me that this was the most important key to survival on a battle field," Jiaming tried to explain further. But he knew this would be very confusing for Nianci to understand.

"That's enough for now. Let's go home! I believe your Mom is waiting for us for breakfast," Jiaming said.

All this conversation took only half an hour, but its contents gave Nianci a lifetime of pondering and searching. From this pondering, he learned how to place his mind into other people's minds and all-natural objects.

CHAPTER 4
DISASTER AND HARDSHIP
災難與困境

UNFORESEEN DISASTER 不可預知的災難

When Nianci was nine years old, there was a celebration on a Sunday for Zunxian's father's 80th birthday. More than 100 people were invited to the big banquet, including Jiaming and his whole family. Jiaming's family were the only foreign province people invited. Since he could speak some of the Taiwanese dialect now, he communicated easily with the other party goers. This improved his relationship with his neighbors, especially once they learned how he had saved the old man's grandson. Jiaming had never met more than half of these people before. They were all extremely curious about his past and how his family had managed to escape from Mainland China.

After dinner when it was getting late, Xiaohua took Nianci home while Jiaming stayed to socialize with the others. Nianci needed to get his rest since he had school the next morning. The party was cheerful, and everyone was in high spirits. Later, when they all had had quite a bit to drink, one of the guests complained about how poorly the landlords were treated by Chiang's party. Soon, this triggered more conversation and discussion. Finally, the forbidden subject, the 2-2-8 Incident, was brought up. Since the government had forbidden the subject to be discussed or talked about, many people, especially the younger ones, did not know the details. Everyone was curious.

One older guest said, "I was a teenager and I know everything in detail."

Now, everyone grew quiet and listened carefully since this was a rare chance to learn the truth.

"It happened between February 27 and May 16 of 1947. You know after the Japanese surrendered and left Taiwan in 1945, Chiang's government sent General Chen, Yi (陳儀) to Taiwan to take over control from the Japanese. However, after the takeover, the conditions in Taiwan got worse every day with corrupt politicians, police, and government workers. There was poor military discipline, and social mores were degrading. The government and military seized people's living supplies. Language barriers, inflation, extreme food shortages, serious unemployment and discrimination against Taiwanese people, and an unfair employment system further complicated things. These all made the atmosphere of hate against Chiang's government and foreign province people quickly get worse."

Old Chen sipped a mouthful of tea and continued, "Then a small incident happened that triggered the people in all of Taiwan against Chiang's party and rule. It happened on the street of Taipei right in front of Tianma Tea House on February 27th of 1947. When a policeman was investigating a case of forbidden private cigarette selling, he beat up the peddler, named Lin, Jiangman (林江邁) till he was bleeding. When people saw it, they circled around to watch the incident. Then the policeman pulled a gun, intending to scare people away. Unfortunately, the gun accidentally discharged and injured a watcher, named Chen, Wen-Han (陳文漢). This led to a big crowd of angry people going to the police station the next day and demanding justice, but the crowd was refused and suppressed. In just a few days, all Taiwanese on the entire island united together against Chiang's government."

All of the audience was quiet and listening carefully since they had never before had a chance to hear the incident described in so much detail. When the Old Chen paused a couple minutes with sigh, they pressed him for more information.

"What happened after that?" someone in the audience who could not wait asked urgently. His eyes were red, and his face wore an expression of great sadness and sorrow.

"General Chen requested support from Chiang. In a short time, the 21st army unit from Shanghai was sent to Taiwan to crackdown on the riot. Many people were killed. Alas! Three feet of ice on the river is not caused from one night of freezing!" His tears rushed out.

"How many people were killed?" another audience member asked.

"Nobody was sure! A rough estimate was between 18,000 and 28,000." Old Chen sighed again.

The entire audience was quiet for a long time. Everyone was angry and sad. They knew that almost all of the civilians killed had been young people.

"I don't think we should talk about it anymore. This incident was forbidden to be talked about by Chiang's government. We may have trouble if we don't stop," someone said with a frightened expression on his face.

"Why can't we talk about it? It is not fair. There is no justice," another one said.

"How about you, Mr. Lin? You were from Mainland China. What do you think?" someone asked.

This triggered everyone's interest and all focused on Jiaming. Actually, he also felt very bad about the incident and felt the injustice of the treatment of Taiwanese people by Chiang's party. However, he was raised under his father's tutelage to be loyal to Chiang's party. He felt awkward and reluctant to express his opinion. However, the pressure from the people around him to answer was so heavy.

Finally, he responded, "I feel very sorry about this incident. Actually, after the Japanese surrendered, it was not better on the Mainland either. The entire society was in a chaotic situation and the government was so corrupt. That was why Chiang's party lost the war to the Communists." He did not want to say much more. His heart was broken, and he felt very sad.

The audience wanted to ask more questions, but he felt too uncomfortable to answer. He simply bowed his head repeatedly in apology. The audience stopped pushing him further.

The meeting and discussion lasted until almost midnight. Finally, the party was over. On the way home, Jiaming had a very uneasy and inauspicious feeling.

Two days later, a mix of military and secret police came to Jiaming's home to arrest him. He knew the arrest was probably related to the discussion at the party a couple of days ago. His face turned pale and he just looked at Xiaohua. Before he could say anything, he was handcuffed and taken away by the military police on a jeep. Nianci was in school at the time and so did not see his father being taken away.

After Jiaming was gone, the secret police divided into two small groups: three men began to search the entire cottage and the other two began to question Xiaohua.

"Does your husband have any connection with the Communists?" they asked her.

"I don't think so. His father was a loyal high rank military officer of Guoming Dang (Chiang's party). I know he is against communism," Xiaohua answered.

"Does he have any connection with the Taiwan Independent Party?"

"No! He does not!" Xiaohua replied again.

The questions continued about when and how they came to be in Taiwan, and other inquiries in that vein. Then one of the secret police came into the room with a pistol he had found in Jiaming's bag.

"Do you know your husband has this pistol?" Xiaohua was asked.

Xiaohua was shocked to see it and to realize that Jiaming had had a pistol that she did not know anything about.

"I don't know where this came from! I have no idea. I never knew Jiaming had a pistol." Xiaohua began to cry. She was very frightened. She could feel that something bad was going to happen to the family. Over the last few years she had heard many stories about how many people, after they were arrested, simply disappeared, and were never seen again. She did not know what to do.

By the time the secret police had finished searching, all they had found was the one pistol with a few bullets, and some documents that proved Jiaming's father's military ranking and his services to Chiang's party in the past.

"You may go to see your husband tomorrow in Muzha military police station. He will be detained there for further investigation," one of the policemen said. Then they left poor, scared Xiaohua all alone.

Xiaohua could not help crying out loud. Her situation was so frightening and worrisome. When Nianci returned home from school in the afternoon, all he found was a pale and anxious mother. She had been too agitated to eat anything since the morning.

"Mom! What happened? What happened? Is Papa OK?" Nianci asked with great concern.

Xiaohua suddenly started to cry again, pulling Nianci closer and hugging him tightly. Nianci was shocked and did not know what to do. He clung to his mother until, after a while, she calmed down.

Xiaohua fiercely held back her tears so that she could tell Nianci what had happened. He needed to know the truth, even though he was only nine years old.

"Your father was arrested by military police this morning. I don't know why! I am just worried and scared."

"But why would they arrest him? He did not do anything illegal. Did he? Mom?" Nianci begged to know more.

"I don't know. I need to go to see him tomorrow at the Muzha military police station."

"Mom! Can I come with you? I want to come with you, Mom!"

"But you have school tomorrow, Nianci."

"Mom, this is a family emergency! If I cannot be there, my mind cannot be in school either. Mom! Please!"

"Alright! I need some courage tomorrow. With your company, I will feel better."

The next morning Xiaohua prepared some steamed buns and took Nianci on the back seat of the bicycle to Muzha. It took them more than half an hour to get to the station. After Xiaohua explained why they were there to the gate police, they were led to an office. There she registered the information required, before they were taken to the back of the building where there were about ten small cages made of wood. Each side of a cage was about four feet long. They saw many prisoners in the cages. When they were led to one cage in particular, Xiaohua noticed that it was Jiaming who was curled up on the bottom of the cage. He had not truly slept the whole night and was almost unconscious with fatigue. In such an uncomfortable cage, a prisoner could neither stand up nor lie down completely. Also, all the prisoner was allowed to wear was underwear. Nothing else.

"Jiaming! Jiaming! Wake up!" Xiaohua called to him.

"Papa! Papa!" Nianci could not help crying.

Jiaming roused himself and when he saw Xiaohua and Nianci, he couldn't speak for the sobs caught in his throat. He moved to the edge of cage and extended his hands to hold Xiaohua's and Nianci's.

"Jiaming! Why did they arrest you? Why?" Xiaohua asked once she had recovered her voice.

"At the party a couple days ago, the group criticized the government. To be easygoing with others, I joined them and said a few complaining words. I should not have said anything. I am so remorseful. I shouldn't have..." Jiaming's voice choked again.

"They also found a pistol in your old travel bag. Is it yours? Where did it come from? They asked me all these questions. I am so scared. Jiaming, I am so scared!" Xiaohua said through her tears.

"The pistol belonged to my Die. When I left the Mainland, I thought it could be dangerous on the way. I took the pistol, just in case we were robbed or in danger."

"Now, they suspect you are a Communist spy hiding in Taiwan with the intent of overthrowing Chiang's government. How can we prove your innocence?" Xiaohua asked.

"I don't know. They already questioned me twice yesterday. They will continue every day until I confess. But I have nothing to confess!" Jiaming replied.

"We just have to wait until everything is clear. You must be hungry," Xiaohua said.

"They only gave me a sweet potato last night. I am very hungry. This cage is so uncomfortable. You can neither stand up nor lie down. They only allow us twice a day to get out and exercise for half an hour. That's all we have and then we are returned to the cage."

Xiaohua took some steamed buns out with some pickles and a bottle of water. When Jiaming saw it, he was touched by her thoughtfulness and very grateful, since he was so hungry.

"Who are these other people in the other cages?" Xiaohua asked curiously.

Jiaming took a bite of a bun before answering, "I recognized three of them that were also from the party. I don't know the others. I believe Zunxian will also have trouble since he was the one hosting the party."

"I will come to see you every morning and bring you some food," Xiaohua said.

"Do we have enough money to support the family and me?"

"Don't worry, Jiaming! Just take care of yourself. I will find a way," Xiaohua answered.

Nianci could not say anything but sat listening to the conversation. He extended his hands to touch Jiaming's legs, like his father would often reach out to touch him when he was sad. After half an hour, the guard came to stop their conversation. They were only allowed thirty minutes to visit each day.

Xiaohua and Nianci left the prison with a great feeling of loss and sorrow. Once they arrived home, Xiaohua sat down to think how she could help the family survive, since there would no longer be any income from Jiaming. Relying just on her tailoring, the income would not be much. Furthermore, she did not have very many customers.

"Nianci, you must go to school again tomorrow. Tell teacher that your absence was because you were sick. Here is a note. Don't say anything about your Papa," Xiaohua said.

"Yes, Mom!" Nianci replied.

Since it was only noontime, after they had eaten some sweet potatoes for lunch Nianci stepped out of the cottage. Whenever he was sad and lonely, he liked to sit under the willow trees on the bank of the creek about a hundred yards away. From listening to the water and the birds, he was able to find a sense of calm and to feel the breeze.

"How can I help my family past this crisis?" he wondered. When he saw the water in the creek, he noticed some fish. "I can catch fish, crabs, clams, and shrimps," he told himself. "I still remember how Papa caught them."

Nianci stepped into the shallow area of the creek and tried to use his hands to catch something but failed. Then he remembered how his father used a net to catch clams. He rushed home and searched for his father's net. After five minutes, he found it. Xiaohua was not at home while he was there.

Nianci returned to the creek with the net and spread one end of it on the bottom of the stream. He used some rocks to anchor the bottom and held it in place. Then he tied up the other end on the branches next to the bank. The flow of water in the stream shaped the net into a big scoop. Now, all he needed to do was wait. According to what his father had said, the clams moved from one place to another by floating and following the current.

As he waited for the net to do its work, Nianci spent some time searching for crab holes along the bank. Soon he found one. He used a branch to dig the hole bigger and deeper. In just a few minutes, he discovered a crab in the hole trying to escape. He immediately caught it.

"I got one! I got one!" Nianci cried out in his happiness. He was so glad that he had gone with his dad many times to catch these small creatures that lived in the creek.

Nianci took his T-shirt off, put the crab inside and wrapped it up to prevent it from escaping. He continued his search for another hole and caught another crab. Within half an hour he had caught four. When he returned to check his net trap, he found that he had also caught nearly 30 clams. He was so happy.

Nianci took his catch home to find that his mom had returned.

"Mom! Look what I caught! We will have a nice dinner," he said with pride. But when he saw his mother's serious face, he knew something was wrong.

"Mom! What happened?"

"Zunxian was also arrested yesterday. He was put in a different location. His whole family is panicky and frustrated. I did not know how to comfort them. They told me, in total, there were about 15 guests arrested from that party. It seemed that someone had reported it to the authorities."

"We just have to wait and see, Mom. Now look what I caught. I think we will have good meals if I have time to catch more," Nianci said.

"But I worry that you have school and that is the most important. It is your future. You have so much homework each day. Promise me that school is your first priority. I also worry about all the poisonous snakes in the creek. You must be very careful! I heard about some people trying to catch fish and crabs in the creek and they got bitten by a snake. If this happens to you, I will not know how to live on."

"Mom, I promise! School first and be careful when I catch seafood."

Nianci and his mom cooked the crabs and had clam soup, saving some for Jiaming to have the next morning. Since Nianci did not have enough time to catch more seafood from the creek and the food ran out very quickly, in just a week Nianci and his mom were facing a serious food shortage. They began to eat just two meals a day, each time saving some food for Jiaming that Xiaohua would take to him every morning.

Due to Zunxian's arrest, his family could not help Xiaohua and Nianci as much as they had before. His entire family was consumed with worry about Zunxian's future. From what everyone had heard, many Taiwanese completely disappeared after being arrested. Nobody knew what happened to them. In addition, because all of their neighbors were afraid of being accused as Communist spies or members of the Taiwanese Independent Party, no one dared to help them. They were left alone to find a way to survive.

After a while, his hunger was so great that Nianci began to steal sweet potatoes from the field on the other side of the rice field in the evening. He would eat some and bring some home for his mom. When Xiaohua asked where the sweet potatoes came from, he simply said the neighbors gave them to him. After a few weeks had passed, Xiaohua realized that the sweet potatoes were in fact stolen from their neighbors. This made her upset and sorrowful. She knew Nianci was hungry, and she could not blame him. She also knew that Nianci was concerned that she and Jiaming would not have food either.

A month later, the rainy season arrived. This made things more difficult. The water level rose in the creek until it was too high for Nianci to catch anything. Until then, Nianci had been able to catch some fish or shellfish during weekends when there was no school.

One rainy night in winter, a strong wind blew away a piece of the aluminum that covered the roof. The entire cottage became inundated with water. Both Xiaohua and Nianci woke up wet and chilly. By the next day Xiaohua was sick with fever. Nianci tried to use his hands and what he knew to fix the roof. At least it stopped the rain from pouring in. He rushed to Zunxian's home to beg for help. Though Zunxian was still in prison and awaiting trial, his father and wife kindly offered some money and food to help during this difficult period.

"Thank you very much, Da Shen (大嬸, Great Aunt). Thank you very much," Nianci gratefully accepted.

Nianci went to a drugstore and bought some medicine to bring back to Xiaohua. They could not afford to see a doctor. The pharmacy worker told him that if Xiaohua's illness was caused from a regular cold or flu, the medicine would help.

The next morning, Nianci went to school and told his teacher the problems his family had encountered. He could not keep the secret about Jiaming being in prison any longer. He needed time away from school to be at home to take care of his mother and father. Once he was back at home, he tried to figure out ways to take care of his family. He went to neighbors and begged for help. They responded with some aid, but it was not enough to survive on. He tried to save food for his parents. But really the only way to survive was to keep stealing sweet potatoes from the field and, whenever, the water in the creek was low enough, to catch some crab and river shrimp. Occasionally, he caught some fish from the rice field, but overall it was much harder to catch anything during this rainy season.

While Xiaohua was sick, Nianci brought sweet potatoes and some salty pickles to his father every morning. Fortunately, after a few days Xiaohua felt better and it seemed the fever had retreated, although she was still weak.

One morning, Nianci called to Xiaohua as he was leaving the cottage, "Mom! I will bring some food to Papa."

"Be careful. Come back soon so I don't worry about you," Xiaohua replied.

"Yes, Mom. I will be back as soon as I can," Nianci answered and left riding the bicycle that was still too high for him. However, he found a way to manage it.

When Nianci passed downtown Muzha on the way to the military police station, he discovered a market place not too far from the main road. He decided to take a look at what was there on his return after visiting his father. Once he had arrived at the station and given his father the food he had brought, Jiaming immediately asked after Xiaohua.

"How is your mom's sickness? Is she better?" Jiaming asked, deeply concerned. He knew if Xiaohua were not sick, she would deliver the food herself instead of Nianci. She would have Nianci going to school instead of coming to the station. Jiaming felt incredibly guilty that he could not take care of his family. Five months had already passed, and he was still kept imprisoned without any further decision or action from the government. He knew he just needed to wait patiently. At least, he had not been taken away for execution yet. He still had hope, although he had gotten very skinny and weak without enough food or health care. There was only one thought that kept him going and wanting to live; that was Xiaohua and Nianci.

"Mom is getting better now. I hope she recovers in the next few days so I can go to school again," Nianci said, looking at Jiaming with all of a son's love.

Broken Hearted Experience 傷心的經歷

On the way home, as Nianci was passing through the market place, his curiosity got the best of him and he decided to take a look. He placed his bicycle under one of the few trees next to the market. As he looked around, he saw hundreds of vendors selling fish, chicken, pork, noodles... all the foods that in his dreams he could have, but in reality, he couldn't. He was very hungry since he had not had anything to eat that morning. Finally, he came to a food stand where there were a lot of steamed buns right in front of him at chest height. His hunger got the best of him, and when he thought nobody was watching, he took one and hid it under his shirt. Unfortunately, the owner spotted his theft and reached out to grab him. There was no room for Nianci to run since there were so many people in the market place. The owner caught him, then bound his hands behind his back with a rope and took him out of the market place. The owner then used a bigger rope to tie up Nianci's body and hang him up on one of the trees.

Nianci did not beg for forgiveness or even cry. He just closed his eyes and said nothing. Deep in his heart he thought, "Why is nature so cruel? Why is the world so cruel? Why are people so cruel? Is this the life I want?" He asked himself these questions over and over.

Slowly a crowd gathered underneath him

"Poor child. He must be very hungry," someone said.

"If he is a thief when he is small, what will happen when he grows up?" someone else wondered.

"Please untie him and let him go," one of the ladies asked the owner.

"No! He needs to be punished. Otherwise, he will commit this crime again," the owner declared.

The owner kept Nianci tied up on the tree for nearly an hour before finally releasing him. When he was untied, he found that his forearms were covered with blue bruises due to the lack of blood circulation. Both of his arms were numb. He slowly took his bicycle and left the scene. He swore that he would never go near that market place again. It would always remind him of the shame of his theft and the punishment by hanging on the tree.

When he arrived home, Nianci did not tell Xiaohua about the event. "Why are you so late? I was so worried about you," his mom told him.

"I met a friend on the street, mom." Nianci did not want to tell his mom about this black spot he had just created on the blank, white slate of his life.

Nianci ran to the willow trees and sat beneath one. He could not stop the tears that flowed as he thought about what had happened.

"I am not a thief. One day, I will prove to them that I am not a thief. I will be a successful man in this world in the future," Nianci swore to himself over and over. This black spot on his clean, white slate would not be easy to erase.

"I need to study hard and try my best for my life. I will be a successful man. I swear, as Heaven is my witness."

FREEDOM WITH DEEP REGRET 悔恨的自由

Sadly, five months after Zunxian's arrest, his father died of a sudden heart attack. Since Zunxian's arrest, the old man had been desolated and heartbroken by what had come to pass because of his 80th birthday celebration. He cried much of the time and deeply regretted all the unfortunate events. When Xiaohua and Nianci heard the bad news, they were very sad. On the day of the burial, Xiaohua took Nianci to participate in the funeral and to try to console the family. They did not tell Jiaming when they visited him in prison. It was just too sad and if Jiaming knew about it, he would be very upset.

Six months after his arrest, Zunxian was set free due to a lack of evidence. This gave Xiaohua and Nianci hope that Jiaming might also be released soon. Unfortunately, the accusation for Jiaming was different from Zunxian's case. Jiaming was accused as a Communist spy. The authorities had found a pistol in his home and his brother had been a Communist. On the other hand, they also knew his father was a loyal, high-ranking officer who had sacrificed his life for the country.

Nianci and Xiaohua's situation improved a bit when spring came, and the rain fell less and less often. Fortunately, Xiaohua's health was better again and Zunxian hired her to do some work. She knew that Zunxian was just trying to help them as much as possible. Nianci was able to catch some shellfish in the creek again. However, because of their off and on starvation and their near constant worry, both Xiaohua and Nianci had developed gastric ulcers. Episodes of stomach pain continued frequently and affected their emotions.

Finally, due to the lack of evidence that he was connected with the Communists, Jiaming was released. He had been in jail nearly ten months and had lost at least 60 pounds in that time. The authorities brought him back in a jeep to the public road nearest his home early one afternoon. As Jiaming stepped out of the jeep, he couldn't hold back his tears.

Xiaohua saw the jeep stopped in the distance on the public road and wondered why this military jeep had stopped there. Then, when she saw Jiaming step out of the jeep she collapsed to the ground. She knelt there and cried out loud, "Thank heavens! Thank heavens for your mercy."

Jiaming was very weak but very happy to be returning home. At first, he walked slowly toward the cottage, but when he saw Xiaohua kneeling down on the ground he sped up as much as he was able. He came near Xiaohua and picked her up and held her. As they hugged each other the love they felt for each other was deeper than ever.

Nianci, returning home from school later that afternoon, felt light and cheerful somehow. The weather was so nice on this April day. Again, his mind felt the birds in the air and the current of the stream. He hadn't had this feeling for some time. He was planning to see if he could find some shrimp or crab for dinner when he stepped into the cottage and saw Jiaming and Xiaohua talking. He was so happy and ran toward his father. The tears in his eyes reflected his happiness and excitement.

Jiaming felt good enough the next day to take Nianci with him to Zunxian's home.

"Mr. and Mrs. Shen, how are you? I came to thank you for taking care of my wife and son while I was in prison," Jiaming said as he and his son bowed deeply to both of them.

"Please don't be so polite. I am so glad that you are free now. I feel so sorry and felt guilty that the party caused so many problems," Zunxian said.

"Actually, I was worried to death. I heard many of the people disappeared after being arrested. When I was in prison, I almost lost hope," Zunxian continued.

"From now on, to keep ourselves safe, we should not talk about 2-2-8 Incident or criticize Chiang's government," Zunxian's wife said.

Jiaming and Nianci just nodded their heads. They knew this was not the era and government for free speech or for expressing personal opinions.

CHAPTER 5
A CHILD'S HEART
童 心

The news of Jiaming's return had spread to the neighbors. Some old landowners, even though they had been allowed to keep only a few acres of land, still needed extra helpers sometimes, especially when the plowing and harvest seasons arrived. Almost all the neighbors treated Jiaming's family as one of the Taiwanese. The neighbors felt much closer to them, especially since Jiaming, Xiaohua and Nianci could speak the Taiwanese dialect fluently. More and more people hired Jiaming and Xiaohua to work during the busy seasons. This improved the family's poor financial condition. When the busy season was over, Jiaming resumed his scavenging work.

From helping their neighboring farmers, both Jiaming and Xiaohua learned how to build a vegetable garden. They cultivated a small garden next to the cottage and planted various vegetables. This was a great help to their food supply, especially for greens.

Occasionally, Jiaming would go to a rich neighborhood to scavenge. Sometimes, he could find something that was useful or valuable for his home. Once, he found an old semi-broken and discarded desk. He had often wished to give Nianci a desk at which to do his studies at home, so he brought it back to the cottage and repaired it. When Nianci saw the desk, he was so happy that his eyes filled with tears. He hugged Jiaming for almost a whole minute. Jiaming could tell how much his son liked the desk.

Not only that, when Jiaming had saved enough money he contacted the electric company to see if they were able to connect electricity to his home. The company came and connected the electricity.

It was quite a surprise for Nianci when he came home from school. He felt like a king living in a palace now. The improvements renewed his determination to study hard every day. His school grades kept going up. This made Jiaming and Xiaohua very happy.

Jiaming also asked his local town government to assign a mailing address to his home. Without their own address, the electric company would have to send their bill to Zunxian's place and then Zunxian would have to bring it to him. Having a home address would also be helpful for all the notifications from Nianci's school. Zunxian had kindly received their mail for so many years already. Jiaming appreciated Zunxian's help, but also felt guilty for disturbing his daily schedule. Once the application was finally processed, the little cottage was assigned an address and could be formally recognized as a home. Since they were semi-isolated from any main residential area and there was no road connected to their home, the address simply read: #1, Creek Pass, Xizikou Mountain, Muzha Town, Taipei. (台北縣木柵鎮溪子口山小溪徑一號).

A Surprise Discovery 一個驚喜的發現

One day in October, Jiaming decided to head to the rich neighborhood again. When he approached it from a side road, he saw a boy who looked like Nianci leaning against a window and peering inside a house. As he got closer, he could see that it was indeed Nianci. Now what, he wondered, had attracted his son's attention? Jiaming drew up close enough to find out that Nianci was watching and listening to a music lesson that was taking place in the house. Nianci hummed with the music and moved his head with the music beats. Inside the house a music teacher was instructing a boy playing violin and a girl playing piano. It was obvious that these two children were the offspring of the homeowner.

From a reflection in the window, Nianci was shocked to suddenly see a shadow behind him. He turned around to find his father standing there.

"Papa, it is you! You almost scared me to death!" Nianci exclaimed.

"Sorry, Nianci. I am on my way home. Do you want to go with me?" Jiaming asked.

"Yes, Papa."

On the way home Jiaming inquired of his son, "Nianci, do you like music?"

"Yes, Papa! Very much, especially the violin. The sound the violin makes touches my heart deeply. I wish I could play it one day."

"Remember, Nianci! The Chinese have a saying that 'Where there is a will, there is a success.' If you would like to be a musician in the future, then you should think as a musician, talk like a musician, walk like a musician, and act like a musician. When the time is right, you will be a musician. Nianci, you should not underestimate the power of your mind."

"Papa, I know! I want to become a great violinist one day."

Although Jiaming thought Nianci was just joking and not serious about it, nevertheless he told Xiaohua what had happened that evening.

"No wonder he always comes back late on Monday and Wednesday. It seems he goes to listen to the music," Xiaohua said.

For the following few weeks, Jiaming went to the same house on Monday and Wednesday afternoons on purpose. He saw Nianci was there every time. He hid himself in the distance and determined to watch for further developments. He realized that Nianci really liked music. Nianci always stayed until the lesson was finished and the teacher had left.

Jiaming wished he could help Nianci fulfill his dream, but he was too poor. Lessons were expensive and a violin was well beyond their budget. The money they had managed to save since he was released from jail would not purchase even a cheap violin.

DESTINY 命運

One Friday, early in the morning before Jiaming went out to work, a military policeman came to visit. Jiaming immediately felt scared and panicked. He thought they would arrest him again. Xiaohua was also very shocked, but the policeman looked at Jiaming with a smile and a complete lack of hostility.

"Mr. Lin, I am delivering compensation for the prison time you served," the policeman said.

"How could this happen, sir?" Jiaming asked.

"If you are found innocent, the government usually will compensate some money to remedy the suffering," the military policeman answered.

Jiaming took the envelope with trembling hands and signed a receipt for it. After the policeman left, he opened the envelope and found there was NT$600. Compared to what he and his family had experienced this would not even remedy 10% of the damage that they had suffered, especially mentally. Nevertheless, it was a welcome surprise.

"Can we afford music lessons for Nianci with this money?" Xiaohua asked anxiously.

"Yes, I think so. We can use this good luck to help Nianci's dream. I will check the cost of lessons and a violin next Monday." Jiaming was very excited but decided not to tell Nianci yet since they weren't sure if it would be possible.

The following Monday Jiaming went to the house where the music lessons took place. Again, he saw Nianci there. He went right up next to Nianci and peeked through the window beside him. Nianci didn't say anything but wondered why his father stayed there with him. They stood silently together, listening until the lesson was over. Ten minutes later, when the teacher stepped out of the house Jiaming took Nianci to meet him.

"Teacher! May I ask you a question?" Jiaming asked.

"Of course, Mr..." the teacher responded.

"Lin, but please just call me Jiaming. This is my son, who is very interested in learning violin. Is it possible for him to join your lesson here? Could you tell me how much it costs?"

"I have noticed his peeking for a while. I did not want to deter him since he had never made any noise to disturb the lesson. Do you really like it, boy?" the teacher asked.

Nianci nodded his head with a big smile.

"I need to ask permission from the master of the house since he is the patron of the lessons. I don't know if he will be happy about this," the teacher said.

"If he agrees, how much will it cost?"

"It will be NT$100 a month, mister." The teacher could see how poor Jiaming was, but he had to give him a price that was also fair to others.

"And how much does the violin cost, Teacher?"

"For very good one, it may cost a few thousand NT, but an average one, for beginner, will be around NT$300 in musical instrument store."

"If possible, could Nianci take your lessons?"

"As I said, I need to talk to the house master about it. I will talk to him this Wednesday when I return. I will let you know Wednesday. By the way, my name is Zhengrong (正榮) and my surname is Zhang (張)."

"My boy's name is Mingde, Mr. Zhang. It is an honor to meet you. See you next Wednesday."

"Papa! Do we have money to pay for lessons and a violin? Do we?" Nianci asked. He was so excited he practically skipped on the way home with his father.

"Don't worry. Mom and I will figure out a way," Jiaming replied.

Nianci could not wait for Wednesday to come. He was both excited and anxious. There was a chance that he might be able to play the violin, his dream! When Wednesday arrived, Jiaming did not go out to do his work. Instead he went to the music lesson house wearing the nicest clothes he had. By the time he arrived, Nianci was already there after school.

When the music teacher saw them from inside the house, he came out to talk to them.

"I asked Mr. Peng, the master of the house, about Mingde. I told him that with three persons, there would be a better ensemble team for practice. Furthermore, a new boy from outside may stimulate his children to have more interest in practice. He hesitated for a while but granted permission. He told me to try it first and see the results," the teacher said.

Nianci could not help the happiness that shone on his face. He gave a deep bow to Mr. Zhang in thanks.

"You may start today. Remember 4 to 5 o'clock every Monday and Wednesday afternoon," Mr. Zhang said. "The boy inside has two violins. I will ask him to let you borrow one today. Mr. Lin, there are no musical instrument stores in this area. If you can, please go to Taipei Symphony Music Instrument store. Here is the address. I know them very well and I knew they had a good used violin on the shelf with a low price. I saw it last week when I was there. Please go to buy it soon. I believe with that quality and low price, it will not last long on the shelf," he continued.

"Nianci, remember what I said! If you really want something, you must pursue it ceaselessly. You will accomplish it when the time comes. Be patient, my boy. I will go now. After you finish go straight home, otherwise, your mom will worry about you," Jiaming said.

Nianci practically glowed with happiness and basked in his father's love. He hugged Jiaming and then went into the house with the teacher.

Jiaming left and went home quickly to tell Xiaohua what had happened. "I need to go to Taipei City to get a violin for Nianci," he said. He did not know how much it would be, so he brought with him almost all the cash he had. Jiaming felt that this was one thing he could do to compensate for Nianci's suffering while he was in prison.

By the time the bus brought Jiaming to Taipei it was dusk already. Fortunately, the store was still open.

"Mister! Mr. Zhang, Zhengrong is my son's violin teacher. He said you have a used violin on shelf for sale," Jiaming said to the store owner.

"Yes. Teacher Zhang. He was here last week and saw that violin. He almost bought it." The owner of the shop pointed with his finger to a violin on a shelf.

"How much is it, mister?" Jiaming asked.

"If this was a new one, usually for this well-known brand, it would cost about NT$1,000. Since this is an old and used one and I got it at a cheap price, I can offer you NT$400," the owner said.

The price took Jiaming by surprise. He had not expecting it would be so expensive to buy just a used one.

"Are there other cheaper ones, mister?" Jiaming asked hopefully.

"Yes, I have. But the sound quality will not be as good. Actually, it is rare to have such a good quality violin with this price," the owner told him. The owner demonstrated by taking the violin from its shelf and playing a short song. Even though Jiaming was not an expert in music, he could hear the quality of the instrument.

"There is no consideration. I want the best for Nianci. He is such a nice boy that I can be proud of," Jiaming thought. He took his money purse out and counted out NT$450. It was all he had.

"I will give you the case free and another set of violin strings. Without the case, this violin will not last long. All of these cost about $100 NT," the owner offered. He could see that Jiaming was not rich but that he had a father's deep love for his son.

On the way home, Jiaming was very happy with his purchase but also hoped that he had made a good investment. He did not know if Nianci would be talented or serious enough in his practice. He knew it would not be easy to reach a high level of proficiency on the instrument.

By the time Jiaming arrived home it was very late. Xiaohua and Nianci were still waiting for him to get back before having dinner. Nianci almost cried when Jiaming handed the violin to him. He could not believe that his father had taken the time to travel all the way to Taipei City just to buy this violin for him.

"This is the violin Mr. Zhang talked about," Jiaming told Nianci. "We are lucky to get it. It is not cheap. Nianci, please take care of it carefully. We cannot afford another one. Now, eat dinner first and then you can try it out."

Nianci finished his dinner very quickly indeed. Unfortunately, due to his excitement and the speed with which he ate, his ulcer acted up. This often happened when he was hungry or right after he ate. Xiaohua also suffered from these episodes occasionally. Nianci did his best to hide his pain and went to his room quietly. He did not want his parents to worry about him.

Xiaohua, however, noticed it and pointed it out to Jiaming. "His stomach pain returns. We should take him to see a doctor," she said.

Jiaming went into Nianci's room to find him holding the violin in its case and lying down on his bed. His face was covered with a cold sweat caused by his pain. Jiaming went over to the bed and gently massaged Nianci's back, helping him to relax. Nianci could feel his father's love in the soothing touch.

Jiaming felt so guilty and sorry that his son had to suffer this pain. He knew Nianci's and Xiaohua's ulcers were caused by the starvation they had experienced when he was in prison. The massage seemed to help Nianci and in half an hour, he fell asleep. Jiaming stepped out of the room and tried to think of a solution.

When Jiaming and Xiaohua woke up, they could hear the quiet sound of a violin far in the distance. Jiaming took a look and saw Nianci was practicing his violin lesson under the willow trees on the bank of the creek about 100 yards from where they lived. It seemed Nianci enjoyed it so much that he had forgotten about getting ready for school. Finally, Jiaming had to go to get him and remind him about school.

"Papa, I really like this violin! The sound generated is so clean and profound. Thank you, Papa," Nianci exclaimed.

After breakfast, Nianci dutifully went to school. He could not wait until his next lesson on Monday. Each day when he returned home after school, he would take the violin to the willow trees and practice. He had four days of practice before Monday. Within just a couple of days he had mastered the basic skills that he was taught in his first lesson. Once he had developed those skills, he tried to put his feeling into each draw of the bow. The sound vibrated in his heart and resonated in his mind and soul. He was so satisfied every day after practice. Jiaming and Xiaohua were very happy to see Nianci's joy and progress. Nianci's playing had brought a lot of joy to the whole family.

The next Monday before he went to the lesson, Nianci went home first to pick up his violin. He did not want to take it to school, in part, because he did not want the other students to know about it, but, in addition, he did not want to risk anything damaging the violin. It was just too precious to him, not just in terms of the money it cost, but also as evidence of the love his parents had for him.

When Teacher Zhang asked his three students to play what they had learned last time, he was amazed that Nianci was not just remembering the lesson but also playing it so well after just four days. Deep in his heart he knew that Nianci would be a very valuable student with a bright future.

Jiaming was waiting outside when the lesson finished. He had not wanted to enter the house and disturb the lesson. Once Mr. Zhang came out, he gave him an envelope with NT$100 inside for the monthly fee. "Teacher Zhang, here is the tuition," he said as he handed it over. Then father and son went home. On the way, they chatted and talked about lesson.

"Nianci! You know what the key secret of success is?" Jiaming asked Nianci.

"Your intelligence!" Nianci replied.

"No!"

"Your wisdom?" Nianci tried again.

"No!"

"Well! What then, Papa?"

"My father told me the most important key to success is your self-discipline. He said 'if you can conquer yourself, you will be able to conquer the whole world. Your self is your biggest enemy.'"

"How do you train your discipline, Papa? I want to train it. I want to be a successful man," Nianci responded.

"To conquer yourself, you must conquer your laziness, learn to be patient and perseverant, learn how to endure what others cannot endure. Chinese have a saying: 'Climbing mountain, must choose the high mountain and carry burden, must choose heavy burden.' The more difficulties you have encountered, the stronger you will be."

They chatted and talked about the past when Jiaming was still young, and before they knew it, they had arrived back home. Nianci felt his father was not just a father, but a teacher and friend.

Nianci continued to display his talent and impressive progress in the following few weeks. This made Teacher Zhang very happy and proud of him. Nianci might turn out to be the best student he had ever taught. He knew Nianci was a precious jade stone that had gone undiscovered and untreated. One day, 25 minutes into a lesson, Nianci suddenly seemed unfocused and absent minded. When Teacher Zhang took a closer look, he noticed that Nianci's face was pale and covered with sweat.

"Are you OK, Mingde?" Mr. Zhang wondered.

"I am very sorry, Teacher Zhang. My stomach is in pain," Nianci replied.

"Did you eat something wrong? What did you eat for lunch?" Teacher Zhang asked with concern. He took Nianci to the couch and let him sit down.

"Mom said I had an ulcer. I feel these sharp pains occasionally. My papa said he would take me to see a doctor one day."

"No! Doctors can only treat the pain temporarily. If you want to heal it from its root, you must learn how to relax and improve the circulation of Qi in your stomach area. Once you provide these conditions, the stomach will heal itself."

"But I don't know anything about how to relax my stomach area."

"I heard practicing Taijiquan could help a person relax his internal organs and improve his Qi circulation. Rest till you feel better. You may skip today's lesson," Teacher Zhang told Nianci.

Nianci was extremely disappointed to have to miss his lesson, but his pain was so severe that it disturbed his concentration. He did not tell his parents about his ulcer episode during the lesson because he didn't want them to worry about him. After dinner, he just went to finish his homework and then went to sleep. He felt depressed that he had not been able to learn anything that day.

The next Wednesday when he went to the lesson, his teacher had some good news for him.

"Mingde! One of my students is from HSNU (The Affiliated Senior High School of National Taiwan Normal University – Muzha Division, 師範大學附屬中學-木柵分部). He told me last weekend that there was an English teacher, Teacher Gao, in his high school who also teaches Taijiquan in the school auditorium early mornings. You may want to check it out and see if he can teach you how to relax your organs," Teacher Zhang told him.

"Do you know when they meet in the morning?" Mingde asked.

"As I heard, they practice every morning except Sunday from 6:00 to 7:00," Teacher Zhang replied.

"Thank you, Teacher. I will check it."

Nianci told his parents about the chance to learn Taijiquan as soon as he got home from his lesson. They realized that HSNU was about 35 minutes from his home and 20 minutes to his school by bicycle.

"May I go to see this Taijiquan teacher tomorrow?" Nianci asked his parents.

"Should I go with you, Nianci?" Jiaming asked.

"It's not necessary, Papa! I want to see their practice first before I ask. I don't know if I will like it," Nianci replied.

"Okay. Then you must get up and have breakfast around five o'clock in the morning. Can you make it?"

"I will make it, Papa."

Learning Taijiquan 學習太極拳

Though he was taller now, especially since he had better food to help him grow, Nianci's feet still barely reached the pedals on his bicycle. The next morning, he got up very early. Jiaming was still sleeping but Xiaohua had also woken up early to make sure that Nianci was up according to what he said he planned to do.

Since there wasn't much traffic on the street at that hour, Nianci actually arrived at the auditorium five minutes early for the Taijiquan class. Five high school students were there stretching. Nianci sat on a bench a little distance away from them, but where he could still see them clearly. He figured they must be there for the Taijiquan class since not many people came to school so early.

Just before six o'clock, Nianci saw a teacher of about 30 years old enter the auditorium. All five students bowed to the teacher.

"He must be Teacher Gao," Nianci thought.

Nianci watched the class stretch and then warm up. Finally, they started on some basic practices of how to move the spine and how to step gently and firmly. After that, Teacher Gao led them in doing some breathing exercises with movements.

"This must be Taiji Qigong," Nianci thought.

The class spent the next 30 minutes practicing slow and soft movements.

"It looks interesting but also a little bit boring," Nianci thought. He was only 11 years old and these movements were so slow that he did not think he would like it. Even so, he continued to watch the class every morning that week. He thought hard about whether he should learn these slow and boring exercises. Then, he remembered what his father had said, "Patience and perseverance are the keys of success."

"This may be a good chance to learn how to conquer myself and build my discipline," Nianci concluded after he had thought it over some more.

At the end of practice on Saturday, Nianci came forward to see Teacher Gao. Actually, Teacher Gao and the other five students had already noticed Nianci's presence during the last few days.

Nianci bowed to the teacher and asked him, "Teacher Gao! May I learn Taijiquan from you?"

When Teacher Gao saw this small boy, he questioned him, "What is your name? How old are you?"

"My name is Lin, Mingde. However, my parents and friends often call me Nianci, my nickname. I am 11 years old," Nianci replied.

"Do you want to learn? You are so young. Not too many young boys your age like to learn Taijiquan, you know," Teacher Gao said.

"I will do my best, Teacher Gao! Please accept me as your student," Nianci begged as he bowed again to the teacher.

Teacher Gao pondered for a moment, then told Nianci, "Okay. Come next Monday."

"How much should I pay for the lesson, Teacher Gao?"

"There is no charge, but you must promise to learn and practice hard. You are my first student at such a young age."

"Thank you, Teacher Gao. I must go now otherwise I will miss school." Nianci bowed one more time and left for school. Thoughtfully he wondered, "Can practicing Taijiquan really help my ulcer problem? I will have to wait and see how it works."

So Nianci began his Taijiquan practice the next Monday morning. Like the other five students, he arrived early before Teacher Gao showed up. He introduced himself to the others. When it was 6 o'clock, Teacher Gao promptly showed up. He was always on time. The students all bowed to Teacher Gao.

"The five of you just warm up and practice by yourself for half an hour this morning. I need to teach Mingde some basic practices," Teacher Gao instructed them, then took Nianci to the side.

"Taijiquan is a soft internal martial style that emphasizes relaxation. When you relax, the Qi in the body will be able to circulate smoothly. If you are tense, the Qi's circulation will be stagnant. Therefore, the first step of learning Taijiquan is to feel your joints. Once your joints are relaxed, then your muscles will be relaxed," Teacher Gao told Nianci.

"Why feeling the joints instead of muscles, Teacher Gao? May I ask?" Nianci wondered.

"The joints are where the tendons and ligaments are located. The tendons are the ends of muscles. If the ends are loose and relaxed, the muscles will be relaxed. It is just like a piece of rope. When the end is loose, the middle is loose as well. That is why Taijiquan emphasizes the feeling of joints." Teacher Gao welcomed the questions since this was a sign of Nianci's curiosity and interest.

"Once you are able to feel your joints deeply, then you learn how to breathe deeply and use the coordination of breathing to enhance the relaxation of your joints," Teacher Gao continued.

"Why is breathing able to enhance the relaxation, Teacher Gao?" Nianci asked, since he saw Teacher Gao was not upset by his questions.

"You see, Mingde, when you inhale you bring the Qi in for storage, and when you exhale you are leading the Qi out for releasing. Breathing is the most important and crucial key of manipulating the Qi's action. That is why breathing is a key strategy in Qigong practice. For example, if you inhale longer than exhale, you feel cool and if you exhale longer than inhale, then you feel warm. Now try it," Teacher Gao explained with a smile. He was happy to know that this boy was different, that Nianci dared to ponder what he was learning and ask about what he didn't understand.

"Now, follow me. Put your hands five centimeters under your navel. This place is called the Dantian (丹田) and means elixir field, since this place is able to produce elixir or Qi for your health and longevity. This cavity is also called Qihai (氣海, Qi Sea) in Chinese medicine. This is because the Qi can be stored and produced here like the sea. Now, inhale deeply and gently push your abdomen out."

Nianci followed the instruction and immediately felt a mixture of warmth and tingling in the groin area.

"Now let the air go out slowly and smoothly. See if you are able to feel the Qi's release through your skin to outside of your body," Teacher Gao instructed.

When Nianci followed the instruction, he could feel a sensational feeling on his skin as the Qi released.

"Wow! Just a simple thing, but I have never paid attention to it. That means if I can use my breathing correctly, I will be able to manipulate the Qi's status in my body," Nianci thought.

"How do you feel? Feel anything?" Teacher Gao asked.

"Yes, Teacher Gao. It is amazing that the feeling of Qi, or the body's sensations, were different when inhaling and exhaling. I never paid attention to this," Nianci replied.

"That is why the mind is the second crucial key of leading the Qi. When your mind generates an idea, the Qi will be led to manifest it into action. For example, if you wish to lift your hand, you must think of lifting and your mind will lead the Qi to the limbs and energize the muscles for action. You see, the principle is very simple. Use your mind to lead the Qi and then manifest it into action. Do you understand, Mingde?"

"Teacher Gao, it is getting too deep for me now. I would like to ponder it and experience it. I hope I will be able to comprehend what you said. Thank you, Teacher Gao."

"Now, I will leave you alone to practice. Remember your mind, Qi, and breathing. They are related, and once you are able to comprehend their relationship and feel it, you will have already built a foundation for Taijiquan practice," Teacher Gao said and went to join the senior group.

Nianci was alone now in the corner of the auditorium. He calmed himself down and practiced his breathing. At the beginning, he needed to intentionally push the abdominal area out when he inhaled and draw it back in when he exhaled. He knew this was because he had never really used his abdominal muscles for breathing before. While he was practicing breathing, he also tried to physically relax, especially his joint areas. After he worked on this for 30 minutes or so, he could begin to feel some amazing phenomenon. He felt, when he breathed, that his joints and skin were also breathing with him. He had never felt this kind of sensation before. Right then, Teacher Gao came to check on him.

"Have you understood what I said? Can you feel your body's relaxation and Qi circulation?" Teacher Gao asked Nianci.

"I began to feel some sensations that I have never felt before. Maybe I just have never paid attention to it. If I practice for a while, I believe I can use my mind, with the coordination of my breathing, to feel the Qi much better," Nianci replied.

"Now, here is the homework that you must practice and feel. Next time, when you inhale, gently push your anus out and when you exhale, draw it upward," Teacher Gao said

"Why, Teacher Gao?"

"There is an acupuncture cavity called Huiyin (會陰, Yin Meeting) between your groin and anus. This cavity is the crucial place for controlling the Qi's manifestation."

"Teacher Gao, I am wondering why we focus on the anus instead of the Huiyin?"

"Good question. When your mind is at the Huiyin, that spot will tense up since you are leading more Qi there. Since the Huiyin cavity and anus share the same muscle, if you use the anus instead of the Huiyin, the Huiyin area will be more relaxed and allow the Qi in and out easily. Other than breathing, the Huiyin cavity is a tricky gate that governs the Qi's intake or release. Go home and try it first and we'll see if you have any questions tomorrow morning," Teacher Gao said and returned to the senior group again.

The class passed very quickly and before he knew it, Nianci needed to go to school. He came to say good-bye and thanked Teacher Gao with a deep bow. There were a lot of things he had learned that he needed time to ponder and experience. The entire day, whenever he had time, he pondered every sentence Teacher Gao had said. He felt like he understood but also did not understand. Right after his violin lesson, he went home and went to the willow tree area. He practiced for half an hour on his violin and then practiced what he was taught by Teacher Gao.

When he returned for class the next morning, Teacher Gao asked him how his practice had gone.

"Have you figured out the principle behind the practice yet?" Teacher Gao asked.

"No, Teacher Gao! It seems that I maybe understand but I am not sure. I need more time."

"That is no problem. These subjects are not easy, especially for someone your age. Keep pondering and practicing for a few days." Teacher Gao left Nianci alone and went to practice with the senior group.

The same situation played out every morning that week. Teacher Gao had not taught Nianci any more but left him to work on what he had already been taught. Nianci did not care since he still needed time to comprehend the meaning behind the practice.

By Saturday, Nianci was not just able to control his abdominal muscles more easily and in a more relaxed way, but he was also able to breathe more deeply and slowly. With the coordination of his anus movements, he could feel the intake and expansion of Qi much more strongly. The most amazing thing was that the more he could feel the Qi, the more he knew how to control it. His feeling got deeper and deeper. When this happened, he started to understand the principle behind the practice. Now, he could feel his joints deeply and use his mind and breathing to let the joints breathe with him. In addition, he could bring his relaxation to a state deeper than he ever had before. However, when he tried to feel his internal organs, except being able to relax his lungs and stomach, he could not yet feel his spleen, kidneys, or other organs. He knew it would take time. He also tried to feel his heart. But whenever he paid attention to his heart, though he could feel the heartbeat, he also felt the heartbeat getting faster and faster.

He stopped putting his mind on his heart. He needed to know the answers to some questions before he continued to feel his heart.

When he went to practice the next Monday and Teacher Gao came to the corner to check on him, Nianci asked, "Teacher Gao, may I ask you a question?"

"Of course, Mingde."

"When I practiced paying attention to my internal organs, I could only feel my lungs, and stomach clearly. I mean, I could make them more relaxed and I could feel it. I still cannot feel the other organs such as the kidneys, liver, or spleen. Ya! One more thing, Teacher Gao! When I pay attention to my heart, I could feel it, but it also increased my heartrate. That made me a little bit nervous," Nianci told him.

"Yes, the hardest organ to feel is your spleen. If you are able feel your spleen, you have reached to a deep level of 'Gongfu of Internal Vision' (內視功夫). That means you are able to observe your internal organs clearly. Since it will take a long time to reach this level, it is called Gongfu. However, there is one organ that you should not place your mind on and that is your heart. Once you pay attention to the heart, you are leading more Qi there and this will affect your heartbeat. Therefore, you should avoid it," Teacher Gao explained.

"May I ask another question?"

"Yes, Mingde."

"If my heart suddenly beats very fast, what should I do?" Nianci asked.

"First, you need to move your mind away from your heart and then use your right hand to slap the inner elbow of the left arm until the area turns red. After that, switch hands and repeat the same thing on the right arm. I learned this method for emergencies from a Chinese doctor, a friend of mine. He told me that this would save a person's life who is having a heart attack," Teacher Gao said.

"Move your mind away, I understand. But why slap your elbows?" Nianci asked again.

"This is because the heart Qi channel passes though the inner side of your elbow and connects to your pinky. If you slap the elbow to stimulate and excite it, you will lead the excess Qi away from the heart to the arms and release the pressure on your heart."

"Wow! The theory is so simple but so logical. Thank you, Teacher Gao."

Teacher Gao left Nianci to ponder and practice and went to work with the senior group. After a while he returned.

"The next thing you should know is Reverse Abdominal Breathing.

That means when you inhale, you withdraw your abdomen and when you exhale, you push it out gently. Naturally, you should also coordinate the breathing with your anus or Huiyin cavity. Now, try that for a few minutes. I will come to check with you again in ten minutes." Teacher Gao left again.

Ten minutes later when Teacher Gao returned, he asked, "How do you feel, Mingde?"

"It seems the Qi feeling is stronger when I use Reverse Abdominal Breathing. For example, I am able to lead the Qi in and out of my joints much better. However, I also feel more tense in my stomach area. I was wondering if this kind of breathing is normal, Teacher Gao? I know if I continue this kind of breathing for a while, I may trigger my stomach tightness and pain," Nianci asked with a worried expression on his face.

"Your question is very good. As you see, we use Normal Abdominal Breathing without thinking. This kind of breathing makes us relax. However, when we have an emotional disturbance or an intention to manifest our power, we change to Reverse Abdominal Breathing without knowing it. Now, place your hands on your abdominal area and laugh loud. You will see when you laugh, you exhale and your abdomen actually expands, pushing your anus out," Teacher Gao explained.

Nianci tried laughing a couple of times. "It is true. I have never paid attention to it," he thought.

"Now, think about something scary or sad. You will see when you inhale that the abdomen is pulled in and the anus is held up. Now, try it," Teacher Gao went on.

When Nianci tried again while imagining he was afraid or sad, he saw the point.

"Now, imagine that you are pushing something heavy or blowing a strong balloon. See what happens to your abdomen and anus?" Teacher Gao asked again.

Nianci tried again with imagining he was blowing up a balloon. Again, he realized that he was using Reverse Abdominal Breathing.

"It is amazing, Teacher Gao. Different actions can affect our breathing behavior and different breathings can trigger different feelings of Qi." Nianci saw the points.

"That is why breathing is considered a key strategy for Taijiquan and Qigong practice. For example, when you practice Taijiquan for relaxation, you should use Normal Abdominal Breathing and if you practice Taijiquan for martial arts, since you need to manifest your power, you use Reverse Abdominal Breathing," Teacher Gao explained again.

"How long should I practice Reverse Abdominal Breathing? I am afraid if I practice too much, it will cause my stomach to ache." Nianci was afraid the stomach tension would trigger his ulcer attack.

"Try it with small scale of abdominal movements. This will not cause too much tension in the stomach area. However, after you practice for a long time and you are able to control your abdominal muscles more efficiently, your stomach tension problem will disappear, and you will be more relaxed. It will take time. Patience and practice are the keys of success," Teacher Gao said.

After this conversation, Teacher Gao left Nianci to practice by himself for the whole week. Nianci practiced different ways of breathing every day after his violin practice. He felt with his intention, focus and Reverse Abdominal Breathing he was able to lead the Qi more efficiently. He was so happy to see his progress each day.

The most amazing thing that resulted from this practice was that when Nianci incorporated his new breathing and feeling techniques into his violin practice, he was able to manage the violin bow more skillfully. Not only that but he found he had a greater feeling for the music and could manifest his feeling into the music, making it more expressive. This in turn had surprised his violin teacher. Teacher Zhang knew the hardest part to teach a student about playing music was how to feel the music and blend it into his own expression. It seemed that Nianci was a natural at this.

Teacher Gao was very impressed with Nianci's progress. He knew that Nianci would be one of his best students. From their question and answer sessions, he could see how deeply this boy thought about things.

"It is not easy for an 11-year-old boy," Teacher Gao thought.

The following Monday, Teacher Gao was anxious to know how Nianci had progressed and was ready to lead him to a deeper practice. When they were in the auditorium corner again, he told him, "Now, you must learn how to incorporate your breathing and coordination of your anus into your body's movements. The first step is to learn how to apply internal feeling to external spine movement. You must learn how to feel and move your vertebrae section by section like a wave from your sacrum to the neck area. Remember what I said in the first lesson? Tell me what the most crucial key in Taijiquan practice is so the Qi can flow smoothly in your body?" Teacher Gao tested him.

"Relaxation, Teacher Gao. If you are tensed, the Qi's circulation will be stagnant. Is it right?" Nianci replied.

"Correct! If you want to relax your body, where should you focus in your relaxation?"

"Joints, Teacher Gao."

"Very good. Now, if you want to relax your joints, which joints of the body are the most important?" Teacher Gao knew this would be a challenging question to Nianci.

"Teacher Gao, the torso. The torso! Right?" Nianci replied.

This had surprised Teacher Gao. He thought Nianci would say arms and legs.

"Why the torso, Mingde?"

Nianci thought for a few seconds and answered, "Well! Since the torso includes all internal organs, if the torso is tense, all internal organs inside will also be tense. This will affect the entire body's Qi circulation."

"Wow! Indeed, this boy is rare and talented. He could get right to the point," Teacher Gao thought to himself.

"Very good. Now tell me, in order to relax your organs, other than to just relax, what can you do to help with relaxation?" Teacher Gao asked again.

"You have to know how to move your spine to enhance the Qi's circulation in your torso. Now, I know that is why I must practice spine movement. If I am able to move my spine section by section, I will be able to relax the torso to a deep level. Is that right, Teacher Gao?"

Nianci was so excited. He could see and feel the whole concept of relaxation.

"Remember what I said last week? Once you are able to feel your internal organs and make them relaxed, then you have reached the stage of 'Gongfu of Internal Vision.' This will offer you the capability of seeing and feeling your health before anything bad happens. This is self-alertness and awareness," Teacher Gao said.

"Wow! Isn't this what Papa said a couple years ago?" Nianci thought.

"When you apply this feeling to your opponent, you will see his intention even before his action. When you apply this feeling to your environment, you will feel everything around you. This is the alertness and awareness of yourself and your surroundings. This will help your spirit evolve," Teacher Gao said, though he did not expect Nianci to be able to comprehend it.

"Teacher Gao! You have just helped me untie many questions about what my father taught me a couple of years ago. I can see and comprehend it much better now," Nianci replied.

"His father must be an amazing person," Teacher Gao thought.

Teacher Gao next taught Nianci how to initiate the spine movements, how to coordinate with his breathing and anus, and how to use the mind and feeling to lead the Qi from the Lower Dantian to the arms. However, the most important thing Nianci learned was how to use the relaxed and gentle spine movements to relax his internal organs, especially his stomach.

Nianci was very excited now that he knew the way to relax his stomach to a deep level. He hoped this would help him heal his ulcer problem. He kept practicing whenever he had time.

"Relaxation and movement were the keys to healing. Deep and soft slender breathing is the key to relaxation. Feeling is the language by which my mind and body communicate," Nianci kept reminding himself when he practiced.

Six months later, Nianci realized that the frequency of his ulcer episodes had been gradually reduced. After one year of practice, it was amazing that he seldom had an ulcer episode. It would happen only if he ate something too acidic or spicy. Now he was much happier since the ulcer that had always bothered him and caused him a lot of pain was almost completely gone.

Within a year, Nianci had also learned the entire sequence of traditional Yang Style Taijiquan.

Teacher Gao had taught him, "Every movement has its meaning and purpose. If you don't comprehend the meaning and understand the applications, then the movements will be shallow and the purposes of practicing Taijiquan will be lost."

Nianci used the same feeling to practice his violin. Soon he realized that every tone had its own energy that caused the body, mind, and feeling to vibrate with it.

"How wonderful to be able to feel all of these!" he thought after nearly two years of learning and practicing with Teacher Gao.

Unfortunately, Teacher Gao eventually moved back to Hong Kong to be with his family. After that, Nianci practiced Taijiquan by himself and continued to search for the deeper feeling of Taijiquan. He hoped through practicing Taijiquan and violin, he could comprehend the meaning of his life. He always remembered what Teacher Gao said, "When you learn and practice Taijiquan, you are not just learning Taijiquan. You are also learning the way of knowing and feeling yourself. That means you are learning the way of life."

"How profound and true it was, what he said!" Nianci was very thankful.

When he was seventeen, Nianci's feeling for Taijiquan and his expressive violin playing had already reached profound levels. One day, after his lesson, his teacher had some news for him.

"Nianci, your skills have already surpassed what I can teach you. I really love your talent, but I cannot be selfish and keep you. You need a better teacher who can direct you to a more proficient level. I have contacted a very professional violinist who just returned from Germany. He graduated from Munich Music Conservatory. He is the one whom I think will be able to teach you further," Mr. Zhang said.

"May I ask, what is his name?" Nianci asked.

"His name is Chen, Qiusheng (陳丘勝). He is the most well-known violin professor in the Department of Music at Taipei City University (台北市立大學音樂學系). He is also one of the main violin players in the Taipei Symphony Orchestra (台北市立交響樂團). I will write a recommendation letter for you. Please go to see him and see if he will accept you as a private student."

"Yes! I remember I read about him in the newspaper a couple times. He is famous," Nianci answered.

Nianci walked home, thinking about the possibility of studying under Mr. Chen. In a way he felt sad to leave Mr. Zhang, but at the same time he was excited that he might have a teacher who could lead him to a higher level of skill.

Nianci talked to his parents about Mr. Zhang's referral and the next day after school he took a bus to Taipei City University. He was hoping anxiously that he could see Professor Chen. He went first to check with the school secretary, who told him that Mr. Chen had left for the afternoon. If he wanted to see him, he could come back after 7:00 that evening since Mr. Chen had a symphony rehearsal at that time. Since it would take a couple of hours to go home and return, Nianci decided to stay and wait. He knew his parents would not worry about him since they knew he was going to see Professor Chen right after school.

This was Nianci's last year of high school. When he turned 18, according to the law, he would be drafted into the military for one or two years of service. What type of service would be decided by a drawing. If he were lucky enough to draw either the Navy or Air Force, he would only serve for one year; otherwise, if his draw was for the army, he would need to serve two years. Nianci had grown quite a lot in the last couple of years. He was taller than his father now, handsome and mature.

"This will be the last year before I enter the military. I must try harder during this precious year," Nianci thought while he waited patiently in the university's music hall.

Fifteen minutes before rehearsal the musicians started to arrive. A couple minutes later, Professor Chen came into the music hall. Nianci recognized him right away since he had seen his picture in the newspaper.

Nianci stepped forward and introduced himself, "Professor Chen, I am Mr. Zhang's violin student. I came to see you and see if you can accept me as your student."

When Professor Chen looked at Nianci, he wondered to himself, "Such a young violinist. How good can he be? Mr. Zhang called me last night and talked about his talent. Yes, let me give him a test."

"Your name is Lin, Mingde. Right? I talked to Mr. Zhang last night. He highly recommended you to be my student," Professor Chen said.

Nianci was surprised that Mr. Zhang had talked to Professor Chen already about him. "He is such a good teacher to be so concerned with my music future," he thought with deep appreciation.

"Can you play one of your practice pieces for me?" Professor Chen asked.

"I am sorry, professor. I did not bring my violin with me," Nianci replied.

"No problem. You may use mine," Professor Chen told him and passed his violin case to Nianci.

Nianci took the instrument out carefully, like a professional, and tuned the strings till they were harmonized. He chose a piece that he loved – the Chopin Nocturne Op.9, No. 2, in E-flat Major. When he played, he put all of his heart into the beautiful piece, and within just a few phrases he had displayed his talent and skill.

"Wow! As Mr. Zhang said, he is talented. It is rare that he is only 17 and already able to place his feeling into the music and pull so much expression from the strings," Professor Chen thought as he was listening. A few musicians also came near to listen to Nianci play. After he finished, they gave him a good round of applause. They were surprised at the skill of this young man.

"Mingde, can you stay for one more hour? We will have rehearsal tonight. See if you are able to blend in with the violin section," Professor Chen said.

"I will try my best, Professor. But I don't have a violin," Nianci replied.

"It is okay. You may still use mine and sit in my place. After one hour, I will take over."

Nianci knew that this was a test, a serious test. He did not know which musical piece they were rehearsing. Now, he had to show how fast he could read the music as well as balance his sound with the group. This was a real challenge. However, he was also excited since he knew that Professor Chen would not have given him this opportunity if he did not think highly about his skills.

The conductor arrived and Professor Chen went to talk to him for a few minutes. The conductor showed Nianci which chair to sit in. In front of the chair was a stand that already had some sheet music on it. Nianci took a look and realized that the piece - J. S. Bach's Symphony #3 - was new to him. He was a little bit nervous. However, he needed to trust himself that he could do it.

In the beginning, Nianci made some mistakes since he was very nervous. However, after about five minutes he started to pick up the feeling of the composer and, his fingers deftly manipulated the strings, he began to skillfully express this feeling.

Professor Chen was very surprised. "This boy would be a precious addition to this symphony team," he thought. It does not matter what, Professor Chen had decided to accept him as a student.

The group took a break an hour into the rehearsal and Nianci came down to the stage to see Professor Chen. From Mr. Zhang, Professor Chen knew that Nianci was from a very poor family.

"Mingde! I would like you to join this symphony group. In this case, you can earn some income whenever we have a performance outside. Part of the income can be used to pay your tuition, and the rest of it you can use to help your parents," Professor Chen said.

"Thank you very much, Professor Chen!" Nianci was so happy since this would be his new future and a challenge.

"I teach my private lessons in the university studio on Tuesday and Friday from 6:00 to 8:00 in the evening. Please come next Tuesday."

The following week, when Nianci arrived, Professor Chen asked him to practice all of the basic drills that he already knew. He was very surprised since he knew these drills very well. When Professor Chen saw the wondering expression on Nianci's face, he explained to him.

"Mingde, you have good skills, but one important thing is missing. You still cannot blend your feeling with the composer's feeling. This is the key to lead you to the depth of the art. Remember, all arts are created by the feeling of the creators. The deeper the feeling, the deeper the art created. Tell me! Do you have the feeling of the composers in these basic drills?"

"I thought all these drills were just used to master your skills. I have never thought that they are connected to deep inner feeling," Nianci replied.

"Well! You see, each note has its vibration and this vibration touches your feelings. Each composer composed the music through his feelings and expressed those feelings into the music. It does not matter how simple or difficult. Only if you are able to blend your feeling with the composer, can you express the meaning of each note to its highest level," Professor Chen told him.

"I understand this theory. But how can I reach that feeling?" Nianci asked.

"Practice is the key. When you learn how to drive, only if you are able to blend your feeling with the car's function can you drive the car smoothly and efficiently! It is the same when you eat rice, can you develop the feeling of rice through taste? When you chew fifty times the taste is different from ten times. Only through practicing repeatedly can you feel the essence of the rice."

"Professor Chen, I will ponder it and practice with this new concept," Nianci said.

After that, Nianci practiced hard until he was able to catch the feeling; his skills had reached to a very high level compared to all other violinists in his age group in Taiwan. He had also become an important key player in the symphony. Within just six months the conductor had asked him to take the role of soloist a few times. His name continued to grow in public. Even though he was just 17 years old, he was hired to be a private violin teacher to the children of some well-to-do families. The money he earned through his music significantly helped his parents.

CHAPTER 6
CHASING THE DREAM
追 求 夢 想

A POSSIBLE FUTURE 可能的未來

Nianci graduated from Muzha High School a few days before his 18th birthday. He knew that when he turned 18, like all others, he would be drafted into the military. One week after his birthday, he received a notice from the military drafting center that he must present himself at the center for his service drawing on June 20th. Jiaming took the day off and went with him. The drawing assigned him to serve in the Air Force for one year and required him to report to the drafting center on August 22nd.

Before his military service would begin, Nianci had one more performance on August 17th. This would be his last performance for a long time. He believed he would not have any spare time for his violin practice while he was in the military.

On August 15, the conductor of The Vienna Boys Choir, Mr. Oliver Stech, and its manager, Michael Gormley, arrived in Taipei to meet with Mr. Huang, the sponsor of the Boys Choir's performance in Taiwan. They wanted to talk about their concert tour that would take place August 24th. Mr. Huang, as an enthusiastic host, invited the conductor and manager to the Taipei Symphony performance. As honored guests they would be seated in the front row. Both guests politely accepted, though they expected the quality of the performance would not be nearly as good as a performance in Vienna or one of the other western European countries. This was due in part to the fact that Taiwan's orchestra program was very young, having had only 15 years of symphonic education and development. However, when they heard

Nianci's violin solo during the concert, Mr. Stech could not believe that there was such a talented boy in the Taipei Symphony, one that was not just skillful but also was able to play his violin with great expression and deep feeling.

Mr. Stech was impressed and enjoyed Nianci's performance very much. During the break, he asked Mr. Huang in English, "This boy is very talented and performs excellently. If he has a chance to train under the best violinist in the world, he could be among the top in the music world."

"Yes, he has been recognized as one of the best in Taiwan, especially given his young age," Mr. Huang replied.

"May I talk to him after the performance, Mr. Huang? Would you be able to arrange that?" Mr. Stech asked.

"I will go to talk to their manager and conductor and see what they say," Mr. Huang said and left to go back stage. Since he had sponsored so many performances of the Taipei City Symphony, he was very well acquainted with both the Symphony's conductor and manager.

Within five minutes he had returned, since the second half of the show would begin soon.

"The conductor said he would talk to the boy and ask him to stay after the show. We can meet him back stage," Mr. Huang informed Mr. Stech.

The symphony's performance was very successful. Immediately after the show, Mr. Huang brought his two guests to the performers' changing room. After Mr. Huang introduced them to Nianci, they all went to a small room to talk.

"Mr. Stech was very impressed with your skills. He would like to talk to you," Mr. Huang told Nianci.

Through Mr. Huang, Nianci realized that the two gentlemen were from the music capital, Vienna. He was very surprised and touched that they had enjoyed his performance enough that they wanted to talk with him.

Mr. Huang spoke to Mr. Stech for a few minutes, then told Nianci, "Mr. Stech suggests that you find a professional high-level teacher to guide you to the deepest level of the violin. He said you have the potential to become one of the world's best violinists. He also knows that there is no such teacher in Taiwan. He would like to see if you are able to go to Vienna for further education."

While Nianci was pleased and very happy to hear that, he had his military service in the way, among other things.

"Mr. Huang, in a couple weeks I will be joining the air force for one year. After that, I don't have any idea of what I will do. Furthermore, I don't have money to pursue an education in Vienna. My parents cannot possibly pay for it. I wish I could make it," Nianci said with an expression of deep regret on his face.

Mr. Huang translated what Nianci had said to Mr. Stech, and they discussed his predicament for a while before Mr. Huang turned back to Nianci.

"Mr. Stech tells me that he could write a recommendation letter for you. When he returns to Vienna, he will also mention it to the school director. He believes that you have a good chance of receiving a scholarship. That means all of your expenses, including your lodging and tuition, will be free. However, you would have to cover your moving expenses by yourself."

When Nianci heard of this, his face shone with joy at the possibility. This was a big chance that brought him great hope for his future. He was so touched and happy that his eyes turned red. Mr. Stech, Mr. Gormley, and Mr. Huang could see his emotion in his facial expression. Mr. Stech spoke some more to Mr. Huang after which Mr. Huang turned again to Nianci.

"Mr. Stech will send you a recommendation letter in the next few days. He said you should request application forms from the school first, and then send in his recommendation letter along with your completed forms. The best chance to be accepted is at the Vienna Conservatory of Mag. Eva Maria Schmid. He knows the school director there very well. You will have to begin your application process next February."

Through Mr. Huang, Mr. Stech gave Nianci the address and then the visitors left.

Since this was the last symphony concert before Nianci's military service, both Jiaming and Xiaohua had been present for the performance and were now waiting for him in the lobby. They did not know what could be keeping him so late - most of the other performers had already left. As they were wondering what happened to him, Nianci came out with a glow of joy on his face.

"Papa! Mama! Sorry for making you wait. I had a meeting with a few important people," Nianci burst out.

Nianci then proceeded to tell them all about the possibility of being able to study in Vienna. Both Jiaming and Xiaohua were very happy to hear the news but, being parents, they also worried that if Nianci went to Vienna they would not see him for at least four years. They were a very close and loving family, and this would be a long separation. Another problem they worried about was how to find the money to pay for the airplane ticket to get him there. They would not be able to afford it. However, they also knew that this was Nianci's future and they would sacrifice anything for him.

Just a few days later, Nianci received a letter. Along with the letter, there was a sealed envelope. The letter was from Mr. Huang telling him the sealed envelope contained the recommendation letter that Mr. Stech had promised. Nianci was happy but also hesitant. He knew that his parents would have a hard time finding the money for his airplane ticket, which would cost at least US$700, the equivalent of NT$25,000. He also did not want to leave his parents alone. He would miss them so much. Reluctantly he put the recommendation letter on the corner of his desk and left it there.

A little more than a week later, Jiaming and Xiaohua took Nianci to the military drafting center to report for his duty. Xiaohua was very sad and worried to have her son going into service. She knew that if there was a war between Communist China and Taiwan, the chance of Nianci's surviving the conflict would be very slim. She still remembered Communist China's attack on Taiwan on August 23 of 1958. In this battle it was estimated that more than 31,000 cannon balls fell on the front line at Jinmen Island (金門), a small island with only 59 square miles. Almost all the Taiwanese soldiers in this cannon battle died. If not for the help that came from the American Navy's Seventh Fleet, the Communists would have already taken over Taiwan. Everyone knew that Communist China could possibly attack again.

"Mom, do not worry! I will come back to visit you whenever I have leave. You know from Pingdong (屏東) to Taipei is about only six hours on the train," Nianci reassured her with tears in his eyes. Jiaming and Xiaohua left with sorrow.

Chinese New Year came five months later, on February 11th, and Nianci was given five days of vacation. He was so happy and very anxious to see his parents. Both Jiaming and Xiaohua were also excited. The little family enjoyed every minute of their five days together. However, there was a shadow in Nianci's heart especially when he saw Mr. Stech's recommendation letter sitting on his desk. He knew it was time to apply for admission and scholarship to the music school in Vienna. If he didn't, he would lose that chance forever. But he also knew he did not have the money to fulfill this dream.

This shadow was soon spotted by Jiaming and Xiaohua. The day before Nianci was to return to the military, Jiaming approached him.

"Nianci, I want to talk to you. Can we take a walk? Let us go to the willow trees. There are so many happy memories there," Jiaming asked.

"Yes, Papa," Nianci responded. He did not know what his father was going to say but walked along with him until they arrived at the spot and sat down on a log.

Jiaming got right to the core of the matter. "Nianci, tell me the truth honestly from your heart. Do you wish to go to Vienna?"

After Nianci hesitated for a moment, he said, "Yes, Papa. It is my dream and would mean great things for my future. But I think it will only be a dream. We cannot afford it, Papa."

"Remember what I told you before? If you really want something in your heart, you must pursue it ceaselessly with firm confidence."

"But Papa! We don't have money to make it happen."

"Nianci, listen to me! Your mom and I have been working very hard the last five months once we knew the possibility of your future study in Vienna. Since then, with our old savings, we have saved about NT$5,000."

"But, Papa! It will cost about NT$25,000 for an airplane ticket and that is far beyond what we can afford."

"Nianci! Listen to me. Go ahead and apply for it. I will find the way. I am confident that this will happen."

Nianci took Mr. Stech's recommendation letter with him when he returned to do his service. He wrote a letter to the Vienna Conservatory of Mag. Eva Maria Schmid and requested the application forms, which he received in three weeks. Immediately, he completed the forms in his poor English and sent them in, along with Mr. Stech's recommendation letter.

In truth, Nianci did not have too much hope of his application being successful as he did not know how to fill it in clearly with the poor English he had learned while in high school. All the same, he waited anxiously for a reply, and worried about the financial difficulty he would encounter should he be accepted. An admission notification arrived from the conservatory at the end of May. The school was offering him a complete scholarship that would cover his tuition and dormitory. In addition, he would also have about US$200 monthly as an allowance. He was very happy and surprised. He had not expected the scholarship to cover so much, so handsomely. Now, the only thing he needed to worry about was his plane ticket.

Nianci wrote a letter home to tell his parents about the good news. He also mentioned his concern about paying for the airplane ticket. Actually, in order to save enough money for Nianci's ticket, Jiaming and Xiaohua had been putting aside every penny they could. They had also enlarged their vegetable garden to double its size from March to August, the best few months for vegetable growing. Xiaohua then took the produce they harvested to the free market to sell. From all of their efforts, they had managed to save NT$15,000. But it was still NT$10,000 short. Finally, Jiaming decided to visit Zunxian and see if it were possible for Zunxian to lend him some money. After he explained the situation, Zunxian went into another room and brought back $15,000 NT.

"Jiaming, please take this. You don't have to return it! It is a gift from me." Zunxian still remembered how Jiaming had saved his son, Nianxiong, in 1951. He thought that without Jiaming's coming to the rescue, his son would have been dead these past 24 years. He also remembered trying to reward Jiaming at the time, and that Jiaming hadn't wanted to accept his money. Now his son was married and had one beautiful daughter.

"No! No! I cannot take it without paying it back. You have already treated us kindly for the last 24 years. I cannot expect more." Jiaming was very surprised about Zunxian's offer.

"Look, when the government took most of my land, I was very angry. Later, I used the compensation money they paid me to make an investment in an import and export business. I have earned more money than I expected. Please take it. I am very happy to help!" Zunxian said. He thought this was the best way to repay Jiaming for saving his son's life.

"No! I can't and shouldn't. Please allow me to pay you back," Jiaming said with red eyes.

"Let us not talk about it further. Only when your financial condition improves, then we should talk about it. Okay?"

Jiaming left with deep gratitude in his heart. Now, he had NT$5,000 extra for Nianci should he need it once he was outside of the country. He wrote a letter to Nianci letting him know what had happened that evening. When Nianci received the letter, he was filled with excitement and happiness. He knew now that his dream would become reality.

Nianci was discharged with honor from the air force on August 23rd.

He had completed his service and could now legally leave Taiwan to further his studies. When he arrived home, the first thing he wanted to do was visit Zunxian and thank him for his help, but when Jiaming and Nianci went to thank Zunxian, Zunxian was not home. He was in southern Taiwan visiting a manufacturer whose factory he was interested in investing in. Zunxian would not be back until the end of August. Unfortunately, Nianci was scheduled to leave for Vienna on August 29th as he needed to be at school a couple of days early for orientation. The semester would begin on September 1st. Nianci and Jiaming just left a message with Zunxian's wife and went home.

Getting Acquainted with Suqin 與素琴相識

When Nianci arrived at the conservatory's registration desk to check in, he discovered there was already a line with about 15 students in it. As he took his place in the line, he noticed a nice-looking Asian girl just two persons in front of him. He was immediately curious about this girl, wondering, "Is she a Chinese? Japanese? Or Korean? There are not too many Asian students around."

As it happened, after just a few minutes this girl also noticed Nianci standing a couple of persons behind her. In her mind, she wondered, "Who is this handsome Asian young man? From China, Taiwan, Japan, or Korea?" As much as she wanted to know more about him, she felt embarrassed to introduce herself. After all, she was a girl. She couldn't help hoping, however, that this young man would come to talk to her.

Unfortunately, Nianci was feeling too shy to approach her, especially since he did not know much English or any languages other than Mandarin and Taiwanese. Instead, he just peeked at her secretly.

"It would be wonderful if we become friends. She is so young and beautiful. I wonder what her favorite musical instrument is?" Nianci's mind kept generating a lot of thoughts like this.

Ten minutes later, this girl used very fluent German to talk to the lady who was registering students. Nianci heard some of their conversation but did not understand any of it. After the girl finished her registration, she decided to stay for a few more minutes and see if she could learn anything about this handsome young oriental man. She sat on the couch next to the registration counter where she could hear what was said.

When it was Nianci's turn, Nianci tried to use his poor English and hand gestures to communicate with the registration lady, but it did not go smoothly. They could not understand each other well enough to get the registration done. Nianci was so embarrassed. When this girl saw it, she laughed in her heart, then stepped up to the counter and used German to tell the lady that she could interpret for them. She said this even though she did not know if Nianci was Japanese, Chinese, or Korean.

"What happens if he does not speak Mandarin? I don't understand Japanese or Korean. Okay, let me try to speak English with him," the girl thought.

"Do you speak English?" she asked Nianci.

"Yes, but very little," Nianci answered.

"Are you a Japanese, Korean, or Chinese?"

"I am Chinese from Taiwan," Nianci replied again.

The girl beamed at Nianci with a big smile full of joy and switched to Mandarin. "Let me help you," she said.

"Xiexie Nin! (Thank you) What is your name?" Nianci asked happily.

"My name is Chen, Suqin (陳素琴). Let us finish your registration first and then we can get acquainted with each other."

Acting as an interpreter, Suqin helped Nianci finish his registration smoothly.

Nianci looked at this beautiful lady and expressed his appreciation. "Thank you very much, Miss Chen," he said with a deep bow. All the people around them laughed.

Suqin was embarrassed, and said in Mandarin, "Let's get out of here quick. Let me take you to your dormitory."

Nianci followed her out of the registration office. "How do you speak German and English so well?" he asked her on the way to his dormitory.

"I came here two years ago. I just transferred from a German music school to this conservatory. You know, Vienna Conservatory of Mag. Eva Maria Schmid is one of the best music colleges in the world."

"No wonder you can speak German so well."

"Actually, almost all Germans and Austrians also speak English, especially the younger generation. Okay, now tell me your name?" Suqin asked.

"My name is Lin, Mingde. However, my parents and close friends call me Nianci, my nickname," Nianci replied.

"Wow! He has already treated me as a close friend and told me his nickname," Suqin thought.

"Your Mandarin has a Taiwanese accent. Are you a Taiwanese?" Nianci asked.

"Yes! But your Mandarin is very standard and perfect. Are you a Taiwanese?"

"No, I am not. My parents were from Mainland China." Nianci used the Taiwanese dialect for his reply.

"I am wondering then how you can speak the Taiwanese dialect so well. I could not tell the difference between you and other Taiwanese." Suqin was very surprised that Nianci could speak the Taiwanese dialect so well.

"Actually, I grew up in a Taiwanese village. My parents speak the Taiwanese dialect very well too."

In Suqin's mind a shadow appeared. She knew that her father did not like foreign province people.

"Why is the hate so strong amongst the older generation against foreign province people?" she wondered. "I need to keep our relationship secret from Papa. He will never approve our friendship."

"Where does your family live?" Suqin asked.

"Muzha! An Eastern suburb of Taipei."

"I know where Muzha is. My family lived in the Yangming Mountain area (陽明山)," Suqin said.

"Wow! Her family must be very rich. Only rich people can afford to live in Yangming Mountain. I was there once on a high school field trip. All the houses there were big and elegant," Nianci thought. "No wonder that she can afford to come to Europe for her musical studies."

They talked and talked until they arrived at Nianci's dormitory. Suqin helped Nianci unpack and settle down, then got ready to leave.

"I need to go to my dormitory too. See you later," Suqin said.

"May I come with you? I enjoyed your company very much," Nianci said with a shy and embarrassed expression on his face.

"Of course! We can use this chance to get to know each other better. You know, we will be here together at least four years," Suqin laughed.

They went to Suqin's dormitory together.

The next day, which was the day before classes would begin, Nianci went to see Suqin at her dormitory.

"I wonder if you would like to go with me to visit a professor. He wrote a recommendation letter for me. I believe that was the reason that I acquired the scholarship here. You know, without the scholarship, I would never have been able to come to Vienna to study," Nianci said. In truth, while Nianci very much wanted to get to know Suqin better, he also would need an interpreter for him to talk with the professor. His German and English were very bad.

"Sure! I am bored and class will start tomorrow," Suqin responded. Actually, she was also eager to spend more time with Nianci. After just knowing each other for one day, she felt that she could stay with him for her whole life.

"What is the professor's name?" Suqin asked.

"Professor Oliver Stech. He was the conductor of the Vienna Choir."

"I know him, he is very famous. But I have never met him. You know, I also just arrived a couple of days ago from Germany. Do you have his address?

"Yes, I do."

Using the address Nianci had, they found Professor Stech's home. They felt a little bit awkward and uncomfortable since they had not made an appointment first. Nianci took a deep breath and rang the bell.

A young man opened the door. "What can I do for you?" he asked.

"Is this Professor Stech's home? If it is, can we see him?" Suqin responded in German.

"Sure! Come in. He is in the living room," the young man said.

The young man directed Nianci and Suqin to the living room and announced, "Pa! You have visitors." Then he returned to the back of the house. This made Nianci more comfortable, as their conversation would be more private.

When Professor Stech saw Nianci, he recognized him right away. He had stayed in contact with the conservatory and already knew Nianci's application as a scholarship student had been accepted.

"It is you! I am glad to see you again," Professor Stech said.

Nianci gave him a deep bow, Suqin followed as well.

"Professor, this is Suqin. She is also a student here," Nianci introduced her with poor English. He then set his bag down and removed a gift he had brought, a nice Chinese engraving of a lion playing with a ball and gave it to Professor Stech.

"I hope you like it," Nianci said. "I want to thank you for your recommendation to come here for advanced study. Without your letter, I believe I would not be here." He bowed again to Professor Stech.

"You are welcome! I am very happy that you were able to come."

They talked for quite a while. The Professor asked many questions about Nianci's plans for his future and about what Suqin's special music instrument was and so on. The three of them had a good time. Nianci and Suqin made sure to leave before lunchtime. It would be impolite to stay too long.

Now that Nianci and Suqin had gotten acquainted, they met each other whenever they had time. Suqin taught Nianci how to speak German, especially those sentences related to music. Without knowing German, Nianci would have a hard time learning in his classes, not to mention he might also upset his professors. Nianci practiced very hard. In one way he liked Suqin as a close friend, but in another way, he treated her as a language teacher.

Eventually, Nianci discovered that Suqin was 18, only one year younger than he was. A few weeks into the semester, they also realized that both of them were chosen to be in the school symphony. Suqin specialized in piano while Nianci focused on the violin. That was so great since just the two of them together could be an ensemble and play together.

When they had time, and there were empty practice rooms available, they would go and play music together, sometimes Chinese and Taiwanese folk songs. They were very happy together. In fact, it was the happiest period of Nianci's life so far. He knew his parents would miss him very much and he wrote to them as often as possible. In his letters he told them that he had become acquainted with a girl who was also from Taiwan. Jiaming and Xiaohua missed him very much, but they knew he was happy in Vienna and they were very happy for him. Occasionally, Nianci would send a photo of himself or with Suqin to his parents.

During the weekends, when they did not have rehearsal, Nianci and Suqin would spend time visiting the old residences of famous composers such as Haydn, Mozart, Schubert, and Brahms. However, the one they were most interested in was Beethoven.

Nianci noticed, when they went to Pasqualati House Museum where Beethoven wrote his famous pieces, Fidelio and Symphonies 4, 5, 7, and 8, that Suqin became very emotional. When she saw the piano Beethoven used to compose his music, she could not help reaching out to touch the piano even though it was forbidden. The music that Beethoven composed in this room played on a sound system. Suqin sat with tears in her eyes while she listened with Nianci. That was the first time that Nianci hugged a lady.

When Nianci and Suqin went to Beethoven's residence at Heligenstadt Testament Museum, they saw Beethoven's hair posted on a wall. That triggered Suqin's sad emotions and tears welled up in her eyes once again. One more time, when they visited Beethoven's tomb in

Central Cemetery, Suqin became so emotional that she could not help crying.

Nianci and Suqin also went to The Mozarthaus Vienna, Mozart's residence from 1784 to 1787. This was the only surviving Viennese residence of Mozart. During all of these occasions, they shared their love of music and appreciation for the composers. Their hearts were together in this.

One day after finishing visiting the museums, Nianci and Suqin went to the park. Suqin was very quiet since her mind was still on what they had just experienced. Nianci pulled her closer and hugged her, then he kissed Suqin for the first time. Now, they knew they were in love.

Whenever Nianci was alone while Suqin had her classes, he would visit music instrument shops near campus. The shops had so many nice, but expensive, violins. He always wanted to have a very good violin to perform with. The violin his father had purchased for him was good, especially since it had been bought with love, but to use it for public performances... the quality of the sound was simply not suitable. To blend with the other high-quality violins in the symphony, he also needed a higher quality violin. Unfortunately, he could not afford it. All he could do was go to the shops and test the violins on display to satisfy his desire for a more beautiful sound.

Three years of happy times at the conservatory passed very quickly for Nianci and Suqin. One evening, when they were together sitting on a bench in the park, Suqin broached a serious topic.

"Nianci! I need to tell you one thing," Suqin said, looking at Nianci intently.

"What! Why you are so serious?"

"My professor told me that if possible, I should stay for two more years to get my master's degree in music. He said with two more years, my skill could reach a level that only a few pianists in the world could match. He strongly encouraged me to do so. He also mentioned that I may be able to acquire a scholarship if I apply," Suqin explained to Nianci.

"Well! That means you will not go back to Taiwan with me next year after graduation? You know, I don't want to be separated from you. But if you go back, you will miss the chance to advance yourself to a higher level. We all know there is no qualified teacher who is able to teach us in Taiwan," Nianci said.

"That's why I am so sad. I don't want to leave you, but I also don't want to lose this chance," Suqin said.

After a while, Nianci thought that if he really loved Suqin, he shouldn't be selfish. He should encourage Suqin to continue her piano training.

"Suqin, listen to me! I don't wish to separate from you either. But I think your future music career is more important. If you lose the chance now, you may never get it again. Furthermore, this will be a good chance to test our love. After two years of separation, if we still love each other, then we can get married." Nianci looked at Suqin with a naughty face.

Suqin could not believe that Nianci was encouraging her to continue and get her master's degree.

"He is not selfish! He really loves me," she thought.

She pulled his head forward and kissed him.

"I will talk to my parents about taking a vacation right after graduation next year. Without you here it will be so boring during summertime," Suqin said.

"That would be so great! I would like you to meet my parents," Nianci told her.

An Unforeseen Destiny One night, Nianci and Suqin took a walk in the famous park in Vienna, Sigmund-Freud Park. It was late and not too many people were around. They occasionally saw some other lovers, but mostly they had the park to themselves. When they came to a corner and sat on a bench to rest, they saw an old man walking slowly under a park light about 40 yards from them. Suddenly, the old man fell to the ground. Immediately they were on their feet and ran to him. They saw that he was clutching the left side of his chest with both hands and that there was a cold sweat on his face. He was in obvious pain.

"He is having a heart attack," Suqin shouted.

"Go to the telephone booth and call an ambulance right away," Nianci told her.

Suqin quickly ran to a telephone booth about 20 yards away, but when she entered the booth, she did not know what number to call. She took a deep breath to calm herself down, then noticed a sign on the telephone stand, "122 Fire Brigade, 133 Police, 140 Mountain Rescue, and 144 Ambulance." She was very happy to see it since the situation was so urgent. She dialed the number 144 and reported the emergency. After that, she returned to Nianci and saw that he had already placed the old man in a more comfortable position. He was using his hand to slap the old man's left inner elbow. Nianci had remembered what Teacher Gao taught him about emergency ways to help a person having a heart attack. After the old man's elbow turned red, Nianci switched to slapping the right inner elbow. A few minutes later, the old man began to feel better and his pain was significantly reduced. He looked at Nianci and Suqin with tearful eyes full of gratitude.

"Don't talk. Just keep taking deep breaths and relax. An ambulance is on the way," Nianci used his German to tell the old man. Suqin was afraid the old man could not understand Nianci, so she repeated it again. The old man closed his eyes and took some more deep breaths. A few minutes later his pale face had regained some color, and just a little after that an ambulance arrived at the park. Nianci ran to the gate of the park and led the ambulance attendants to the place where the old man lay. One of them took a look at the old man and gave him an injection. After that, they put him on stretcher.

"Are you his family?" one of the ambulance attendants asked.

"No, we are not, sir," Suqin replied.

"Could you please come with us? We need you to fill in a report about this. It will not take too long," the attendant requested.

Since it was still early, Nianci and Suqin agreed and got into the ambulance with the old man.

In the ambulance, the old man was doing much better already. He smiled at Nianci and Suqin. "Thank you very much for saving my life. Without you, I don't know what would have happened," he said.

"You are welcome. We are music students from Taiwan. My name is Mingde and her name is Suqin. We hope you get better soon. Please rest. It is important for you now." Nianci used his German to respond to the old man. After three years in Austria, Nianci's German was much more fluent than when he had first arrived.

"My name is Christoph Müller. Thank you again," the old man said, then closed his eyes and paid attention to his breathing and relaxation.

As soon as the ambulance arrived at the hospital, hospital staff took the old man away immediately. It took a long time for Nianci and Suqin to fill in the report since they did not know many of the German medical terms. They had to keep asking the lady at the service counter to help them. Finally, they finished.

"Should we take a final look at the old man? I hope he is okay," Suqin said.

"I think he should be okay. He is in good hands now," Nianci replied. They were getting ready to leave the hospital when a nurse came out to talk to them.

"Hello, Mister and Miss. If possible, Mr. Müller would like to see you for a few minutes. Is that okay?" the nurse asked.

"Of course," Nianci replied. They were wondering why the old man wanted to see them again.

"I think he just wants to thank us again," Suqin thought.

When they entered the emergency room, they could see the old man was feeling much better already. The old man used his hands to welcome them.

"The doctor will see me in a few minutes. I am alone in Vienna. Can you do me a favor? If possible, can you come to visit me tomorrow? I may need further help over the next couple of days. I would appreciate that very much," Mr. Müller asked them.

"Since tomorrow is Saturday, we can come to see you tomorrow. Just rest and we'll be back tomorrow, Mr. Müller," Nianci said.

The old man was relieved to hear they would come back the next day.

The next afternoon when Nianci and Suqin returned to visit Mr. Müller, the old man beamed at them with a big smile as soon as they entered the room. It seemed that he had been waiting for them for the whole morning.

"I am so happy to see you again! I was afraid you would not be able to come. I am a stranger to you, and you offered me so much help," the old man said.

"No, no! You are just like a grandpa to us now. We could not come this morning because we had a rehearsal that we had to attend or we would have been in big trouble," Suqin said with a laugh.

"The doctor said that one of my coronary arteries was almost sealed. They need to conduct an angioplasty procedure to open the blocked vessel. They will do this procedure tomorrow morning. I am very scared," Mr. Müller explained.

"Do you have any relatives in Vienna?" Nianci asked.

"No, not in Vienna. I already called my sons last night about this and told them I am stable now. They will arrive here tomorrow after-noon. I have two sons. The older one is an engineer who married a French girl and has one boy. His wife is expecting a second child, a girl. My younger son was just married last year and moved to Italy with his wife. Both he and his wife are teachers. He is teaching German in Italy." The old man said all of this with a happy smile on his face. It was obvious that he missed his sons and grandson very much.

"It sounds like you have a wonderful family. Why don't you live with your sons?" Suqin asked curiously. Since her German was much better than that of Nianci, she wanted to talk more and get better acquainted with this old man.

"You see, after my wife's death from cancer last year, I was thinking about moving to Paris and staying with my elder son, Phil. But I don't speak French. And frankly I don't feel comfortable leaving Austria. I have so many memories here," the old man replied.

Suqin and Nianci chatted with the old man for quite a while. By the time they left, they all felt they knew each other much better and the feeling of being strangers had disappeared. The old man thought both Nianci and Suqin were very kind. They were like his own children to him.

"Sorry, but we need to go. We have to practice tonight again. What time did the doctor say the procedure would take place?" Suqin asked.

"Nine-thirty tomorrow morning. Will you come? It would give me a lot of courage," the old man said. He felt so much more comfortable with them around.

"Sure! We will be here tomorrow morning about 9. Don't worry! I have heard that though angioplasty is a newly developed medical technology, it is very safe and effective." Nianci tried to comfort Mr. Müller with his poor German.

The next day, Nianci and Suqin arrived at the hospital at 9 o'clock. They just sat with the old man and chatted about many things to try to ease his worry.

"We will wait here until the procedure is finished," Suqin told him.

"Thank you very much. Without my sons here, you are just like my family offering me so much comfort and courage." Mr. Müller looked at them with deep appreciation.

Two and half hours later, a nurse came to see Nianci and Suqin in the waiting room, "Mr. Müller is in the recovery room now. You can see him if you wish to."

Nianci and Suqin nodded their heads and followed the nurse to the recovery room. Mr. Müller was awake and smiling at them.

"Actually, the procedure was pretty easy and smooth. I was awake the whole time since they only anesthetized my right thigh at the joint area. They explained to me what they were doing. From their explanation, I could understand how they did it clearly. It was amazing for today's medical technology," Mr. Müller told them.

"How do you feel now?" Nianci asked.

"I feel great! The tightness in my chest and stiff feeling have suddenly disappeared. I had had that feeling for a couple years," Mr. Müller replied.

Everyone was very happy that everything turned out so well.

"We cannot stay too long since we have another rehearsal tonight. Since we have regular classes during the weekdays, the only days we have for rehearsal are Saturday and Sunday. I'm sorry that we cannot stay with you or come to see you this afternoon," Suqin explained.

"I understand, Suqin. Right? Did I say it correctly? My sons will be here this afternoon. The doctor said I could go home in two days. Will you come to my home next weekend? Please. It will mean so much to me." Mr. Müller pleaded with them.

As they already felt like comfortable, old friends, Nianci looked at Suqin and smiled.

"Of course, we will come to visit you. Where is your home?" Suqin asked.

Mr. Müller handed Suqin a piece of notepaper with his address and telephone number on it. It seemed he had had this note already prepared before they came. It was obvious Mr. Müller's invitation was sincere.

Nianci and Suqin bowed down and hugged Mr. Müller before they left. This was the first time they had hugged him, and it made him feel very warm and close to them.

As promised, Nianci and Suqin went to visit Mr. Müller the following Sunday morning. They had an entire day off without rehearsal as Saturday's rehearsal had gone so smoothly and satisfactorily that the director gave the group a little break. Mr. Müller opened the door right away, as soon as the bell was rung. It seemed that he had been waiting and expecting their arrival. He was very happy to see them and announced that he was almost entirely recovered from the procedure.

"Welcome to my home," Mr. Müller said as he showed them inside.

Nianci and Suqin looked around the apartment with great curiosity. It was located in a very rich area near the park where they had rescued Mr. Müller. The inside of the apartment was decorated with expensive furniture, and when they stepped into the big living room, they could see a beautiful grand piano in one corner of the room. This piqued Suqin's interest and curiosity since she loved the piano and had spent so much of her life becoming an expert pianist. She saw that the piano was made by Steinway, one of the most famous piano producers.

"This piano must cost US$10,000," Suqin thought. "It would not be possible for any Taiwanese pianist to own it." Her fingers itched to play the Steinway, but she knew it was not polite to ask immediately. She could not stop herself from looking at it, however, and wondering how such an expensive piano had come to be there.

Mr. Müller noticed Suqin's interest and said, "This piano belongs to my elder son. He loved to play piano since he was a child. I bought this piano for him on his 18th birthday. Unfortunately, after his marriage, he seldom plays. I keep it in tune at all times. You know, I was an importer of the best musical instruments from the best factories in the world. I distributed them in Austria and some European countries until I sold my business when I turned 70 years old."

"What is your age now, Mr. Müller? Oh! I am sorry to ask," Nianci said politely.

"I am 75 now. I am getting too old," Mr. Müller sighed.

"No wonder he could afford this luxury piano," Suqin thought.

"Are your sons still in Vienna? May we meet them?" Nianci asked.

"No, after three days they needed to go back due to their work. Besides, I felt much better already," Mr. Müller replied.

Mr. Müller showed Nianci and Suqin around his apartment. There were three bedrooms, all large and comfortable. When they came to a room in the corner, he told them, "This was my second son's room. His name is Ben. Now, they are all gone, and the apartment is empty. I feel very lonely sometimes. I miss the old times." Mr. Müller's face took on a depressed expression.

In Ben's room, Nianci saw a violin case and became curious to know what kind it was. "May I take a look at this violin, Mr. Müller?" he asked.

"Naturally! This violin belongs to Ben. He loved it. I gave it to him when he was 18 years old. You like the violin, Mingde, right?"

"Yes, Mr. Müller. Suqin is good at piano and I am more interested in violin."

Nianci took the violin case and opened it carefully. He was shocked to see that the violin was made by the most famous Italian violinmaker, Antonio Stradivari. He kept looking at it and wishing he could play it, even if only for a few minutes. He knew that the sound produced by this violin would be fantastic.

When Mr. Müller saw Nianci's expression, he suggested, "Bring it to the living room. I will be very happy to hear you play this violin and Suqin play the piano. One of my most enjoyable things many years ago was listening to my sons play. Oh! Time passes so fast!" he said with a sad expression on his face.

"Is Ben still playing? Why didn't he take this violin with him? It is easy to carry around," Nianci asked curiously.

"When he was 25 years old, he went to ski with his friends. When they were competing downhill his left leg suddenly cramped. He hit a tree and broke his left arm. Since then he cannot move his left arm and fingers as comfortably as he used to. Ben quit playing after that accident. How I yearn to hear their practice again. They used to play together, one at the piano and the other on the violin. It was a great time. My wife and I would just sit there and listen." Once they were back in the living room, he pointed to a nice big couch. "Can you play for me? Please. I miss the old times," Mr. Müller said.

"Naturally, Mr. Müller," Suqin said and looked at Nianci. She knew from Nianci's greedy expression that he wanted to play that violin as much as she wanted to play that piano. They found some well-known classical music scores beside the piano and looked through them, talking to each other for a minute. Suqin sat down on the piano bench and hit an A so that Nianci could tune the strings of the violin. Then they started to play.

Nianci and Suqin grew more and more excited as they played, they could not believe how beautiful the sound of these two instruments was.

"The sound of this violin is far better than any of the violins I have played in the music shops," Nianci thought. He felt like a child holding a very precious tool in his hand.

Suqin was also very impressed with the sound the piano produced.

"I wish I had a nice piano like this one. I believe even if my father wanted to buy one for me, there is no place you can buy one in Taiwan. Most families cannot afford this kind of expensive piano," Suqin thought. She played with her superior skills and blended with Nianci's violin perfectly. They had practiced together like this very often at the music conservatory, since this was one of their favorite pastimes, especially when they played Chinese or Taiwanese music.

After Suqin and Nianci finished playing a piece by Chopin, Mr. Müller sat on the couch lost in thought and memory. The music had taken him back to the past and his eyes were full of tears. Suddenly, he realized that the music had stopped.

"I have not had such a good time in many years," Mr. Müller said. "Thank you. Can you play more? Please don't worry about me. I could listen to you play all day."

Since this was a rare chance to use such good instruments, Nianci and Suqin were very happy to continue. They interspersed classical pieces with some Chinese music and folk songs. Mr. Müller was deeply touched and listened quietly.

After nearly three hours, Suqin said, "I need to take a break."

Suqin and Nianci stopped and each of them went to the bathroom.

"I am so happy today. Let me treat you for lunch," Mr. Müller said when they returned.

"It is so impolite to disturb your life. Now, you want to treat us to lunch." Nianci felt a bit uneasy.

"Nonsense! Nonsense! You just don't know how much I appreciate your visit and music. Come on, my children!" Mr. Müller said, treating them like he would his own children.

The three of them went to a very fancy Austrian restaurant that was not too far from the apartment. This was the first time Nianci and Suqin had been to such an elegant and luxurious restaurant.

"Wow! Every dish is so expensive. The food must be great!" Nianci thought as he looked at the menu.

Suqin and Nianci did not know how to order. They relied on Mr. Müller's suggestions to choose their food and drinks.

As they were waiting for their meals to arrive, Mr. Müller asked with some concern, "How long will you be in Vienna?"

"We will graduate in June next year. Suqin has decided to stay two more years for her master's degree. After graduation, I need to go home to help my parents," Nianci replied.

"May I ask an unreasonable request?" Mr. Müller looked at them with a longing expression on his face. When Nianci and Suqin motioned for him to continue, he asked, "Would you please come to my home more often or at least every weekend? I enjoyed your company so much, and especially listening to your playing."

Nianci and Suqin looked each other. Suqin knew that Nianci would like to play that violin as much as he could. In addition, she also liked to play that piano, especially with Nianci.

"We will come to visit you as much as we can. As you know, we will be very busy in classes during weekdays and often have rehearsal on weekends. However, we will try our best to come to visit you," Suqin said. This made Mr. Müller very happy.

"I may move to Paris and stay with my son next year. I will enjoy playing with my grandchildren. I wish my wife were still alive and could enjoy them with me. Please come as much as you can."

They enjoyed a very elegant and nice lunch, after which Suqin and Nianci said good-bye to Mr. Müller. They still wanted to have their private time together. They knew they would be separated starting next year for at least two years. But as they promised, they went to visit Mr. Müller almost every weekend and enjoyed their time with him. Often, Mr. Müller took them out for lunch or dinner. Sometimes, Nianci and Suqin cooked Chinese food for him. Suqin had learned to be a very good cook from her mother.

Meet Suqin's Parents

Time continued to pass quickly. Three months later, while they were having breakfast in the campus cafeteria, Suqin mentioned that her parents were coming to visit.

"Nianci, you know my father exports goods produced in Taiwan and distributes them to the world. He and my mom will come to Europe in two weeks. They will stay here for three days. Since I will be busy during weekdays, they arranged their time to arrive on Friday and leave on Monday," Suqin told him.

"That's great! You must miss them very much," Nianci said.

"My mom knows I have a boyfriend in Vienna, but my father does not. You know, I am from a Taiwanese family and my father does not like foreign province people. I don't know how to tell him. I really want to introduce you to him, but I am afraid that he will be against our relationship," Suqin said with a worried look.

Nianci knew that many Taiwanese did not like foreign province people because of the 2-2-8 Incident that had happened more than 30 years ago. Now, he more fully realized how deeply ran the animosity and hatred created by that event. He remembered he was also a victim of the incident when his father had been put in a military prison when Nianci was nine years old. He still could not tell anyone about how he was hung on the tree due to his stealing of a bun. That black spot and scar on his spirit had never disappeared or healed. Whenever he looked at himself internally, he still felt uncomfortable. This continued to make him humble.

"Don't worry, Suqin. Let us arrange something so they will know me without prejudice. Did you say they would stay for the weekend?" Nianci asked.

"Yes, from Friday to Monday," Suqin said, curious to know what Nianci had in mind.

"How about if you invited them to Mr. Müller's home? You can tell them Mr. Müller has looked after you for a few months and you often go to his home to play for him since he has such a precious piano," Nianci said.

"Then, how do I introduce you though?" Suqin asked again.

"Just tell them there is a very good piece of music that is an ensemble for piano and violin together and you will bring a friend from Taiwan to play with you. Just don't mention that my parents were from Mainland China with President Chiang," Nianci said.

"You know? You are smart but also cunning!" She looked at him and gave a big laugh. "Okay. I will arrange it," Suqin continued.

When Suqin's parents arrived in Vienna, because Suqin had class in the afternoon, they hired a taxi to take them directly to her dormitory and then waited for her in the lobby. Suqin's father, who had to travel very often, could speak English fairly well. Suqin was expecting that her parents might be waiting for her when she finished class. Sure enough, she saw them as soon as she stepped into the lobby of her dormitory.

"Mama! Papa! It is so good to see you. I missed you very much," Suqin said as she hugged her parents with teary eyes.

"Are you well, Suqin?" her mom asked with concern.

"I am very good. Where are you staying, Mom?"

"I have a reservation in a hotel near campus. It is not too far," Suqin's papa said.

"Why don't we go to your hotel first and check in? I have missed you so much and have a lot of things that I want to tell you." Suqin held her mom's hand. She was always Mama's girl. Her father always had a solemn face. Suqin, in one way, respected her father, but in another way was a little afraid of him.

Suqin's parents told her the name of their hotel. "I know exactly where it is. Not too far from here," she said, picking up her mother's luggage and beginning to walk with her mom. Her father just kept quiet and followed them. He knew that they missed each other very much.

After they were checked in, they went to a restaurant next to the hotel for dinner. Suqin took advantage of the moment to start to implement the plan for introducing her parents to Nianci.

"Mom, you know what? I accidently became acquainted with an old man and we became good friends. He has often looked after me. He has the best piano in his home! Now I often go there to play the piano for him. He treats me like his daughter. You know, I am a stranger here and very happy to know him. He loves music so whenever I go to his home to play piano, he is very happy," Suqin said.

Her parents were very shocked to hear this. They thought Suqin was falling in love with an old man.

"I hope he is not taking advantage of you, Suqin. When you travel outside, you must be careful," her father said.

"Papa, this is Austria, a very peaceful country! I have seldom heard about any crime since I have been here," Suqin argued.

"But your papa is right. You should be more careful, with high alertness and awareness," her mom said.

"Mom, he is 75 years old! What advantage can he take of me? I believe I can take care of myself. How about we all visit him this Sunday? I will not have rehearsal in the morning.

"Mr. Müller likes to listen to my playing, and you want to see if I have made progress. Right?" She looked at her parents like a spoiled girl.

"Well, one purpose of my visit here is sight-seeing, especially those famous composers' homes," her papa said.

"No problem, Papa! I know all of them, but you will be so tired after visiting so many places. You know, so many famous musicians have been here in the past such as Beethoven and Mozart. After tomorrow, you will be so tired!" Suqin joked with a naughty look on her face.

"Then, we will have a nice concert performed by a great musician next day, Suqin. Am I correct?" her mom joked back. She was very happy to see that Suqin was healthy and happy but was also worried that Suqin might fall in love with an old man. But she did not want to say it.

"No sweat! I will show my best," Suqin answered.

Since Suqin had a rehearsal in the morning until 11 o'clock and her parents still had jetlag, they rested in their hotel in the morning. Suqin arrived at the hotel around 11:30 and they all went to lunch. Then, Suqin spent all afternoon showing her parents around Vienna. This was their first visit. They were very impressed with how beautiful the city was.

By the time they had finished dinner, both Suqin's parents were tired. Suqin said good-bye and told them she would come to pick them up at 8:30 in the morning. She said they had an appointment with Mr. Müller at 9:00.

Right after she left, Suqin went straight to Nianci's dormitory and chatted with him for a couple of hours. Everything was arranged for the next day, she said. She explained what type of person and personality her father was and reminded Nianci to arrive at Mr. Müller's home at 9:00, right on time.

It would be a big and important day for Nianci since he had to face Suqin's parents. Whether or not they could continue their relationship depended on the success of the next day. He was somewhat nervous.

Sunday morning Nianci shaved his face and trimmed his hair short. He even put on a necktie. He seldom wore a tie, usually only when he performed. By the time Suqin and her parents arrived at Mr. Müller's apartment, Nianci was already there waiting for them.

"Nianci, you are early," Suqin greeted him.

"Suqin, how are you? Yes, I came a little bit early. These two must be your Papa and Mama." He used the Taiwanese dialect to talk to Suqin. Since his Taiwanese dialect was so perfect, Suqin's parents thought this handsome, young man was Taiwanese who had also come to Vienna to study music. They were very happy to see that Suqin and Nianci were so close. As they greeted each other, Suqin's mom could not help sneaking looks at Nianci.

"He will be a perfect man for Suqin," she thought, as all Taiwanese mothers do.

Suqin rang the bell and Mr. Müller promptly opened the door. He had actually been waiting, but when he heard his guests talking outside of his door, he did not want to open it and disturb their conversation.

"Hi, Mr. Müller! This is my dad and mom," Suqin introduced her parents.

"Nice to meet you, Mr. Müller," Suqin's father greeted him in English.

Mr. Müller showed his company into the living room. Once they had all sat down, Suqin's mother took from her bag a very elegant tea set and some tea, which she then handed to Mr. Müller.

"Thank you for taking care of my daughter," Suqin's father said.

"No! No! You know how happy I am that I know Suqin and Nianci. They come here to play music for me almost every weekend. I should thank them," Mr. Müller said.

Since Suqin's mom spoke neither German nor English, she remained quiet as the others spoke. Suqin, who was sitting next to her, occasionally translated the conversation so her mom wasn't left entirely out. After they had chatted for a while, Suqin's mom was ready to hear something other than the foreign languages spoken around her. "Suqin, don't you want to play piano for us?" Suqin's mom asked.

"Yes, Mom. Actually, I asked Nianci to be here so we can also play some ensemble music for you. His violin skills are very good. We come here to play for Mr. Müller together."

Suqin sat on the piano bench and began to play. Since the living room was specially designed for listening to music, and the piano was one of the best, her playing filled the room with beautiful sound. After that, Suqin asked Nianci to play a violin piece with her accompaniment. They played so very well together, and their styles complemented each other perfectly. Next, they played some Taiwanese folk songs. Suqin's parents could not help smiling and laughing. They had never had such a nice and private recital, especially from their daughter. However, Suqin's mother could sense the relationship between Nianci and Suqin was more than they were making it appear. It was deeper than just friends. She was happy to see that. They had a very good time.

After the performance, Mr. Müller insisted on taking everyone out for lunch. By the time lunch was finished, Suqin's parents were ready for a rest. So Suqin and Nianci walked them back to their hotel.

"Nianci, can you go back by yourself? I would like to stay with my parents for a while. They will leave tomorrow. See you tonight in rehearsal," Suqin told Nianci.

Nianci said good-bye to Suqin's parents with a deep bow and left. Suqin went into the hotel room with her parents.

"I need to take a nap. I am tired. Let me rest. I have an important meeting once we arrive in Paris tomorrow," Suqin's father said.

"It is okay, Papa! Mom and I will talk in the lobby. We can have some coffee or tea there." Suqin took her mom downstairs to the lobby where there was a small coffee shop inside the hotel. She purchased a cup of coffee for herself and a mint tea for her mom. Her mom did not like coffee.

Once they were seated, Suqin's mom asked what was uppermost in her mind. "Suqin, do you like Nianci? I could see from both of your eyes, you love each other. Am I correct?"

"Wow! After all, my mom knows me best," Suqin thought. Still, she kept her head down without saying a word.

"If you love each other, I am very happy for you. It looks like Nianci is a very good boy. I was so impressed with his violin skills."

"Mom, there is one thing that I need to tell you though." She looked at her mom with serious look.

"What is so serious, Suqin? He does not love you? He has a girl-friend already?"

"No, Mom! He likes me a lot. Actually, we like each other a lot. We can talk whole days without feeling bored."

"Then, what is the problem?"

"Mom, he is not a Taiwanese. His father and mother were from Mainland China recently," Suqin said.

"But his Taiwanese dialect was so accurate, just like a Taiwanese," Suqin's mom wondered.

"Actually, he grew up in a Taiwanese village. His parents raised him up in a Taiwanese environment. But you know Papa! He hates foreign province people," Suqin said.

"I don't know. I like Nianci a lot. He is polite, humble, handsome... And talented! Let me see if I can convince your papa," her mom said.

As Suqin had expected, there was no obstacle from her mom. Nianci was a good boy who made her daughter happy, and that was all that mattered. They continued to chat for a while before returning to the room, where Suqin's father had just woken up.

"Don't sleep too much, otherwise, you won't sleep again tonight," Suqin's mom reminded her husband.

Suqin enjoyed visiting with her parents until suddenly she noticed the time.

"Papa! Mom! I need to go. Rehearsal begins at 6:30 and I need to find something to eat. Rehearsal usually lasts till 9:00. It will be too late for me to eat dinner afterwards," Suqin said.

"Why don't we eat something now? We can still be together for a while. Furthermore, I don't like to eat late. I know we are not quite hungry after that big lunch. But we can eat a little, just to keep our stomachs busy," Suqin's mom suggested.

"That's a great idea," her father agreed.

During the dinner, Suqin asked, "Mama, Papa, will you come to my graduation next year? It will be great if you can."

"It depends on your papa. You know he is a busy man." Suqin's mom looked at her husband and smiled.

"Well, if I arrange my European business trip earlier, I think we can make it. Like this time, business and seeing you, one stone, two birds," Suqin's papa laughed. Actually, he would very much like to come for the graduation ceremony as it would be a significant event in his daughter's life.

"Papa, Mama, after graduation, can I go back to Taiwan with you for summer vacation? You know, I will be here for two more years. I miss Taiwan. Especially the food there." Suqin looked at her mother with a pleading expression

"Well, if you are a good girl, no problem," her father joked.

"Thank you, Papa."

Actually, in Suqin's mind, she was anxious to meet Nianci's parents and to have a good time with him. After dinner, Suqin rushed back to her dormitory to pick up some music scores and then go to rehearsal. She would not see her parents anymore this trip, since they were leaving for Paris early the next morning.

On the airplane, Suqin's mom noticed her husband was in a good mood. "Do you like that boy? What is name? Nianci? Right?" she asked him.

"Yes. It seems that he is a very nice and talented boy. Do you think he and Suqin like each other?"

"I believe so. But there is a problem that may upset you though."

"What will make me upset? Don't be ridiculous. You like him also, don't you?" Suqin's father said.

"Yes, I like him very much. Suqin and I are just afraid that you won't like him."

"Why? I cannot think of any reason," Father said.

"His parents came to Taiwan with Chiang in 1949."

"What? Are you sure? His Taiwanese dialect was so perfect."

"Yes, he grew up in Taiwanese village and environment."

Now, Suqin's father was quiet. His mind was in conflict because he did like Nianci. After a while he said, "We'll wait and see how their relationship develops."

Suqin's mom knew that at least he was not against it now.

GRADUATION 畢業

One day before the Friday graduation, the conservatory's symphony had a major performance at the school. All students who were going to graduate were up on the stage. Each one of them would show what talent they had. Naturally, Nianci and Suqin were part of the concert. During the program, Nianci was to play a solo accompanied by Suqin on the piano. It was a great honor for them. They were chosen because their playing was more skillful than anyone else at the conservatory.

Suqin's father and mother arrived on Thursday to attend the

concert. It was very important for them to be there. The performance was so beautiful that Suqin's mom almost cried, especially when she heard Nianci's solo with Suqin.

"I wish Mama and Papa were able to come to see this show and participate in my graduation. But it would have been too expensive for them to come," Nianci thought with regret. He envied Suqin that her parents were there.

Mr. Müller had also been invited to the concert and to graduation the next day. After the ceremony, Mr. Müller invited everyone to his home for a celebration. He knew that they would all be leaving in the next two days. Suqin's mom and dad decided to not go to Mr. Müller's, but to stay at the hotel since they were so tired after three weeks of traveling. Furthermore, Suqin and Nianci believed that Mr. Müller might wish to have some private time with them, and they hoped to give him one more long performance.

In the evening when Nianci and Suqin arrived, Mr. Müller told them he would miss them.

"Nianci, I feel sad that I may not see you again soon. Also, Suqin, even though you will be here for another two years, I have decided to move to Paris within the next couple of months and stay with my son after I take care of some matters here. I miss my grandchildren very much. Besides, I don't know when I will have another heart attack. I am getting old and I am lonely." Mr. Müller looked sad as he spoke.

Nianci and Suqin also felt sad that they might not see Mr. Müller again in this lifetime.

"I will miss both of you very much. You have given me a year of good times," Mr. Müller continued.

"I will see if I can come to visit you in Paris. I will still be here for two more years," Suqin said.

"Please play one last time for me. I will remember this forever," Mr. Müller asked.

Without saying a word, Suqin went to sit at the piano and Nianci took the violin from the living room shelf. Nianci thought to himself, "This will be my last chance to play this violin. I really love this violin. I will play with all my heart this time."

They played many pieces. They could see the old man's eyes were red with unshed tears. When the last piece was played, Mr. Müller had one more surprise for them.

"Nianci, I want to tell you one thing. I talked to my second son last night about how much enjoyment I have received from both of you.

He wants to give you this violin as a gift."

"Really, Mr. Müller! But this violin is so expensive and precious," Nianci gasped with surprise.

"I know it is a very good violin, but that's exactly why you should have it. You know how to play it and take care of it. I will feel more comfortable if it is in your hands rather than anyone else's. Now, give me your Taiwan address. I may write you sometimes when I have time," he laughed. Then he looked at Suqin.

"You too! Give me your address in Taiwan. I may also write you after you return to Taiwan. Of course, if I am still alive," he laughed again.

"All right! You have to give me your son's address too. We may come to visit you if you keep yourself healthy and happy for the next 100 years. Is that a deal?" Nianci joked back. He really liked this violin. He swore that he would take good care of it with all his heart. Now, he had a truly superior violin for his future performances. This was another happiest day of his life indeed.

RETURN TO TAIWAN 返回台灣

Two days later when the four of them had arrived in Taiwan, an employee from Suqin's father's company came to pick them up with a company car. They would drop Nianci at a bus stop where he could get a bus to Muzha. On the way from the airport to the bus stop, Suqin's mom kept asking Nianci questions. She felt much closer with him now since this was the second time they had met.

As Nianci and Suqin's mom spoke in the Taiwanese dialect, Suqin's father thought again, "This boy speaks the Taiwanese dialect just like a Taiwanese."

Suqin's mom asked a lot about Nianci's family and family history. She needed to know him better since she knew that her daughter was very serious about him.

"Mom! It seems like you are questioning a prisoner. We just arrived and are tired," Suqin scolded in a playful way.

"Suqin, it is okay. I enjoy talking to your mom very much. I am not that tired," Nianci said. He wished Suqin's father would join the conversation so that they could get better acquainted with each other. However, Suqin's father seemed to keep a distance from him.

Nianci thanked them and said good-bye after he stepped out of the car at the bus stop. He was anxious to see his own parents. Originally, his parents had wanted to meet him at the airport, but Nianci persuaded them not to go since the airport was so far from Muzha. Furthermore, he did not think it was the right time yet for his parents to meet Suqin's parents.

"It's been four years!" Nianci thought. "I wish I had had the money to come back to visit them in the last four years. It just costs too much money." He was so happy when he stepped off of the bus in Muzha village. He knew he had another two miles to walk from the bus stop to his home next to the creek, but when he stepped out of the bus, he saw his father and mother were waiting for him.

"Mama! Papa! You are here." Nianci was very surprised.

"Yes, your mama could not wait to see you. She kept urging me and wanting to come earlier," Jiaming said. He was overjoyed to see Nianci again and held his son in a tight embrace.

Nianci looked at his mother, who just could not help the tears that ran down her cheeks.

"Four years, Nianci. Four years. How much I have missed you!" Xiaohua hugged Nianci tightly.

"Mama! I missed you too. I never want to separate from you again," Nianci said.

As they walked home, Xiaohua peppered Nianci with questions about Suqin. She was very interested in knowing more about this girl that her son had mentioned so often in his letters.

"Mama, I will bring her to meet you and Papa! She has two months of vacation. After that, she will return to Vienna for two more years of study."

Nianci was elated to see the familiar rice field and creek again. All his memories of his childhood came pouring back to him.

"Papa, do you remember I caught a big crab there? I also caught a big eel in this rice field." He mentioned all these unforgettable good memories.

"You were only seven years old at that time. Remember, once you saw a poisonous water snake, you were so frightened?" Jiaming laughed.

It had been a good time. Now, it was over and both parents were getting older and Nianci had grown up into an accomplished young man.

"How fast the time passed!" Nianci thought. Then he thought of how much suffering his parents and he had endured during his childhood, especially when he was nine years old.

"Life is precious. I must use the rest of my lifetime to appreciate my parents and what they have given me. Oh, Mama! Papa! How could I ever repay you?" Nianci thought deeply.

When he arrived home, he saw, that in the four years he had been gone, his father had improved a lot of the living conditions. Though compared with Vienna, and living in the dormitory, this cottage was not nearly as comfortable. But this cottage, his home, had the most important things that he could never find in Vienna, his parents' love and the memories of his childhood.

Nianci found his father had made his room bigger and added screens to all the windows and doors. He remembered that one of the biggest headaches they had were the mosquitoes - mosquitoes were everywhere! They had to use cheap mosquito repellent incense to keep the bugs away in the evening, otherwise they could not sleep. He also discovered that the roof and the kitchen had been renovated.

"Your papa just finished last week to welcome you home. He was afraid you could not get used to our poor living conditions after four years in Vienna," Xiaohua said.

"Mama, I love it here! This is my home. I don't care how bad or how good it is. I just want to be with you," Nianci said.

Xiaohua reached out to her son and hugged him again. She was so grateful that heaven had given her this son. She felt so happy and deeply grateful for her life.

The next weekend Nianci went to Muzha City and used a public phone to call Suqin.

"You just woke me up. Today is Sunday. Why do you get up so early?" Suqin asked when she answered the phone.

"I just want to ask you if you want to go to visit my old symphony team with me. I miss them very much. I don't know how many of them are still there. Do you want to go? It will be so great if you meet them. They are all musicians," Nianci told her.

"Okay, I will meet you in the Taipei Train Station. But why are you in such a rush? We can meet them some other time, can't we?"

"They will be in rehearsal today. Today is Sunday. They are usually busy during weekdays. The only time they can get together is Sunday afternoon," Nianci said.

"Okay. I will meet you at 10 o'clock under the big clock of Taipei Train Station," Suqin instructed and hung up.

Actually, after one whole week of staying at home, Nianci missed Suqin and wanted to be with her. He also wanted to introduce Suqin to his old teammates. Nianci brought along the violin that he had received from Mr. Müller. He wanted to know how the violin would sound with the rest of the instruments.

Nianci arrived ten minutes early. While he was waiting, he kept thinking, "How can I create a future in music in Taiwan? It has been four years now. Will the symphony team welcome me back? I miss my old teammates very much.

"How lucky I am! Almost all musicians in Taiwan are from rich families. Only rich families can afford the lessons and musical instruments when their children are still small. But I am from a poor family, and yet I can still fulfill my dream.

"Now, I really love Suqin. I hope to marry her after she comes back from Vienna in two years. Will her parents be disgusted by my family since we are so poor?"

While Nianci was deep in thought, a voice came from behind him.

"Hey! Wake up! What are you thinking? Yes, I know... you are thinking of me, right?" Suqin laughed and roused Nianci from his reverie.

"I do miss you. Very much. Don't you miss me, my queen?" Nianci joked.

Suqin did not reply. She just stepped forward and wrapped her arms around him.

"Rehearsal is at 2:00 this afternoon at Taipei City University. We have some time before then. We can be together and have a nice lunch first," Nianci said.

"How about we go to Muzha to visit your parents? I always wanted to meet your parents and see the place where you grew up."

"Really? My parents wanted me to bring you there. They are also very anxious to meet you. They have mentioned it twice already since we returned. Today is Sunday. My father should be home. He always uses Sunday to take care of the garden," Nianci told her.

"Wow! You father works hard," Suqin said.

"My mom too. Usually, she is the one taking care of the garden. However, if there is any heavy work my father will handle it on Sunday."

"What is your father's job?" Suqin asked since Nianci had never mentioned it.

Nianci hesitated for a long time while Suqin looked at him with curiosity.

"Usually, my father is a scavenger. However, whenever the local farms need help, they will also hire him. My mother has poor health from an illness in the past. However, she does some tailoring for the neighbors," Nianci admitted with uneasiness and a look of shame on his face. He hoped Suqin would not despise him now that she knew the truth.

Suqin had never thought about Nianci's family being so poor. "How could he afford to learn music and go to Vienna?" she wondered.

"Your parents must be so great! I know it is not easy for you to learn music with such a background. They must have sacrificed everything for you," Suqin said after pondering for a while. "Let's go to meet them. I want to meet these two great parents," she continued.

Nianci was touched and very happy. He had thought that Suqin would look down on him and his family.

They took a bus to Muzha village and set off toward Nianci's home. As they walked from the village, passing through farms and along the big stream, then coming to the rice field, Suqin thought how wonderful it all was.

"Nianci! How beautiful this place is! It gives me such a peaceful and calm feeling. See those white cranes on the bamboo trees? Aren't they beautiful? See the water in the stream. It is so clear!" Suqin had grown up in the city. She had seldom seen such beauty and serenity.

When they neared the creek, Nianci told her about how to catch crab, shrimp, and clams. Jiaming was in the garden and saw them in the distance.

"Xiaohua! Xiaohua! It is Nianci and his girlfriend. They are coming!" Jiaming rushed to the door and shouted.

Xiaohua, who had been preparing some lunch, called out in a panic, "What? Nianci and his girlfriend? Why didn't he tell us first? How can we prepare some lunch for her? She is from rich family and will not be used to our simple food." She did not want to bring shame to Nianci and was frantic about what to do.

"Just be yourself, Xiaohua. If she cannot accept our poor condition, then their relationship will not last long. Don't panic! We should just be casual," Jiaming reassured her

When Nianci and Suqin stepped in the cottage, Xiaohua looked at Nianci with exasperation. "Why didn't you tell me that you were going to bring your girlfriend home today?" she complained.

"Mama! Papa! This is Suqin. The girl I mentioned to you so many times. It was her idea to come here today. She wanted to meet you," Nianci told his parents.

"But I don't have anything prepared! There is nothing much to treat her."

"Da Bo! Bo Mu! Please don't be so polite! It is very nice to meet you," Suqin said.

"Nianci, let's go catch some crab and shrimp. It is still the dry season. We should be able to catch some," Jiaming suggested.

"Really! I miss the old times when we caught shellfish in the stream. Suqin! Come watch us. It is fun," Nianci said.

Nianci changed his pants into shorts. His father had already taken a fish cage, a fish net, and two small shovels out from a room.

"It takes too long to trap clams and shrimp. However, we may be able to catch some fish and crab," Jiaming said.

Suqin could see Nianci was very excited since he had not done these things for four years. They came to the creek and Jiaming and Nianci went into the water. Within five minutes Nianci was shouting.

"I caught one, Papa! This is a big crab. No wonder the hole was so big." Nianci was excited by his luck. Suqin had never seen people catching crab before. She felt like a child watching a Walt Disney movie.

Soon, Jiaming caught one too. After just 30 minutes or so, they had six big crab.

"That's enough for crabs. Let us see if we have any luck catching Wuguo fish. There should be a lot this time of year. Nianci! Pull that side of net. See that spot? We may have luck there," Jiaming said.

They went to an area where a few branches dipped into the water. Both Jiaming and Nianci opened the net and slowly circled the area against the flow of water in the stream. Gradually, they then moved the net to a shallow area of the creek.

"Look! Look! There are some fish jumping in the net!" Suqin shouted in her excitement. But just a few seconds later, she shouted again in a panic.

"Watch out! Watch out! There is a snake on your left, Nianci!"

"Don't worry about it, Suqin. My father always told me, if you don't bother them, they don't bother you. Just leave them alone. Actually, the snake is probably more scared of us," Nianci laughed. Sure enough, after a minute or so the snake swam far away from them.

When the circle of the net had been narrowed down, they found they had caught three good sized Wuguo fish.

"That's our lunch." Jiaming looked at Nianci and Suqin with smile.

Suqin had never had so much fun out in the country. It warmed her heart to see how close Nianci and his father were.

Back at the cottage everyone had a nice lunch with sweet potatoes, fish, crab, and various home-grown vegetables straight out of the garden.

"Wow! This is the most delicious meal that I have ever had. Everything is so natural here," Suqin complimented Xiaohua.

While they were eating, Jiaming and Xiaohua asked Suqin many questions. Suqin did her best to avoid mentioning how rich her parents were. She was humble and very polite. She felt a deep respect for Nianci's parents in her heart.

Once they were done eating, Suqin asked "Do you still want to see your old symphony friends?"

"It is 1:30 already. If we leave now, we may catch them in the last half hour of rehearsal," Nianci replied.

"Then let's go right away. We don't have too much time."

Nianci and Suqin arrived at the university's music hall while the musicians were rehearsing the last movement of Chopin's Symphony No.5, Op.67. They went in quietly and sat in the last row, listening to the rehearsal patiently and wishing they could play along. When the last notes were played, both Nianci and Suqin stood up and walked toward the stage.

"Hey, everyone! See who it is? It is Nianci, our old teammate," a young musician shouted. He and Nianci had always enjoyed each other's friendship in the past.

"Hi, everyone. How are you? I want you to meet Suqin. I met her in Vienna. She plays piano," Nianci said by way of introduction. When he looked out at them, about one-third were new faces, but the other two-thirds were good friends. Professor Chen, his old teacher before he went to Vienna, was also there. Nianci bowed to him deeply.

"Nianci! It is good to see you back. Are you ready to rejoin us?" Professor Chen asked with a smile. He was very proud of his old student.

"That is why I came - to see if I am still welcome," Nianci joked with a laugh on his face.

Conductor Dong said, "Why don't we stay a little bit longer and give this guy a test? We will see if he wasted his time in Vienna or not?"

Everyone laughed.

"Can Suqin join us too, Conductor Dong?" Nianci asked.

"Of course! She can take the place of Naona. Naona had a stomach flu last night," Conductor Dong said.

Actually, Naona was feeling very tired due to her flu. She had come for rehearsal because she was the only one who could play the piano part for the Chopin Symphony. She was more than happy to be relieved at the piano and went to the side to sit down.

Nianci took out his violin while Suqin went to the piano and sat on the bench. Conductor Dong tapped the music stand with his baton to get everyone's attention.

"Let us repeat the last piece we rehearsed today. It is not quite polished yet."

Since both Nianci and Suqin had practiced this piece in Vienna and were familiar with it, they fitted in easily and blended in musically with the others. All the musicians could hear that their skills had been honed to a very high level. However, the most amazing thing to them was the tone of Nianci's violin. The sound he created from it was so profound, clear, and touching. They all knew that this was not a regular violin, the kind easily acquired in Taiwan.

After the piece was finished, Conductor Dong just could not believe the excellent performance they had just had. Everyone came forward to shake Nianci's and Suqin's hands.

"Will you both join us from now on?" Professor Chen asked them.

"Yes, I will," Nianci replied, "but Suqin must return to Vienna next month for two more years of study. I am sure that she will be very happy to join us when she comes back. Right, Suqin?" Nianci looked her with a funny face.

"No problem! When I come back, I would enjoy very much to be part of the team," Suqin said.

"Will both of you come to practice with us before Suqin returns to Vienna?"

"Naturally! We would love to," Suqin said.

"Nianci, when will you be back formally?" Professor Chen asked.

"From September 1st. After that I will be here all the time," Nianci replied.

A SURPRISE GIFT 一個驚喜的禮物

On the fourth Monday after Suqin's return to Taiwan, she was sitting in the living room with her mother. They were planning something secret when suddenly, the doorbell rang. Suqin rose and went to answer the door

"Is this the residence of Chen, Suqin?" the deliveryman asked.

"Yes, I am Chen, Suqin. What can I do for you?" Suqin replied.

"There is a delivery from Vienna for you. A piano."

"What! Have you made a mistake? I did not order any piano from Vienna," Suqin said in confusion.

Her mother, who had become curious, also came to the door. "Yes, I am pretty sure that it is for you. Yes, you can see this letter that came with the piano is addressed to you," she said.

When Suqin took the envelope, she was surprised to see that it was from Mr. Müller. She opened it and read.

> *Suqin! How are you? I hope you are having a good time in Taiwan. I am almost ready to move to Paris. Actually, right after you and Nianci left, I had a talk with my eldest son, Phil. Phil said he would like to give you this piano. He was very happy to think that you would be able to make use of it.*
>
> *Thank you and Nianci for saving my life and also for giving me a very happy year. I will remember our time together the rest of my life.*
>
> *Wishing you the best.*

Suqin just could not believe this was happening. This piano was so precious and expensive. The shipment of a grand piano through an instrument delivery company was also expensive. This was a very big surprise indeed.

The deliveryman carefully and professionally reassembled the piano in the living room. Once he was gone, Suqin gently stroked her fingers across the piano's glossy lid.

"Mom, I really love this piano! It is such a surprise."

Suqin opened the piano and played a few songs. She was overwhelmed by the thoughtfulness and generosity of the gift. Since there was a six-hour time difference between Taiwan and Austria, Suqin waited until 3:00 p.m. to call Mr. Müller. At that time, it should be 9:00 a.m. in Vienna. Unfortunately, there was no answer on the other side. Instead, she listened to a message saying the telephone line had been disconnected. It seemed that Mr. Müller was not in Vienna anymore, so she wrote him a formal thank you letter and sent it to his son's home in Paris. She also asked Mr. Müller to thank his son, Phil.

Suqin would have liked to tell Nianci about this surprise right away, but Nianci's home did not have a phone. She had to wait until the next day when they met again.

A Birthday Surprise 一個驚喜的生日

Ever since Suqin and her parents had returned to Taiwan nearly a month ago, Suqin's mom, Qionying, and Suqin often talked privately. They were planning something that had to be kept secret from Suqin's father.

"Mom, how about if we give Papa a nice concert? We have the best piano, Nianci's incredible violin, and two highly skilled musicians. I believe between the two of us, we can give a very nice concert first and then, right after that, a banquet. With, of course, a large birthday cake," Suqin suggested.

"Do you think that will be adequate? You know your father has a lot of close business friends and relatives. If all of them come, that will be nearly 50 people," her mom worried.

"I know that! That is why a concert would be so good. They will hear what I have learned in Germany and Vienna over the last six years."

"You have to talk to Nianci first and see what he says," Suqin's mom said with concern.

"I don't think he will have a problem with it. I can take care of that. However, to be polite, we should also invite his parents to the party," Suqin said.

"Will they feel okay since all your father's friends and relatives are Taiwanese?"

"I think it will be all right since they can speak the Taiwanese dialect fluently. Mom, let's do it!"

"Then we better begin to prepare everything now. You know your father turns 50 in just three weeks. We should have the party on the last Saturday before you go back to Vienna."

"Yes, Mom! I will take care of the concert side and inviting Nianci's parents. You, please take care of notifying all his friends and relatives and arranging the banquet. I am so excited. I cannot wait!" Suqin was very animated.

"Remember to tell all the friends and relatives to keep it a secret from Papa! If we do it right, Papa will be surprised since his birthday is two days after the party. He will not suspect anything," Suqin continued.

Nianci and Suqin met each often since they returned. They wanted to spend as much time as possible together before Suqin went back to Vienna. They had traveled to almost every known tourist place near Taipei City. Actually, they enjoyed being with each other more than sightseeing. Now they were planning to go to a village of a native Taiwanese tribe, Wulai (烏來), not too far from Taipei City, on the coming Tuesday.

When Tuesday arrived, they met each other in Taipei Train Station. From there they would take a bus to Wulai.

When they met, Nianci could feel that there was something making Suqin very excited and happy. "Why are you so happy today? Is there something funny on my face? Or are you just so happy to see me, my Queen!" he asked her.

"No! No! I just have two big pieces of news that I want to tell you," Suqin said.

"If it is good news, tell me quick. But if it is bad news, keep it to yourself." Nianci looked at Suqin with a naughty expression. Actually, he knew from Suqin's behavior that the news must be pretty fantastic. They sat down on a bench in the station.

"Guess what I received?" Suqin asked.

"An angel's kiss, right?" Nianci replied.

"Yes! From Mr. Müller. He sent me the piano in his living room!"

"What? Don't tease me. That piano would be too expensive to send to Taiwan," Nianci exclaimed.

"Well, remember his old business? Importing expensive music instruments from all over the world? Obviously, he still has some connection with those delivery companies. They delivered it very professionally," Suqin told him.

This reminded Nianci of the violin that he had received from Mr. Müller's family as well.

"I cannot wait to play with you again, my violin and your piano," Nianci said. But suddenly he felt uncomfortable, thinking of going to Suqin's home since it was in a rich area. As soon as he said it, he was a little bit awkward.

Suqin could sense his uneasy feeling and thought it best to move on.

"Guess what the second piece of news is?" Suqin said.

"You decided to marry me, right?" Nianci joked with a laugh.

"Maybe! If you behave, maybe in the future. It is too early." Suqin laughed too.

"Actually, my father's 50th birthday is coming up soon. You know, it is a big deal to turn 50 in Chinese tradition. It is half of 100," she continued.

"When is his birthday?"

"August 27th, the Monday before I leave. You know I have to leave on August 30th."

"Should I give him some gift for his birthday? Gosh! I don't know what to give him." Nianci began to worry.

"Don't worry, my King! He has everything materially that he could want or need. We can never find any material things that he doesn't already have," Suqin said.

"Then what should I do? Give me a suggestion, please, my Queen," Nianci begged.

"Mom and I are planning to give him a surprise party with a concert and banquet afterwards on Saturday, two days before his birthday. He usually stays at home Saturday afternoon," Suqin said.

"A concert! Who will be playing?"

"Guess who? It will be you and me! Now that we have our wonderful instruments, we should be able to give the audience an excellent performance," Suqin said.

"Where will it be? How many people will be there?" Nianci asked.

"It will be in my parents' home. Mom estimated that there would be around 50 guests coming including my grandparents, my uncle's family, and my father's closest friends."

"Wow! Fifty people can fit in their house! It must be a very big house," Nianci thought. He could not imagine a house that big.

"By the way, your papa and mama are also invited to the party. Remember to tell them. It will be so great for our parents to meet and know each other," Suqin continued.

When Nianci heard this he felt uneasy, since he knew all the guests would be Taiwanese and socially high-class. He did not know if his parents would feel comfortable or fit in with them. Furthermore, he did not know how many of the guests might still be hostile against foreign province people. Suqin could feel Nianci's uneasiness.

"Don't worry! Your parents speak perfect Taiwanese dialect. They will fit in just like that." Even as Suqin said so, she also worried deep in her heart. "Please talk to your parents and persuade them to come, okay?" she asked.

"Let's go to Wulai and we can talk about details later," Nianci answered.

They spent the rest of the day having fun in the Wulai native village. This village was so beautiful, located in a deep valley with a nice waterfall cascading into the river.

Nianci told Jiaming and Xiaohua about the birthday party and invitation as soon as he got home. At first, Xiaohua felt that it would be very awkward to participate in an elegant, high-society party. She was afraid to bring shame to Nianci. But, Jiaming countered her worry.

"If we don't meet Suqin's family and their friends, there will always be a gap between their family and our family. This will be a cheerful situation. It will provide us a chance to introduce ourselves in a joyful setting. It does not matter if the consequences are good or bad, we must face it for Nianci's sake. I know he is deeply in love with Suqin," Jiaming said in an attempt to convince Xiaohua to accept the invitation.

The date of the party was coming soon. Suqin's mom had notified everyone who was supposed to be there. They had managed to keep the party a secret from Suqin's father. Though Nianci and Suqin had played together many times when they were in Mr. Müller's home, they still rehearsed together a couple times right after symphony rehearsal.

After lunch on the day of the party, and once Suqin's father, Jinxian, had woken up from a nap, Suqin innocently asked him, "Papa, would you like to take a walk with me in the park? You know I am leaving next week, and I have not had a chance to talk to you personally. I would like to spend some time with you. Is that okay?"

"Naturally! Sorry that I have been so busy and did not spend too much time with you," Suqin's father said. He felt that Suqin wanted to talk to him about Nianci and her future. He did not know that it was a trick to get him out of the house so guests could enter. When they arrived at the park, Jinxian was surprised that Suqin did not start talking about Nianci or her future. All she wanted was to know more about her childhood. She wanted her father to tell her every detail. She also wanted to know more about her father's childhood and how he could have become so successful in business. They spent nearly two hours in the park. It was a precious time for both Suqin and her father.

When Nianci and his parents rang the bell, a young cousin of Suqin's opened the door.

"How can I help you?" The cousin saw a young man with two elders in casual dress standing outside the door. He had never met them before. He was wondering why they were there.

"I am Suqin's friend. We were invited to join tonight's birthday party," Nianci said politely in Taiwanese dialect.

"Please wait a minute. Let me notify the host," the cousin said and ran into the house.

"Aunt! There are three persons outside of the door. They are dressed very casually. They said they are here for the party." The cousin was curious as to why these three strangers wearing not-too-nice clothes were here.

"Oh! They must be Nianci and his parents," Suqin's mom said and rushed to the door.

"Welcome! Welcome! I am so glad that you were able to come. I was worried that you might not," and saying that, she shook Jiaming and Xiaohua's hands enthusiastically.

This surprised Suqin's cousin. "Who are these people?" he wondered.

When Nianci and his parents entered the house, they saw a big living room that could fit 60 people easily and comfortably.

"Please be yourself! Treat it like home. I am sorry that I am very busy right now arranging everything. You know, Suqin tricked her father into going to the park so all of the guests could arrive unnoticed." Suqin's mom laughed and left.

Nianci and his parents went out into the back yard. There they were surprised to see a big garden and a nice yard with a cement patio. There were five banquet tables covered with red cloths. On top of the tables, beautiful settings of china, silverware and glassware were arranged. At the corner of the yard was a chef with two assistants busy preparing food.

Nianci and his parents re-entered the living room and found a couch in a corner where they sat and chatted amongst themselves. They didn't know how to greet the others. They felt so awkward.

Back in the park, Jinxian told Suqin, "We should go home now. It is almost 5 o'clock. Your mom must be worried about us."

"Okay. Let's go home. Mom should begin preparing dinner soon. I should help her." Suqin knew it was about time.

When they arrived home, Jinxian wondered why there were so many cars parked on their street tonight. He thought that someone must be having a party. Suqin could barely keep from laughing when he mentioned this to her. Then he entered the house.

"Happy birthday!" All the guests were shouting and laughing.

Jinxian was confused for a little while. Suddenly, he realized that this was a surprise party for him. "No wonder there are so many cars on the street," he thought.

His parents and his brother's family were there. His wife's whole family was there as well. All his best friends and business partners were there. He could not help laughing out loud, "You have tricked me. It is not my birthday yet! I am not that old yet. I have two more days. Ha! Ha! Ha!" He was very happy.

After twenty minutes or so, Jinxian noticed a couple of strangers sitting in the corner with Nianci. As he walked toward them, Nianci and his parents stood up and bowed to him.

"Bo Bo! How are you? Congratulation on your birthday!" Nianci said.

"Are these...?"

"My parents, Bo Bo! My father, Jiaming and my mother, Xiaohua."

Jinxian extended his hand, "Welcome! Welcome!" He tried to use his Mandarin to express his welcome.

"Don't be so polite! Please don't be so polite!" Jiaming said in the Taiwanese dialect to answer.

Actually, Jinxian felt a little worried and uneasy, and wondered how these foreign province people could fit in in a Taiwanese group. However, he did not know what his wife and daughter had planned so he just did his best to be hospitable and chatted with them. After a few minutes, he left them to go greet other guests.

Nianci and his parents continued to sit watching everyone else greeting and chatting with each other. Twenty minutes later, they noticed that Suqin was having some young folks arrange 12 nice chairs in front of the piano, with two other rows behind the first one. Then, she asked her grandparents and her uncles and aunts to sit in the front row. There were two seats empty.

Suqin approached Jiaming and Xiaohua, "Bo Bo! Bo Mu! Please come with me and sit in the first row."

"No! No! We are okay here. Thank you," Jiaming and Xiaohua protested. They just felt that they were not fitting in at such an elegant party.

"Bo Bo! Bo Mu! I insist today. Please cooperate with me this time. You have to be there since Nianci is going to perform tonight," Suqin persisted.

It would be impolite for them to refuse, so they humbly stood up and followed Suqin over to be seated in the empty seats. When the other guests saw them, they were very surprised and wondered who these two guests were that were being honored in such a way.

Suqin hit a glass with a spoon to get everyone's attention.

"Hi, everyone! Grandpas and grandmas, all uncles and aunts! Welcome to the party. It is my father's 50th birthday. Those who are over 40 please sit in the second and third rows. Those young folks, sorry, please stand around us." In this way Suqin arranged the seats for the elders. After everyone was seated or had found a place to stand, Suqin addressed the group.

"As you know, I have spent six years learning piano in Germany and Austria. I will return to Vienna next week. Tonight is a good chance for me to show off and demonstrate what I have learned," Suqin bragged with a laugh in her voice, since she knew almost everyone there. Everyone laughed.

"First, I want to play a piece by Beethoven and after that my best friend, Mingde, who also graduated from the Vienna conservatory, will play a few songs with me to entertain you. I hope you enjoy our playing. If you don't, please cover your ears." At this, Suqin stuck out her tongue and made a face.

"By the way, I forgot to introduce Mingde's parents, Mr. Lin, Jiaming and Mrs. Lin, Xiaohua," Suqin said, making a graceful gesture toward them. When Jiaming and Xiaohua saw that, they immediately stood up and faced the guests.

"It is very fortunate to be here and to get acquainted with all of you" Jiaming said with perfect Taiwanese dialect. No one suspected his origins and assumed his family was Taiwanese.

After everyone was quiet, Suqin sat on the piano bench and began her piano solo while Nianci sat next to her to turn the music score pages for her. It was a beautiful scene. The sound generated from the piano was fantastic, and the technique Suqin displayed was of such a high degree of proficiency that the guests could not believe it. When the piece ended, they applauded with great enthusiasm.

Suqin stood up and bowed to the audience. Her parents smiled with satisfaction. They knew now that Suqin had not wasted her six years studying outside of the country.

"Next, Mingde and I will play a few ensemble pieces. He plays violin." Suqin sat down again and Nianci took his violin out from its case. He adjusted the strings to be in tune with the piano.

After a few minutes of piano introduction played by Suqin, Nianci began to play his violin. Within moments the guests were staring in astonishment. They could not believe what they saw and heard. The music being created from the Stradivarius violin by Nianci's skillful use of the bow was so amazing and fantastic.

As Suqin and Nianci finished their first piece there was a moment of quiet while everyone was gripped by the spell of the music. Suqin's grandpa broke the silence and began to applaud. Immediately, the entire room filled with applause.

Suqin's grandfather on her father's side looked at his son, Jinxian. "He is fantastic! I can't believe that he plays so well. Is he Suqin's boyfriend?" he asked curiously.

"Mingde was Suqin's classmate, Papa!" Jinxian replied.

"It would be so nice if they were boyfriend and girlfriend," Jinxian's father said.

Suqin had always been her grandfather's little angel. He had loved her since she was a baby. She was so cute and knew how to cheer him and his wife up.

Once the audience had quieted down, Suqin and Nianci began to play another piece, one even harder than the last. Their audience admired both performers very much. A deep respect emerged from their hearts.

After that, Suqin and Nianci played a few short Taiwanese folk songs. Some people began to hum or sing with the music. Everyone was happy. The concert lasted for 45 minutes before Suqin and Nianci made their final bows. Some guests came to congratulate Jiaming and Xiaohua on their son's achievement. Many others went to talk to Nianci and Suqin.

"Look! I am almost 76 years old. I would like to see Suqin find a good husband before I die. I wish they were boyfriend and girlfriend," Suqin's grandpa said.

"But, Papa! They are foreign province people," Suqin's father said.

"What! Really? I can't believe that they can speak Taiwanese just like Taiwanese."

"Yes! They live in a Taiwanese village and Mingde grew up there."

"In this case, they are no different from Taiwanese," the grandfather said. He really liked Nianci and hoped the feeling of dislike for foreign province people would not become an obstacle to the relationship between Suqin and Nianci.

Conversation was interrupted when one of Suqin's cousin's announced, "Dinner will be served in ten minutes."

Suqin's grandpa went to talk to Jiaming and Xiaohua. He asked them a lot of questions. In just a few minutes, he could already see what a kind and lovable couple they were. While they were talking, a few more people came to join them.

"It must have been very hard for you to escape from Mainland

China in 1949. You must have suffered greatly to raise up your child. He is such a nice and talented boy. You should be proud of him," Suqin's grandpa said.

Jiaming and Xiaohua were taken off guard. They had not expected that Suqin's grandpa would know their origins. Now their secret was out. They were a little bit nervous. But from the expression on Suqin's grandpa's face, they could see only real concern and no hostility. However, this news had surprised the other guests standing around them. The guests had become very curious and the grandfather's words gave them an opening into the conversation. Many of them showed compassion about Jiaming and Xiaohua's past and praised their success in educating Nianci to become such a talented young man. In just a few minutes, both Jiaming and Xiaohua felt much better. It seemed the gap between them and the other guests was getting narrower every minute.

All the guests were asked to sit at the round tables for the banquet. Jiaming and Xiaohua were treated as honored guests and seated with Suqin's grandparents, parents, uncles, and aunts. Nianci was seated with other young people around his age. Naturally, Suqin arranged herself to sit next to Nianci. She acted as a guardian angel protecting him. She was determined not to allow anyone to look down on him because of his origins or background. As the evening progressed, she realized that she had worried too much. Everyone admired and respected Nianci from their heart and extended their friendship sincerely.

This made Suqin very happy. "After all, the hate in the younger generation's mind is not as severe as the older generation," she thought. She knew that if Nianci wished to marry her, the guests invited to the party tonight must accept him first. In just thirty minutes or so, Nianci was getting along with everyone like they were old friends. They started to call him by his nickname, Nianci, instead of his formal name, Mingde. This was a sure sign of their acceptance of him, and that the gap between him and them had narrowed significantly.

At the honored guest table, Jiaming and Xiaohua felt uncomfortable and awkward at first. However, Suqin's grandpa kept talking with them and the conversation piqued the other guests' interest. Soon, everyone knew they were from Mainland China recently. Fortunately, because of their fluent Taiwanese dialect, and after listening to Nianci's performance, it seemed any potential feelings of hostility had disappeared. Instead, many of the guests were interested in knowing about the situation around 1949 when Jiaming and Xiaohua had escaped from Mainland China. By the time the banquet was over, most of the guests were fairly tipsy. The curiosity of the company at the honored guests table had them following Jiaming and Xiaohua to the living room to continue their conversation.

In the living room, the group around Jiaming and Xiaohua became bigger and bigger. Someone asked what they thought about the 2-2-8 Incident. Someone else asked about the situation when Chiang's party ruled China around 1949, and how could the Communists have defeated Chiang. This reminded Jiaming of Grandpa Shen's 80th birthday party. He tried to avoid the politics. He was so afraid it might bring him another disaster.

Jiaming dodged the sensitive topics about politics. He talked about how they had escaped and how his mom and he had helped Xiaohua to get out of China. Though this brought them more attention, it also triggered Xiaohua's memory of the past. Soon her tears began to fall.

When it got late, guests began to leave. This lifted the pressure-off Jiaming's shoulders. It was a relief to know that this small Taiwanese community had accepted his family. Suqin's mom asked the company's driver to take them back to Muzha. Once they had left, Suqin's father came to her while her mom was helping to clean the place.

"Suqin! Thank you for this surprise party. I had a very good time. I am very lucky to have you as my daughter. I am very proud of you." Jinxian paused for a moment, then burst out, "When are you and Nianci going to get engaged?"

This surprised Suqin. She was afraid that her father would not approve her marriage to Nianci.

"Papa, it is still early. I am still young. I know! I know! You don't like me and are trying to get rid of me, right?" Suqin laughed and stepped forward to hug her father.

"No! No! I want to keep you forever. But I also want to play with my grandkids. You are my only child. I hope you have many kids," Jinxian laughed.

"We may get engaged after two years when I return to Taiwan."

Now, Suqin knew that the feared obstacle from her father was gone. She was very happy.

Nianci and Suqin met for the last time during Suqin's vacation the following Wednesday. Suqin would take off the next day and her parents would take her to the airport.

"Suqin! Please take care of yourself. I will miss you," Nianci begged when they were together in a cafeteria.

"Nianci, I will miss you too! I feel very sad to be leaving Taiwan. And without you in Vienna, it will be less fun and meaningful for me."

"This will give both of us a real test. If we really love each other and miss each other continuously over the next two years, then we will be very sure that we want to spend our lifetime together. I am ready to take this challenge, aren't you?"

"Okay! I will concentrate my whole heart on study and practice. We will keep in touch," Suqin promised.

CHAPTER 7
REUNION
團圓

GREAT REUNION 大團圓

After Suqin left to return to Vienna, Nianci became the major soloist for almost all of the public orchestra performances. Usually, the orchestra had a couple of national performances and many smaller local performances each year. The income from performing was not much. But Nianci did not care since he had such a great love for the music. It was also good for his playing proficiency to be continuously practicing. During this time, due to Nianci's prodigious talent, the Taipei Symphony Orchestra's reputation increased rapidly.

During the first six months of Nianci's return home, more and more wealthy families hired him to be a private music teacher for their children. He began to contribute more money to his family. Even though he was only 25 years old, he gave private lessons almost every day. Jiaming continued his temporary jobs helping the local farmers. Since Nianci was able to bring in better income, Jiaming did not have to continue his scavenging career that brought in only a little income. When they had extra money, they continued to improve their rustic cottage and make it a more house-like dwelling. Over time the roof was completely redone and the walls more tightly sealed.

At the end of his first year back at home, Nianci received an appointment letter from Taipei National College of Arts. The college wished to hire him as an assistant music professor. The position was open due to one of the old professor's decision to retire, and Nianci was the best candidate to fill this position. The entire family was very happy. However, they would have to move to Guandu (關渡), where the college was located.

A month later, Nianci and his parents moved from their old home to a professor's dwelling in Guandu. The housing facilities there were rented to college professors for a very low rent. The apartment was very nice and comfortable compared to their old home that had been continuously improved upon for over 30 years. This new apartment had two bedrooms, a living room, a bathroom, and a good-sized kitchen that was connected to the public gas supply. Their building also had two public phones in the hallway of each floor for families living on that floor.

Nianci had been a professor for a full semester when he first noticed a section in the newspaper, United Daily News (聯合報), that specialized in searching for people missing after 1949. He became excited at the thought that this might help his mom to find her family with whom she had lost contact. He got in touch with the newspaper and put in a notice. It said simply, "Peng, Xiaohua, 53 years old from Zhenjiang City, Jiangsu Province, looking for Peng, Zhigang, Peng, Xiuzhen, and Peng, Ronghua. Please contact Peng, Xiaohua, with address below." Then Nianci added his name on the bottom of the announcement and, since they didn't have a telephone at home and he would be in school or having rehearsal most of the time, he put in his office phone and the symphony secretary's phone number. He knew if he could successfully find his mom's family, it would be a huge surprise for her. Deep in his heart, however, he did not have much hope for this search.

After thinking about it, Nianci also put his notice in several other popular newspapers. He did not tell his mom about this since he knew that if his mom knew what he was doing, she would become expectant and emotional. If he then could not find her family, she would be very disappointed and frustrated. Nianci also made sure to let the symphony secretary, Miss Mai, know that he had used her phone for a contact number.

Nianci's anxiety rose as the days passed slowly for nearly two weeks without any news. He almost gave up hope. Then one morning, when he went to the symphony hall for rehearsal, the secretary, Miss Mai, called to him.

"There was a gentleman who called my phone yesterday looking for Xiaohua. I almost hung up because he did not mention your name."

"Really, Miss Mai? Did he leave any message? Remember I told you that I was looking for my mom's family. The call might be from them," Nianci said excitedly.

"Yes, he told me to ask you to call him. Here is the number. His name is Peng, Ronghua." Miss Mai handed Nianci a slip of paper with the telephone number on it.

"Thank you very much, Miss Mai."

Nianci could not believe he was going to contact a person that might be his uncle - his mom's missing brother. He was so excited. When he took a look at the number, he recognized that it was a Hong Kong telephone number. He had not realized that many of the Taiwanese newspapers also distributed in Hong Kong.

In his eagerness, Nianci begged, "Miss Mai! May I use the symphony's telephone to call Hong Kong? It is very important to me."

The secretary could see how important the news was to Nianci and how earnest he was. "Yes, you may," she replied, "but keep this between you and me. You know, this is a long-distance call and this line belongs to the symphony and is not private. No more than 10 minutes. It is expensive." Miss Mai tried to look at him sternly but could not help breaking into a laugh. She had never seen Nianci so animated.

"Thank you very much! Please let the conductor know that I will be a few minutes late for rehearsal due to a family emergency. I am so excited. I know if I don't make this call, my mind will not be on the rehearsal anyway," Nianci said with a grin.

Miss Mai stepped out of the office to give Nianci some privacy. He picked up the phone and dialed the number, waiting expectantly for the other side to answer.

"Hello! My name is Lin, Mingde. May I speak to Mr. Peng, Ronghua?" Nianci asked when someone came on the line.

"This is Peng, Ronghua. May I help you?" the voice replied.

"I wonder, do you know a lady named Peng, Xiaohua, from Zhenjiang City, Jiangsu Province?" Nianci asked.

"Yes, she is my sister. Ya! Are you the one who put the person-searching announcement in the newspaper? What is your name again?"

"My legal name is Mingde and my nickname is Nianci. My mom's name is Xiaohua and my grandpa's name is Zhigang."

"Aaah! I cannot believe we found each other." Ronghua said but then broke off and couldn't continue. Obviously, he also was happy and emotional to have made this connection. He could not believe he would finally have contact with his sister, who had been lost for more than 30 years. After Ronghua had his voice under control again, he began to ask Nianci a lot of questions. Nianci could only give brief answers since he was allowed only 10 minutes for the call and the whole symphony was waiting for him.

"Uncle, I will call you again later today," Nianci apologized. "I have a rehearsal that I need to go to now. I will call you again around 4 o'clock Taiwan time. Sorry!" With that he hung up and rushed to the rehearsal hall where he saw everyone was waiting for him. He apologized with a deep bow and a delighted smile that made the whole team realize the 'family emergency' was a happy surprise.

Around 4 p.m., Nianci went to the telecommunications office in the city to make a long-distance call. As soon as the operator connected the number for him, the other side picked up their phone immediately. It seemed that his uncle had been standing right by his phone waiting for this call.

"Hello! This is Ronghua."

"Uncle! This is Nianci. I have more time to talk to you now. Sorry about the earlier call that I needed to cut short!"

They talked and exchanged news for nearly half an hour.

"Nianci, I have arranged a flight to arrive in Taipei this Friday evening around 7 o'clock. Do you mind picking me up? I will wear a blue shirt and wear a hat. My son, Wenxiong, will come with me."

"Really, Uncle! That will be such great news to Mom. Should I tell her about your coming or should we give her a surprise?" Nianci wondered.

"You should tell her! It will be too cruel to keep this news a secret. Furthermore, a surprise like that may shock her and trigger a heart attack!" Ronghua joked.

When Nianci returned to their apartments, Xiaohua was waiting for him.

"Why did you come home later than usual? I was so worried about you," Xiaohua asked with concern and love.

"Mom! I have big news that I must tell you." This announcement also caught Jiaming's attention, especially when he saw the excitement on Nianci's face.

"Mom, I have found Uncle Ronghua and I talked to him today," Nianci said.

"What did you say? Is it real or you are just making a joke?" Xiaohua couldn't believe what she had heard.

"Mom, it's true! Uncle and his son, Wenxiong, will come to see you this Friday."

When Xiaohua heard this news, she could not believe that it was true. Tears rolled down her face as she was caught up by the excitement and old memories.

"How about grandpa and grandma?" Xiaohua asked.

"Uncle told me that grandpa passed away two years ago. Grandma is 77 years old now and still healthy. Uncle has two children, one boy, Wenxiong (文雄) and one girl, Yijuan (怡娟). Wenxiong is 9 years old and Yijuan is 12. I don't know any other details."

Xiaohua cried out loud upon hearing that her father had passed away already. That evening, she could not sleep all night in her anticipation of seeing her brother. A lot of old memories kept appearing in her mind.

Friday afternoon the whole family went to Taipei airport to wait for Ronghua and his son's arrival. They were standing anxiously at the arrival gate for China Airlines. Xiaohua was so eager to see her brother that she had a hard time breathing with her abnormal lungs' diminished capability. Her eyes were full of tears.

When Ronghua and Wenxiong stepped out of the gate, even though it had been decades since she had seen him, Xiaohua recognized Ronghua right away. Her legs trembled due to the excitement. Ronghua and Xiaohua looked at each other for a moment, drinking in the sight of their beloved faces, before crying out loud and hugging each other tightly. This was a very emotional moment. After a couple minutes, they calmed down and introduced each other to their families with much laughter and joy. Finally, Nianci had some close relatives.

All the way home from the airport, Xiaohua kept asking Ronghua about her mom and the past. However, it was too emotional to talk about it in the car. Ronghua just held Xiaohua's hands.

"Let us talk about it later; we have three days. I am tired and feel a little dizzy right now. It is too much and too emotional to talk about it now," he told her.

Ronghua looked at Xiaohua and could not believe the time had passed so fast. He just said, "When Niang (Mom) knew that we had re-connected with each other, she was so excited and cried for a couple days. She also laughed a lot. It seemed that some shadow hidden behind her had suddenly disappeared."

After dinner, Xiaohua brought Ronghua into the living room. The rest of the family followed to listen to the incredible story that they had never known.

"I was only 9 years old," Ronghua started. "When I saw Die and

Niang were so panicky, I was scared and worried so much. All I did was hold Niang's hand tight and followed. We were afraid to be pushed off the side of the road. I did not notice that you were missing. I did not know how long you were gone. When I discovered you were not behind me, I kept pulling Niang's hand and shouting. When Niang realized what had happened, she was so frightened and worried. After she told Die, Die was also panicky, especially since there was such a big crowd that kept pushing us forward. Mom almost fainted." Ronghua mentioned what had happened in 1949.

"Actually, I lost my shoe and I had to find it," Xiaohua explained, "otherwise, I would be barefoot on one foot. I kept shouting at Niang and Die, but the crowd moved forward so fast and it was so loud, you did not hear me. I thought I could find you, Niang, and Die after I found my shoe. It took me about five minutes to find it. When I returned to find you, I couldn't. I was so scared and panicked. I stood beside the road and stood on a pile of discarded furniture. I hoped I could see Niang and Die. I remember, it was getting dark quickly and soon I lost all of you."

"We had to squeeze ourselves out of the crowd and we waited for you. Die and Niang kept calling your name. But their shouts were covered by the crowd's noise. There was a fork in the road ahead and we didn't know what to do. After waiting for an hour in the dark, Die knew that the chance of finding you was so slim. Furthermore, if we didn't get to Shanghai soon, we might lose the chance to escape. Die decided to follow the crowd and finally we reached Shanghai port the next day. I remember when we were near Shanghai, the rain was pouring, and the weather turned so cold. Niang could not help but crying about losing you," Ronghua said.

"Actually, I walked the whole day in the rain. When I arrived in Shanghai, I realized that I was very sick with a fever. I was so weak and could not continue to search for you, Niang, and Die. I found a place under the eaves and waited there to die. I did not know what to do. There were so many people, and all was in panic. No one came to help me until Niang and her son. I was so lucky to have them to help me." When Xiaohua talked about the past, she could not help crying.

"We were also looking for you. But there were so many ports in Shanghai and people were packed everywhere. After we searched two ports, we were so tired. When Die found there was a fishing boat going to Hong Kong, Die believed that was the last and only chance to get out of China. Die had to pay three bars of bullions for three of us," Ronghua said.

"Why did Die decide to go to Hong Kong instead of Taiwan?" Xiaohua asked.

"People around us said that sooner or later, the Liberation Army would take over Taiwan. However, if we went to Hong Kong, since it was under the rule of the British Government, it would be safer. Furthermore, the boat spaces were limited. If we did not take them, the chance might be gone forever. Niang was so sad and did not want to leave without you," Ronghua said.

"Jiaming and his Niang looked after me and found a way to take me with them to Taiwan. On the boat, my cold turned into pneumonia. When we arrived in Taiwan, my sickness got worse. Jiaming and his Niang converted all of the jewelry they had to money for penicillin. That saved my life, but by then the pneumonia had damaged my lungs severely. Without them, I would have been dead a long time ago," Xiaohua explained. "What happened after you arrived in Hong Kong?"

"As you know, Die took all 35 bars of bullion we had with us when we escaped. Three of them were used to pay the fishing boat. After we arrived Hong Kong, Die used ten of them to buy an apartment. Later, he sold the remaining bars and bought two more apartments to rent out. All of the houses and apartments were cheap at that time due to the chaos of the war. Though the rent he made was not much, we could survive without too much problem."

Ronghua took a sip of his tea, then picked up his story again. "Five years later, the situation was more stable and all of the real estate's value increased. Die used three apartments as collateral and bought two more apartments. In just ten years, we owned more than six apartments for rent. You know, after 1949 to 1957 the border between Hong Kong and Mainland China was still not completely closed. More and more people escaped from China during this period. The income from apartment rental brought us better income each month.

"Once it was more stable, Die put an advertisement in the newspapers both in Taiwan and Hong Kong to look for you. He did this for six months, but we never received any response. Die and Niang were so sad and frustrated. We all thought we had lost you forever," Ronghua paused.

"Actually, we did not have any access to newspapers. You know, Jiaming was only a scavenger and we lived isolated from others," Xiaohua told him.

"Later," Ronghua continued, "a couple of years later, Die sent me to school, and finally I received my bachelor's degree of Business. I married my college classmate, Meihui (美惠) when I was 27 years old.

Now, I have two children, a girl, Yijuan (怡娟), 12 years old, and this boy, Wenxiong (文雄), only 9. This boy likes to follow me anywhere if possible. I also like him to keep me company." Everyone looked at Wenxiong, but he was shy and ducked his head down to avoid their gaze.

"How did Die pass?" Xiaohua asked.

"He worked too hard, even at 79 years old, and refused to retire and pass the entire real estate business to me. One night, he was taking a shower and fell. When we discovered him, he was already dead due to a heart attack."

Even though Xiaohua had already known her father had passed away two years ago, when she heard of this incident she could not help crying.

Xiaohua and Ronghua talked until midnight, long after the others had grown tired and gone to sleep. Xiaohua told Ronghua briefly what had happened to them since they arrived in Taiwan. They continued talking the next day. It seemed they wanted to use these moments to catch up on all of the time they had missed together. However, Wenxiong was bored.

Nianci did not have class in the afternoon. When he saw Wenxiong was bored, he made a suggestion to his family.

"Why don't we take a walk and see some of the neighborhood around campus? You may still talk to each other. Some areas are very beautiful. You can see Guanyin Mountain (觀音山) and Danshui River (淡水河)."

This idea made Wenxiong very excited. Fortunately, the day was cloudy and not too hot, comfortable for walking. Jiaming decided to stay at home, since he knew that Xiaohua and Ronghua wanted to share this precious time alone.

First, Nianci brought them to the beautiful campus and then they followed a small path to a wider area outside of the campus where they could see the mountain and river. There was a nice breeze blowing. They found a big tree and sat down on the lawn underneath it. Near to the tree was a large and nice-looking house with a sign out front that showed the property was for sale. The house captured Nianci's attention and he wondered curiously how much the property cost.

"It would be a very good location for a home with its nice view, near the college and with convenient transportation to Taipei City. This place makes you feel like your heart is wide open," Nianci thought. He really missed the feeling of the old home next to the creek, where there was a wide rice field and a beautiful mountain.

"Mom! Don't you like this place? It gives me a feeling similar to our old home. It has a beautiful mountain view. The only difference is that this river is big and the creek we had was small," Nianci said out loud when he saw his mom and uncle had stopped talking.

"Yes, Nianci. I miss our old home too. Whoever buys this property will be lucky," Xiaohua replied.

When it got dark, "Let's go home to prepare dinner," Xiaohua said.

Early the next morning, when Xiaohua woke up, she could not find Ronghua. His son, Wenxiong was still sleeping. She knew that Ronghua might go out to take a morning walk. Actually, morning time was the best time to walk around campus and in the neighborhood. Xiaohua decided not to worry about Ronghua and started to prepare breakfast.

By the time Ronghua returned about thirty minutes later, everyone was up already. Nianci did not have rehearsal until the afternoon. The family took advantage of the time to enjoy each other and chat. Ronghua was especially interested in the old place where they used to live. Unfortunately, it was too far from Guandu (關渡) to Muzha (木柵) to go in one day, and Ronghua and his son would depart the next morning.

Since Nianci had to teach at school the next day, Jiaming took Ronghua and his son to Taipei Train Station first and then hired a taxi to take them to the airport. Xiaohua stayed at home since she had not rested for many days. All of the excitement and talking had made her very tired.

Before they left, however, Xiaohua charged her brother, "Ronghua! Please take care of Niang. She is very old. I want to see her very much. I will see if Nianci is able to arrange a trip to Hong Kong for me to see her." Then she said good-bye to Ronghua and his son. This had been an emotional reunion, bearing a combination of sadness and happiness.

Visiting Hong Kong 訪問香港

Because of Nianci's teaching schedule, he could not find time to leave. He had been trying to find a way to take his mom to see his grandma, but he had only a couple of days of holiday from December 30th to January 2nd, and that would be too short to visit. However, he would have a longer vacation during Chinese New Year which was also the college's winter vacation. Nianci and his parents decided to visit Hong Kong on January 25th. Nianci would have at least two weeks of vacation then before he needed to return for rehearsals.

A few days before Chinese New Year, Nianci, Jiaming, and Xiaohua took off from Taiwan to go to Hong Kong. They were so excited, especially Xiaohua. She had not seen her Niang for 33 years. When they arrived at Hong Kong International Airport, Ronghua and his son, Wenxiong, were at the gate to welcome them. He took them home in his car.

As they entered the private parking lot for Ronghua's apartment, it truly hit Xiaohua that she was going to see her Niang soon. She became very agitated and her breath and heartbeat sped up. Her eyes were red.

Ronghua opened the apartment door, and shouted, "Niang! We are home!"

Xiuzhen was sitting in the living room waiting anxiously for them. As soon as Xiaohua saw her mother she rushed toward her, knelt down in front of her, and held her mother's legs. Jiaming also knelt down next to her while Xiaohua cried aloud, "Niang! How much I missed you, Niang!"

"Xiaohua! Jiaming! Stand up and let me take a look at both of you. My poor child, you have suffered so much in your life." Xiuzhen's tears were unstoppable. She had heard the entire story of Xiaohua's past from Ronghua.

Xiaohua and Jiaming stood up and when Nianci started to kneel down to show his respect to his grandma, Xiuzhen stopped him.

"This must be my grandson, Nianci. Oh, heavens! He is so handsome!" Xiuzhen pulled Nianci closer and gazed at him with a big smile.

"How happy I am today! This is the first time I meet my son-in-law, Jiaming, and grandson, Nianci. How happy I am today!" She kept laughing through her tears. The reunion brought relief to the more than 33 years of guilt and regret that she had hidden deep in her heart.

"Oh! I wish your Die was still alive. If he was, he would be as happy as I am today. Come! Come! All of you come to worship your grandpa and ancestors." Xiuzhen stood up and held Nianci's hand, leading him to a worship room where a tablet had been placed. Inside the tablet, the names of all the family's ancestors had been concealed.

Ronghua rushed to the incense storage drawer and brought out some incense. He lit their tips and gave three sticks to each member of the newly reunited family. Xiuzhen stood in front while everyone else knelt down behind her.

"Zhigang! You see? We found Xiaohua! We have found our Xiaohua!" As Xiuzhen spoke her tears streamed from her eyes.

Xiaohua was also in tears behind her mom. She prayed, "Die! Die! I have returned. I am safe and fine. Please rest in peace, Die! I miss you very much."

Over the next few days Ronghua showed Xiaohua and her family around Hong Kong and took them to various attractive places. Whenever Xiuzhen and Xiaohua were not tired, they talked about the past and present. They had a few wonderful days together. When Chinese New Year arrived, they all sat down together for a traditional New Year's dinner. The family felt enveloped in so much love and happiness. Wenxiong and Yijuan felt maybe they were happiest, since they received so much lucky money in their red envelopes. Jiaming and Xiaohua also gave Xiuzhen a red envelope out of respect for her.

On the third day after Chinese New Year, Ronghua and Xiuzhen came to see Xiaohua in her room.

"Da Jie (Big Sister), I am so happy you and your family were able to come to see Niang. I am so happy to see her smile again. After returning from my visit to you a few months ago, I talked to Niang. Niang and I decided we wanted to compensate you for your suffering in the past." With that, Ronghua handed a red envelope to Xiaohua.

Xiaohua was filled with curiosity, since New Year and the time for red envelopes had already passed three days ago. When she opened the red envelope, inside she discovered the deed to a house and a few keys. She just stared at them, wondering what this was all about.

"Remember that house next to campus? You and Nianci liked it so much. I bought it for you. It is under your and Jiaming's name," Ronghua explained. This just confused Xiaohua even more.

"Remember that Sunday morning, one day before my departure? I went to that house and looked around. I wrote down the contact number. After I returned to Hong Kong, I talked to Niang and we decided to buy that house for you. I negotiated with the Taiwan Real Estate Company and I finally got it a week ago."

"No! No, Ronghua! You don't have to give me this. We are fine and very happy!" Xiaohua protested when she understood what her brother was saying. She looked at Ronghua and her mom with deep appreciation for their gift and thoughtfulness.

"Listen to me, Xiaohua!" Xiuzhen said. "Remember your father took 35 bars of gold bullion from China? Three were used for paying the fishing boat that helped us escape. There were still 32 left. Your father, before he died, told me to find you. He told me that you and Ronghua should have 11 bars each. The other ten was for our pension. It was a pity that he died only a few years after."

"Da Jie (Big Sister)!" Ronghua added, "Die and I used all the money for real estate investment, and we were very successful. This is your share. You must take it. This is Die and Niang's wish."

"Xiaohua! You must take it; otherwise, I will always feel very bad about your suffering. We shouldn't have left you behind and come to Hong Kong without you." Xiuzhen extended her hands to hold Xiaohua's. Xiaohua was again deeply touched by her mother's love. Her eyes filled with tears.

That evening, Xiaohua told Jiaming about the house she had received from her brother and mother. Jiaming couldn't believe what had happened. The next day the family left and returned Taiwan. On the way, Xiaohua and Jiaming told Nianci about the new home they had.

Nianci was very surprised. Actually, in his mind, he had been planning to own a bigger house. He wanted to marry Suqin when she returned and they would need a bigger living space for the whole family, especially once a few kids were added.

Once they returned to Taiwan, they went to the house and used the key to open the door. They could not believe how luxurious and pretty it was inside. There was a big window in the living room facing Guanyin Mountain and Danshui River. It said in the deed that the property also included five acres of land. This was surely a huge surprise. They did not know how much Ronghua had paid for it. Xiaohua knew that if she asked, Ronghua would not tell her anyway.

Over the next two weeks the little family moved into their new home. Xiaohua and Jiaming just could not believe they now owned such a fancy property. Compared with where they had lived next to the stream, this was a palace. But they would never forget the small, simple, and crude cottage that was their first real home together. So much joy and tears had happened in that cottage.

MARRIAGE 結婚

Nianci kept waiting anxiously for Suqin's return from Vienna. All of the time they were apart they never stopped missing each other. They were pretty sure that they would be happy to share their life together. Finally, Suqin graduated on May 29th with a master's degree in Music.

Her parents went to Vienna to participate in the graduation ceremony and returned to Taiwan with Suqin on June 1st.

Other than teaching, Nianci and Suqin saw each other every day. Every day they made plans for their future together. In the very first week Suqin was back, Nianci had presented her to join the symphony group. The director and conductor were very happy to have her with them, since her skill at the piano was among the best in the world.

Two weeks after Suqin's return, Nianci invited Suqin and her parents to their new home for dinner. Nianci was very excited and happy. He felt he was the luckiest person in the whole world. When they arrived, Suqin's parents were impressed to see the place where Nianci's family was now living. They had expected it to be a simple and awkward house because Nianci's teaching income was not a great amount.

The dinner was only the second time that the two sets of parents had met. The atmosphere was joyful and happy, and during the meal the parents got a little bit tipsy on some high-quality Cognac.

When Nianci saw all the parents were in a very good mood, he saw his opening.

"Da Bo (大伯), Da Niang (大娘), I would like to ask your permission to marry your daughter," he said, looking into their eyes with a touch of anxiety.

Actually, everybody already knew Nianci and Suqin were deeply in love. And they also had expected that this dinner night was to be a special night. Now they realized they had been maneuvered into getting together to meet and talk about their children's future.

"Ha! Ha! Ha! So, to speak! I am very happy that Suqin has found a nice person she can trust. There is no problem, no problem at all. Ha! Ha!" Suqin's father said.

"In that case, Papa, Mama, please accept my respect and drink this cup of wine," Nianci said as he lifted his cup to honor them.

"Everyone! Everyone! It is a good time to celebrate," toasted a very happy Jiaming.

"When do you plan to get married? Have you talked to each other about that yet?" Suqin's mother asked with concern.

"If everything goes smoothly, we think we will get engaged on July 31st and have the wedding on October 10th," Nianci replied.

"That will be next month already. It seems that we will be very busy for the next few months," Suqin's mother responded excitedly.

The engagement ceremony was arranged to be held at the Taipei First Grand Restaurant. Since Suqin's family had many relatives and friends, they reserved 100 seats for it. Nianci's uncle would not be able to come to the engagement, but he promised to be present for the October 10th wedding.

As estimated, more than 110 guests would be coming to witness the engagement. Many others promised that they would be there for the wedding; to many, an engagement was more of a private family event. To support his side of the family, Nianci invited the old landowner from next to the creek, Mr. Shen, to their engagement. Surprisingly, Zunxian and his son, Nianxiong (年雄) promised to come.

Soon the engagement date arrived. Everyone was kept busy in arranging everything. In Nianci's family, there were only Jiaming, Xiaohua, and their friends, Zunxian and his son. All of the other guests belonged to Suqin's family. Nianci appreciated Zunxian and his son's presence so much that he offered them the great honor of being seated at the main dining table with Suqin's family.

In conversation during the banquet, Zunxian mentioned the events that had happened in 1950 when Nianxiong was only five years old.

"If not for your help, Nianxiong would not be here today," Zunxian said as he looked at Jiaming with a smile.

"I wish your father was still alive to join us," Jiaming said with a sigh.

As they talked about old times and all the suffering Nianci's family had endured in the past, Suqin's parents listened with a great deal of interest and curiosity. They wanted to know how Zunxian's family, a Taiwanese family, could have gotten along so well with a family from a foreign province. That was truly a rare thing in the 1950s.

"It would be great if we could see their old place. Is the cottage still there?" Suqin's father asked.

"Yes! It is there. Jiaming's family moved to Guandu Town only a couple of years ago. The cottage is still there, but I heard the government might take it down soon. They are talking of building a water channel connected with Shimen Reservoir (石門水庫) for irrigating the fields. They said it might happen next year," Nianxiong informed them.

"If you would like to see it, why don't you come to visit us, and I will show you around. It is in Muzha (木柵), not far from here. How about next Sunday? You will be our honored guests," Zunxian kindly invited them.

"That will be great! This will help us to know our new relatives better. We will come with Jiaming's family about 9 o'clock. Is that good for you?" Suqin's father replied.

"Wonderful! We will have lunch at my house, a typical Taiwanese farmer's meal," Zunxian said with a laugh.

The following Sunday Jiaming, Xiaohua, and Nianci took a train to Taipei to meet Suqin's family. Actually, Suqin's father had made arrangements for a mini bus to take the group from Taipei to Muzha, since his company car was too small for so many people. In total there were six people: three from Nianci's family and three from Suqin's. The group arrived at Zunxian's home right before 9 a.m. They were all very happy to see each other again.

First, Jiaming took everyone to his old home and showed them where he used to catch fish, crabs, river shrimp, and clams. He also showed them the open area under the willow trees where Nianci had practiced his violin from the time he was ten years old. Suqin's parents could not believe how simple and rustic their living condition used to be. From what they saw, they could feel the suffering Nianci's family had had in the past. Jiaming also mentioned how much Zunxian's family had helped them to get through many difficult times.

"Where is the place that Jiaming saved your son?" Suqin's father asked Zunxian curiously. He wanted to see the site of the crucial turning point in their relationship.

Zunxian then took everyone to the old stream. Though the bridge had been rebuilt with concrete, from Zunxian's description they could roughly picture what had happened there 32 years ago.

After a very nice lunch of delicious Taiwanese cooking, the visitors left and drove back to Taipei. Suqin's parents invited Nianci and his parents to stay for dinner, but Jiaming demurred in a friendly way.

"Xiaohua is very tired. You know, her health is not great. We should go home and rest. However, Nianci can stay so you can get to know your future son-in-law better," Jiaming laughed.

They returned by train to Guandu, where Nianci went to Suqin's home for dinner. At the house, Suqin's father went upstairs to take a shower while Suqin's mom went to the kitchen.

"Mama, anything I can do?" Suqin asked.

"No! You and Nianci just prepare the dining table, chairs, and tableware. I can handle things in here," her mother said. Actually, she liked seeing her daughter and husband-to-be together, and the dinner should be easy for just four people.

When Nianci and Suqin were setting up the table, Suqin said, "Nianci, my parents were very surprised and impressed by your success. You came from such a poor environment and from poor conditions, and yet you've been able to achieve so much!"

"Suqin! Honestly, my parents, music teachers, and my Taijiquan teacher influenced me the most. Without them, I could not have come as far as I have today."

"I know that! But there are thousands of young kids like you. They also suffered and were influenced by good parents and teachers. But most could not conquer themselves and build up their self-discipline and confidence. My parents' question is, how did you conquer yourself? You know, knowing how might be easy but to then do it is not easy. I have seen many people who like to talk big, but they could not even conquer their own laziness."

"Suqin, since you will be my wife, I need to tell you a dark secret of mine. Please keep this between you and me. I have never even told my parents," Nianci confided.

"What is your dark secret?" Suqin was very curious.

"Look! When I was born, my life was just like a piece of white paper, plain and clean. However, I created a black spot on this paper. Throughout my life, whenever I looked at this spot, I became humble and pushed myself up and up. I tried to wipe it out, but I couldn't. The more I wiped it, the worse it became. Eventually, I learned to downplay this spot and focus my efforts on making the white part whiter. Now, the white part is so shiny and bright, nobody can see this black spot anymore. But seriously, this spot is still deep in my heart and still bothers me sometimes."

"Would you share your secret with me about this black spot?" Suqin asked.

"Of course! But again, please keep it between you and me. I will reveal it to others when I am ready. Please," Nianci pleaded.

"I promise. If I want to share my life with you, I want to share everything, including both good and bad," Suqin told him.

They finished setting the table, then went to sit on the couch near the window. There Nianci told Suqin about what had happened in the market place when he was nine years old.

"Since then, everyone thought I was a thief and I also thought of myself as a thief. The shame of that moment created my black spot. I swore that I would never go near that place again in my life," Nianci said.

"But Nianci! Have you thought about it? Why did it happen?

Without that incident, you would be like any other kid. You were different because of that spot. In my opinion, this black spot is not black at all. It is a star that shines and directs you on your path of self-conquest. Don't you think?"

"I have thought so! But I still also feel there is a shadow deep in my heart," Nianci said.

"Why don't we go to that market place tomorrow? I want to see the place. I want to feel what you feel. Can we go?" Suqin asked.

"I don't know, Suqin. I swore that I would never go back to that place!"

"Come on! You were only nine years old, Nianci! Furthermore, you were hungry! I think it is time for you to face that moment and untie this knot tangling your heart. Let's go tomorrow. Please! For me! Okay?" Suqin begged.

"Okay. I believe I am ready to face it again after more than 15 years. I will meet you at Taipei Station at 2 o'clock tomorrow afternoon. I have to teach tomorrow morning."

"Let's take a taxi," Suqin said the next day when they met. "It will be faster than a bus."

"But won't it be too expensive?" Nianci still retained the habit of saving money.

"Look, how much time do we have? If we take a bus, we would still have to walk for quite a distance once we are there. It is more time saving and efficient to take a taxi because the taxi can take us directly to the place. Don't be stingy, Professor!" Suqin shot back.

When they arrived at the place where Nianci had had his shameful encounter, he was shocked to see that there was no market and there were no trees. Even the road was different – it had been widened and paved. The entire place had been renovated. If there weren't still a couple of old buildings standing, he would never have recognized the place. A 12-story apartment building had replaced the marketplace and there was no trace of the trees. He could not even tell where the shop had been whose owner had tied him up on a tree.

"They are all gone, Suqin! All gone!" Nianci said with wonder.

"See? It only exists in your mind. You have kept the shadow of what happened in your heart, but the place is no longer here," Suqin said with smile.

"It is time to make this black spot fade away! It is time to let the shadow disappear," Nianci thought. He felt lighter to be rid of the stigma he had carried, but still appreciated what had happened there.

Without that incident, he would have had a different destiny and been a different person.

October 10th is the birthday of the country of Taiwan and almost all of the restaurants were booked up for that day months in advance. Luckily, Nianci and Suqin had managed to reserve a restaurant with a big hall for their wedding. They estimated more than 250 people would be coming. Most of them were Suqin's relatives and family friends. Nianci's uncle's whole family would be coming, including the 78-year-old grandma, Xiaohua's mother. Her mother arrived in a wheel chair since she could not walk due to severe arthritis. In addition, Zunxian and his entire family also came for the celebration. It was a great wedding including many of Nianci and Suqin's musician friends. During the banquet immediately after the wedding, there was a small concert for the guests performed by the happy couple's symphony friends. Naturally, Nianci and Suqin also performed a couple pieces. Xiaohua looked up to see her mother laughing and was filled with happiness.

By January 20th, Suqin realized she was pregnant. This brought another joyful time to the family. On October 18th, a baby boy was born. Nianci asked his mother to name the new baby.

Xiaohua said, "I miss Mainland China very much. How about if he is called Lin, Sihan (思漢)."

"It is a good name. I like it. I also miss Mainland China as well," Jiaming said.

Both Nianci and Suqin agreed.

CHAPTER 8
RESONANCE OF LOVE
愛 的 迴 盪

AN UNFORTUNATE SHOCK 不幸的消息

In February of 1984, Xiaohua caught a cold and because of her limited breathing capability, the cold triggered pneumonia again. With her weak immune system, even though the pneumonia was suppressed with antibiotics it caused more damage to her lungs. Her illness made the whole family extremely worried.

"Xiaohua! I am very concerned about your health. You know, since pneumonia damaged your lungs in 1949, your health has never completely recovered." Jiaming was holding the newborn baby, Sihan, with the satisfied feeling of a grandfather. Nianci and Suqin were at rehearsal that night. Their symphony was scheduled to have a big performance in public on October 27th.

"Jiaming, please don't worry about me. Actually, I am very happy with my life. I had you and your mom to take care of me while I was sick in 1949. I also got to marry you! A husband that I could never have dreamed of. Furthermore, I have found my family and seen my Niang. Now, I can also see the success of Nianci and my grandson, Sihan. I don't have anything to regret. I am very happy about my life. My dear husband, please don't worry about me. I will be okay." Xiaohua looked at Jiaming with a smile.

Truthfully, Jiaming also appreciated the good things they had achieved out of their past tough times. They were so proud of Nianci's success and delighted to see his happiness and bright future.

Two months later, after dinner, Xiaohua had a severe cramp in her stomach. Within just a few minutes, the pain became so severe that she could hardly breathe and broke out in a cold sweat. Fortunately,

Nianci and Suqin were home. Immediately, Nianci called an ambulance to take Xiaohua to a local hospital. Jiaming and Nianci went to the hospital with the ambulance while Suqin stayed home to take care of Sihan.

After emergency treatment and being administered with pain medicine, Xiaohua felt better. However, the doctor asked Xiaohua to stay until the next day while he conducted a more detailed examination. It seemed the cause of Xiaohua's pain was not just a common problem.

Jiaming came to the hospital alone the next day, since Nianci had to teach at the university and Suqin needed to stay home to look after the baby. Jiaming stayed with Xiaohua all morning. Xiaohua was given a gastroscopy, and in the afternoon the doctor showed Jiaming the photos they had taken of the inside of her stomach.

"Mr. Lin, you can see how many scars she has in her stomach. They were caused by starvation many years ago."

Jiaming realized that this might be the result of his ten months in the military prison. Xiaohua must have saved all of the available food for him and Nianci. His eyes turned red and his tears fell.

The doctor waited for Jiaming to gather his emotions and calm down before continuing, "If you see this photo, there is something developing in this area. It may be the beginnings of stomach cancer."

This was very shocking news to hear since everyone knew once you received a cancer diagnosis, you were essentially given a death penalty. Jiaming just looked at the doctor numbly.

"Is there any hope to save her, Doctor?" Jiaming asked.

"One possibility is to cut out the affected part of the stomach as soon as possible and hope the cancer does not spread to other places."

Jiaming looked at the doctor with deep sadness. He did not know what to do.

The next morning, the day of his mom's surgery, Nianci went to the hospital with his father. He had been able to take the day off from teaching, but Suqin still needed to stay at home with little Sihan since he was only a few months old. An hour later, Suqin's parents arrived at the hospital. They had heard the bad news from Suqin the night before. Suqin's father, Jinxian (進賢) and his wife, Qiongying (陳瓊英) gave Jiaming an envelope. Jiaming knew it was money; that they were trying to help. His eyes turned red.

"Jinxian, you are too kind and generous. But Nianci said we should have enough money to cover the cost," Jiaming refused the gift politely.

"Jiaming, please take it, for my daughter's sake. You and your wife have treated her like your own daughter. She is very lucky to have you as parents-in-law and we are very happy. Whenever we see our new grandson, Sihan, we cannot help but laugh. Please accept it as close relatives. We are very happy to help." Jinxian looked at Jiaming with a sincere face.

"Thank you very much. Let's treat it as a loan. When I can afford it, I will return it to you."

"Please don't worry about it. We can talk about it in the future."

Since Suqin's parents had another engagement, they had to leave. Once they were gone Jiaming looked inside the envelope and found NT$10,000, more than enough to cover the cost they needed to pay. Both Nianci and Jiaming were touched deeply.

Nianci and Jiaming had a light lunch in the hospital cafeteria while they waited for news. Xiaohua had gone into surgery at 10:00 in the morning. A little after 1:00 in the afternoon the surgeon came out to see them.

"The surgery was successful. I believe we have removed all of the suspected cancer. Now we just hope she recovers soon," he said.

"When can she go home, Doctor?" Nianci asked.

"In about three to four days. She is in the recovery room now. You may go to see her."

Both Jiaming and Nianci quickly rushed to the recovery room. They saw Xiaohua was resting. She looked like she had not completely recovered from anesthesia yet. Nianci held his mom's hand and looked into her pale face. He could feel all of the suffering she had borne in the past. Xiaohua opened her tired eyes. When she saw Nianci and Jiaming, she revealed her smile.

"Both of you are here!" Xiaohua said.

"Mom, the doctor said you might be able to go home in three days. It depends on the progress of your recovery. He said the operation was successful!" Nianci assured her.

"How are Suqin and the baby?"

"They are fine, Mom."

Jiaming, for his part, just stood there and listened to the conversation between his wife and son. All of his old memories ran through his head. He just could not believe how quickly the time had passed and how short a human life could be. He looked at Xiaohua with all the love and concern in his heart.

Three days later Nianci hired a taxi and went with his father to bring his mom home. They were happy to have the whole family together again.

Nianci and Jiaming decided not to tell Xiaohua's brother what had happened, since they didn't want Xiaohua's old mother to worry about her. They believed Xiaohua would recover completely very soon.

But four months later Xiaohua's stomach pain returned, bringing with it even more pain in other places. Nianci and Jiaming took her to the hospital again. After his examination, the doctor came to the waiting room to see Nianci and Jiaming.

"I am sorry to tell you that your wife's cancer has returned and spread to her liver and spleen. She is in the third stage. I don't think we will be able to help her much this time. The cancer's spreading is too aggressive." The doctor looked at them sadly.

"How long will she be able to live?" Jiaming asked with worry and in tears.

"Probably six weeks to two months. I am very sorry, Mr. Lin. You may take her home any time you wish. Here is a prescription for pain. Whenever she has pain, she can take this to ease it," the doctor said.

This shocking news threw a deep shadow over the whole family. They decided to take Xiaohua home right away since the doctor had said he could not do anything more.

When they arrived home, Xiaohua tried to comfort her husband.

"Jiaming! I already know that I will not stay too long. I don't want you to feel sad for me. I have had a good life with good family. I am able to go peacefully without regret. Just let us live happily now until I pass away. I want to enjoy my last limited time with cheer instead of sadness."

Jiaming stayed near Xiaohua almost all of the time. They talked about the past and the present. Often, they just sat quietly without talking. They were very comfortable and happy just to be together. Since Nianci and Suqin were busy with teaching and symphony rehearsals, whenever Xiaohua and the baby were both awake, Jiaming would bring the baby to visit with his grandma and play with her. Xiaohua was most happy when she had a chance to tease Sihan and make him laugh.

During weekends, if there were no rehearsals, the whole family would go to the park, along the river, or to the zoo. It was the most enjoyable thing for Xiaohua when she held the baby against her chest as she sat in her wheel chair while Jiaming and Nianci took turns pushing it.

One Sunday morning, Nianci took his mom in the wheel chair for a walk on the campus of the Taipei National College of Arts. Though the campus was located in beautiful Guandu down next to the Danshui River, Nianci and Xiaohua missed the old creek and rice field next to their old home. In the far distance, a misty fog was still covering the river and field. Occasionally, you could hear birds calling or a crane's shouting. Xiaohua always loved this early morning atmosphere and air. It was still early on the Sunday morning and the campus was empty and quiet. Nianci had brought his violin with him. When they came to a place with a far view of the river, Nianci took his violin out and played for his mom. She closed her eyes. As she listened to the music, she felt so satisfied with her life.

When Nianci and Suqin had gotten married, they had moved Suqin's piano from her parents' home to the new home. Now whenever Nianci had time on rainy days, he and Suqin would play for Xiaohua. Xiaohua enjoyed so much listening to the music with the baby in her arms.

That same morning, Jiaming was home looking after the baby while Suqin was preparing some breakfast. Suddenly the telephone rang.

"Hello! This is Jiaming. Who is it, please?"

"This is Ronghua. I have not talked to my sister for a few months. May I talk to her? My mom likes to hear her voice. She misses her a lot." Xiaohua's brother was on the line calling from Hong Kong.

"I am sorry, Ronghua. She went out with Nianci for a walk. I will tell her you called," Jiaming said.

"Is she well and happy? My mom said she had a nightmare that something unfortunate had happened to her," Ronghua persisted.

Jiaming paused a while and could not believe that Xiaohua's mom was able to feel her daughter's sickness. It was said, 'A mother's heart is always connected to her children's.' "How true it is!" Jiaming thought.

"Ronghua, to tell the truth, Xiaohua has had cancer since more than four months ago," Jiaming admitted. "According to the doctor, she may have only a few more weeks to live. I am so sad." Jiaming broke off in tears.

"What? My heavens. Why has heaven kept torturing her? I cannot tell my mom this. She is 81 years old and will not bear this shock. Please keep this news from her. My son and I will come to Taiwan next weekend to see her. But please don't tell Xiaohua. I want to surprise her," Ronghua said with sadness.

An hour or so later Xiaohua and Nianci returned. After breakfast, Xiaohua felt tired and went to her room to rest, leaving only Jiaming, Nianci, Suqin, and the baby in the dining room.

"Nianci, your uncle from Hong Kong called earlier and I told him about your mom's situation. He will come with his son to see your mom next weekend. He may call your office about his flight itinerary," Jiaming said.

"Really! Uncle Ronghua and his son are coming to see Mom? This will be a big surprise to her. She has mentioned her mom and brother several times since our wedding."

"Yes, that is why you should not tell her. It is a surprise," Jiaming said.

Tuesday morning, when Nianci was in his office he received his uncle's phone call and was given the flight itinerary. The following Saturday afternoon, Nianci went to the airport to pick up his uncle and cousin. They were happy to see each other but all of them deeply felt the shadow of the reason for this meeting.

Xiaohua had no suspicion her brother was coming since Nianci had told her he needed to meet a musician about a rehearsal matter. When the taxi arrived home, she was sitting in the living room and playing with the little baby. Teasing him until he laughed made her very happy. She was laughing when Ronghua and Wenxiong stepped into the living room. She could not believe what she saw, her brother and her nephew. She looked at them with surprise and her tears came out helplessly. She missed her mom and brother so very much.

"Ronghua! It is you and Wenxiong. I did not know that you were coming. Nobody told me!" she said with a big smile.

"Yes, I told them not to tell you. I wanted to give you a surprise. Niang misses you very much. She mentions you constantly. You know, she is 81 years now."

"Ronghua, I miss her very much too. I wish I could still fly to Hong Kong to see her." Xiaohua recognized that Ronghua already knew about her condition. She looked at her brother frankly. "Let us have a nice chat and a good time before I am gone. But please, don't tell Niang about my illness. Just tell her that I am happy and fine. Please!" she continued.

"I know. I will not tell her," her brother reassured her. "Let's have a few days of good times. Wenxiong and I will need to go back by next

Tuesday."

The day before they left, Ronghua gave Jiaming an international bank draft.

"I hope this money can help you during this difficult time," Ronghua said.

"No! No, Ronghua! We are okay. We have enough for everything," Jiaming politely refused.

"Please accept it. That will make me feel better. My business has done great over the last two years. And this will help Nianci for his future. Please accept my money."

Jiaming looked at Xiaohua who was sitting on the couch.

"Jiaming, since Ronghua is offering his help with a sincere heart, we should accept it. This will be my gift to my grandchildren. I hope Nianci and Suqin have a few more children. Unfortunately, I will not see them," Xiaohua sighed.

Ronghua and his son were leaving on Tuesday morning's flight. As they got ready to depart, Xiaohua looked at them with tears in her eyes since she knew this was probably the last time they would see each other.

"Please pass my love to Niang! I will miss her forever," she said.

Time passed very quickly, especially when the days were happy. However, Xiaohua's condition continued to get worse and worse. The week before the October concert, her condition became critical. This made the whole family sad. But they tried not to show it in front of her.

"Jiaming! I wish I could still be alive to see Nianci and Suqin's last performance. It would be so wonderful to hear them before my passing." Xiaohua looked at Jiaming with anxiety and hope on her face.

"You will! You will! You will see their performance. Two TV stations will broadcast the performance live! You will see them on the TV," Jiaming told her.

"I am so glad that we have TV today. Otherwise, it would be a great regret to me," Xiaohua said, and smiled at him.

On October 27th of 1984, the audience filled the entire National Concert Hall, since there were three very famous young violinists performing with the Taipei City Symphony Orchestra that night. Tickets had been sold out a couple of weeks ago. This was one of the biggest events in Taiwanese music society.

After the orchestra played a couple of classical symphonies, the first violin soloist performed with the entire symphony group. The pieces were so fantastic that the entire audience remained quiet to enjoy the music. After the first soloist, the symphony performed again. Then the second soloist played and was again followed by the symphony. Finally, the last part of the concert program was Nianci's solo performance with Suqin at the piano. First, he played Paganini's *Caprice No. 1*. The audience was stunned by Nianci's ability to play this very difficult piece with so much dexterity and feeling. His second piece was *Zigeunerweisen*, Op. 20 (流浪者之歌), by the Spanish composer Pablo de Sarasate. While Nianci performed his second piece, his mind was thinking about his parents' hardship and suffering when they escaped from Mainland China to Taiwan and faced all kinds of difficulties. He thought about how lucky he was to have such nice and kind parents. He also thought about his mom's condition. All of his feelings and deep emotions he channeled into the music, which emerged from his violin with touching expression and great skill.

When Nianci finished his second piece, all the audience stood up and applauded his excellent performance. He, Suqin and the entire symphony kept bowing to the audience, but the applause continued for more than a minute.

Finally, they shouted, "Encore! Encore! One more song! One more song."

Nianci looked at Suqin and told her a few words with a smile. Then he took the microphone on stage, "Thank you! Thank you, my dear audience. My last piece is dedicated to my dear mother. She is in the last moments of her life right now. Mom! I love you! I don't know how I can repay you." When he said this, his voice trembled with emotion. The audience quieted down quickly.

Xiaohua and Jiaming were watching the concert on TV. They both started to cry at Nianci's announcement.

Suqin began with a little introduction, then Nianci began to play. Everyone in the audience recognized this well-known Chinese song immediately, "Mother! How great you are." Some of the audience members even began to sing with the music.

母親你真偉大！
Mother, how great you are!

母親像月亮一樣，照耀我家門窗。
Mother is like the moon that shines on our house.

Resonance of Love

聖潔多慈祥，發出愛的光芒。
So holy and kind, that beams out shining love.

為了兒女著想，不怕烏雲阻擋，賜給我溫情，鼓勵我向上。
For children, (she is) not afraid of blockage of dark clouds (difficulty). Offers warm kindliness and encourages us to go upward.

母親啊！我愛您。
Oh, Mother! I love you.

我愛你，你真偉大！
I love you; you are really great!

母親像星星一樣，照耀我家門窗，
Mother is like the stars that shine on our house.

聖潔多慈祥，發出愛的光芒。
So holy and kind, that beams out shining love.

不辭艱難困苦，給我指引迷惘，
(She does) not avoid difficulty and hardship to direct us when we are confused.

親情深如海，此恩何能忘。
Mother's affection is so deep like the sea! How can we forget this kindness?

母親啊！我愛您。
Oh, Mother! I love you.

我愛您，您真偉大！
I love you; you are really great!

When the song was repeated for a second time, the entire symphony joined in. Within seconds, almost the entire audience had joined the singing. Many of them had tears in their eyes.

At the end of the song, the atmosphere in the concert hall was calm, quiet, and deeply reflective. Finally, someone began to applaud, triggering the entire audience's applause. It took nearly two minutes for all the performers to complete their bows and finally, the performance was ended with great success.

Once the concert was over, Nianci and Suqin did not join the celebration dinner but instead hired a taxi and rushed home. Their mind was on Xiaohua.

"Mom! Wait for me, Mom! Wait for me." The thought repeated in each of their minds.

When they finally arrived home and entered the house, they could feel something long awaited had happened. Jiaming looked at them with the baby in his arms.

"Your mom passed away peacefully and happily. She saw your entire performance," Jiaming said through his tears.

Nianci and Suqin entered their mother's room and knelt down next to the bed. They saw that she had died with a smile, satisfied with her life.

"Trees wish to be calm, but the wind does not stop blowing. The son wishes to repay to his parents, but the parents cannot wait."

漢・韓嬰・韓詩外傳・卷九：「樹欲靜而風不止，子欲養而親不待也。」

ABOUT THE AUTHOR

Dr. Yang, Jwing-Ming was born on August 11, 1946, in Xinzhu Xian (新竹縣), Taiwan (台灣), Republic of China (中華民國). He started his wushu (武術) (gongfu or kung fu, 功夫) training at the age of fifteen under Shaolin White Crane (Shaolin Bai He, 少林白鶴) Master Cheng, Gin-Gsao (曾金灶). Master Cheng originally learned taizuquan (太祖拳) from his grandfather when he was a child. When Master Cheng was fifteen years old, he started learning White Crane from Master Jin, Shao-Feng (金紹峰) and followed him for twenty-three years until Master Jin's death.

In thirteen years of study (1961–1974) under Master Cheng, Dr. Yang became an expert in the White Crane style of Chinese martial arts, which includes both the use of bare hands and various weapons, such as saber, staff, spear, trident, two short rods, and many others. With the same master, he also studied White Crane qigong (白鶴氣功), qin na or chin na (擒拿), tui na (推拿), and dian xue massages (點穴按摩) and herbal treatment.

At sixteen, Dr. Yang began the study of Yang-style taijiquan (楊氏太極拳) under Master Kao Tao (高濤). He later continued his study of taijiquan under Master Li, Mao-Ching (李茂清). Master Li learned his taijiquan from the well-known Master Han, Ching-Tang (韓慶堂). From this further practice, Dr. Yang was able to master the taiji bare-hand sequence, pushing hands, the two-man fighting sequence, taiji sword, taiji saber, and taiji qigong.

When Dr. Yang was eighteen years old, he entered Tamkang College (淡江學院) in Taipei Xian to study physics. In college, he began the study of traditional Shaolin Long Fist (Changquan or Chang Chuan, 長拳) with Master Li, Mao-Ching at the Tamkang College Guoshu Club (淡江國術社), 1964–1968, and eventually became an assistant instructor under Master Li. In 1971 he completed his MS degree in physics at the National Taiwan University (台灣大學) and then served in the Chinese Air Force from 1971 to 1972. In the service, Dr. Yang taught physics at the Junior Academy of the Chinese Air Force (空軍幼校) while also teaching wushu. After being honorably discharged in 1972, he returned to Tamkang College to teach physics and resumed study under Master Li, Mao-Ching. From Master Li, Dr. Yang learned Northern-style Wushu, which includes bare-hand and kicking techniques as well as numerous weapons.

In 1974 Dr. Yang came to the United States to study mechanical engineering at Purdue University. At the request of a few students, Dr. Yang began to teach gongfu (kung fu), which resulted in the establishment of the Purdue University Chinese Kung Fu Research Club in the spring of 1975. While at Purdue, Dr. Yang also taught college-credit courses in taijiquan. In May 1978, he was awarded a PhD in mechanical engineering by Purdue.

In 1980 Dr. Yang moved to Houston to work for Texas Instruments. While in Houston, he founded Yang's Shaolin Kung Fu Academy, which was eventually taken over by his disciple, Mr. Jeffery Bolt, after Dr. Yang moved to Boston in 1982. Dr. Yang founded Yang's Martial Arts Academy in Boston on October 1, 1982.

In January 1984, he gave up his engineering career to devote more time to research, writing, and teaching. In March 1986, he purchased property in the Jamaica Plain area of Boston to be used as the headquarters of the new organization, Yang's Martial Arts Association (YMAA). The organization expanded to become a division of Yang's Oriental Arts Association, Inc. (YOAA).

In 2008 Dr. Yang began the nonprofit YMAA California Retreat Center. This training facility in rural California is where selected students enroll in a five-year to ten-year residency to learn Chinese martial arts.

Dr. Yang has been involved in traditional Chinese wushu since 1961, studying Shaolin White Crane (Bai He), Shaolin Long Fist (Changquan), and taijiquan under several different masters. He has taught for more than forty-six years: seven years in Taiwan, five years at Purdue University, two years in Houston, twenty-six years in Boston, and more than eight years at the YMAA California Retreat Center. He has taught seminars all over the world, sharing his knowledge of Chinese martial arts and qigong in Argentina, Austria, Barbados, Botswana, Belgium, Bermuda, Brazil, Canada, China, Chile, England, Egypt, France, Germany, Hungary, Iceland, Ireland, Italy, Latvia, Mexico, the Netherlands, New Zealand, Poland, Portugal, Saudi Arabia, South Africa, Spain, Switzerland, and Venezuela.

Since 1986 YMAA has become an international organization, which currently includes more than fifty schools located in Argentina, Belgium, Canada, Chile, France, Hungary, Iran, Ireland, Italy, New Zealand, Poland, Portugal, South Africa, Sweden, the United Kingdom, the United States, and Venezuela.

Many of Dr. Yang's books and videos have been translated into other languages, such as French, Italian, Spanish, Polish, Czech, Bulgarian, Russian, German, and Hungarian.

For more books by Dr. Yang, Jwing-Ming, please go to the YMAA Publishing website.
https://ymaa.com/publishing

Dr. Yang, Jwing-Ming

.